HIDDEN MOTIVES

Four Romances Emerge from Mysterious Shadows

CAROL COX
GAIL GAYMER MARTIN
DIANN MILLS
JILL STENGL

BARBOUR
PUBLISHING

Introduction

Watcher in the Woods by Carol Cox
Laurel Masters is thrilled to receive an invitation to visit the grand-mother she's never met. But instead of a cozy cottage, Grandma's house turns out to be a center for New Age studies. Bolstered only by her growing relationship with Jason Wells, a visiting computer consultant, Laurel's resolve is tested when a cyberstalker begins sending threatening E-mails. Then the stalker leaves cyberspace to become a very real—and dangerous—presence.

Then Came Darkness by Gail Gaymer Martin
Gerri (Seward) Ward, a housekeeper at Emory Estates, hopes to vindicate her grandfather's imprisonment for murder. Gerri strug-gles without the Lord's help until the estate's groundskeeper, Rich Drake teaches her a lesson in faith. While Gerri finds clues in the gloomy mansion, she draws closer to the Lord and to Rich, but when the estate owner realizes her motives, can Rich save her from danger and will God bless their growing love?

At the End of the Bayou by DiAnn Mills
Shelby Landry travels to her vacant childhood home in Louisiana to find a key to reoccurring migraines, although she doesn't remember her life there. She meets Chad LeBlanc, a developer who wants to restore the antebellum home to its original grandeur. With Chad's gentle guidance, he helps Shelby unlock the mystery of her tragic childhood. She discovers her grand-father's hatred and a fire that claimed her sisters' lives.

Buried in the Past by Jill Stengl
American widow Stephanie Keller hopes to begin life anew at Haverstane Cottage. Although Pastor Dudley Larkin welcomes her warmly, Stephanie wonders if England can ever feel like home. She plans to renovate the historic church on her property despite anonymous threats. . .until the night mysterious lights appear in its windows. A secret lurks beneath the vestry floor, and a murderer plans to kill again.

ISBN 1-59310-257-7

Scripture quotations marked NIV are taken from the HOLY BIBLE, NEW INTER-
NATIONAL VERSION®. NIV®. Copyright © 1973, 1978, 1984 by International
Bible Society. Used by permission of Zondervan Publishing House. All rights
reserved.

Scripture quotations marked NASB are taken from the New American Standard
Bible, © 1960, 1962, 1963, 1968, 1971, 1972, 1973, 1975, 1977 by The Lockman
Foundation. Used by permission.

Scripture quotations marked KJV are taken from the King James Version of the
Bible.

Cover image © Kamil Vojnar/Photonica

Illustrations by Mari Goering

This book is a work of fiction. Names, characters, places, and incidents are either
products of the author's imagination or used fictitiously. Any similarity to actual
people, organizations, and/or events is purely coincidental.

Published by Barbour Publishing, Inc., P.O. Box 719, Uhrichsville, Ohio 44683,
www.barbourbooks.com

*Our mission is to publish and distribute inspirational products offering exceptional
value and biblical encouragement to the masses.*

Member of the
Evangelical Christian
Publishers Association

Printed in the United States of America.
5 4 3 2

Watcher in the Woods

by Carol Cox

How, then, can they call on the one
they have not believed in?
And how can they believe in the one
of whom they have not heard?
And how can they hear without
someone preaching to them?
ROMANS 10:14 NIV

Chapter 1

The change in pitch of the plane's engines drew Laurel Masters's attention from the letter she'd been reading. She glanced out the window and saw a thick belt of forest below. They'd be landing at Pulliam Airport in a few minutes.

She looked again at the letter in her hand. Over the past few weeks, its message had become embedded in her brain, but she needed the tangible reassurance of the words written in clear, flowing script. She picked up where she left off.

> *We can't make up for a lifetime of separation in the course of a mere day or two. I hope you will consider coming to Capstone for an extended stay.*
>
> *Your grandmother,*
> *Millicent Reed*

Laurel folded the letter along its well-worn creases and tucked it into her purse. Her grandmother! After all these years, she would finally have contact with a member of her mother's family.

Snippets of memory tumbled through her mind: herself as a child of seven, staring at her mother in dismay. "Megan and Amy both have two grandmothers. Why don't I?"

Her mother pulling her into her lap and holding her close while she explained, "The one you have loves you enough for twenty grandmothers. You don't need another one. Trust me on this, darling."

And that had been that. No amount of cajoling dislodged so much as a morsel of information. Given her mother's usual forthright behavior, Laurel never understood her reticence concerning her side of the family. All future questions were met by noncommittal answers, then silence. Laurel didn't doubt that her mother had her reasons for such evasiveness; she'd just never been convinced she would agree with them.

The pilot's voice filled the cabin. "Ladies and gentlemen, we'll be landing momentarily. Thank you for flying with us, and we hope to see you again soon."

Laurel offered the passing flight attendant a bright smile, even though she struggled with the twinge of guilt that beset her every time she thought of how coming here violated her mother's wishes. But she needed closure, needed to understand. *Why couldn't Grandmother have found us six months sooner, before Mom died?* Surely her mother would have relented and welcomed the opportunity for reconciliation.

Buoyed by that thought, Laurel braced herself for the landing. She waited until the plane stopped rolling to gather her belongings and stand in line with the twenty or so other passengers to exit the plane. Quite a difference from the crowded 737 she'd taken from Dallas to Phoenix before catching this commuter flight to Flagstaff.

She stood at the top of the steps and gave her eyes a moment to adjust to the intense Arizona sunlight before descending to the tarmac. The other passengers streamed ahead of her and went their various ways. A lone man remained at the gate. Laurel lifted her hand in a tentative greeting.

The man removed his Stetson and walked out to meet her. "Miss Masters? I'm Garrett Harper. Your grandmother asked me to pick you up." His deep blue eyes crinkled at the corners when he smiled.

"She said someone would meet me but didn't tell me who. Please call me Laurel." Garrett's smile deepened, and she felt warmed by more than the summer sunshine. She pointed out her luggage, then followed him to a gleaming white SUV where he swung her bags into the back with ease. The pungent scent of pine tickled her nostrils, and she drew in a deep breath.

Garrett maneuvered the heavy vehicle out of the parking lot and onto the interstate. "Is this your first visit to Capstone?" he asked minutes later when he left I-17 and joined the westbound traffic on I-40. At Laurel's nod, he grinned. "I thought so. If you'd been around during my time here, I would have remembered."

Laurel felt her cheeks flush at the compliment and tried to change the subject. "What do you mean 'your time here'? Do you live near Capstone?"

"Not near. . .at. Didn't your grandmother tell you? I work for her."

"Oh." Apparently, she would have to revise her image of a lonely grandmother in her cottage in the woods. "I just hadn't thought of her needing an employee." Her lips stretched wide in an unexpected yawn, and she clapped her hand over her mouth. "Excuse me."

Garrett chuckled. "Don't worry about it. At seven thousand feet, most people feel the difference in altitude the first day or so."

Laurel stared out the window at the scenery rolling by. "I keep thinking of Arizona as desert. I never dreamed there'd be so many trees."

"We're driving through the largest Ponderosa pine forest in the world," Garrett said. "It stretches out for miles on end."

Laurel settled back and watched the towering trees flash by. Her eyelids drifted shut. She roused briefly when the SUV slowed and bumped across a cattle guard, then changed direction.

"We're turning off the interstate," Garrett explained. "The road won't be quite as smooth the rest of the way."

Laurel murmured acknowledgment and dozed until a series of turns woke her again. She sat up, her mind fuzzy from sleep, and tried to take stock of her surroundings.

The SUV wound up a steep hill through more of the forest giants. "My grandmother said she lived out of town, but I didn't expect anything quite this remote."

"It is pretty secluded," Garrett agreed. "But it suits her purpose."

The vehicle emerged from the pines at the top of a broad mesa. Laurel caught her breath and stared at the scene before her. Gone was the rustic cottage of her imagination, replaced by a massive log structure with wings angling off on both sides. The soaring A-frame roof crowned the central part of the building and framed the towering windows that dominated the entrance.

"This—is Capstone?"

"Home sweet home." Garret slowed when he drove beneath the entrance sign and pointed overhead.

Laurel craned her neck to make out the words carved in the wooden arch: THE CAPSTONE CENTER FOR SPIRITUAL STUDIES.

Garrett pulled up in front of the lodge and helped Laurel out. "I'll start unloading your luggage. She'll be out to greet you in a moment."

The carved wooden doors swung open before he finished speaking, and a blond woman about Laurel's age stepped out onto the flagstone-paved porch. "It's about time you got here."

"It didn't take a moment longer than expected." Garrett set Laurel's bags near the door, then tipped his Stetson to her. "It was a pleasure getting acquainted. I hope to see more of you while you're here." He drove off toward a low building Laurel assumed must be the garage.

She turned back to the blond woman, ready to introduce herself, when a man and an older woman emerged from the lodge. The woman captured Laurel's fascinated stare. Her mother would have looked much the same in another twenty years.

But where her mother would have glowed with delight, this woman's face seemed fixed in a look of disdain. This was no grief-stricken elderly lady. Every inch of her spoke confidence, from the elegantly coifed hair to the beige linen suit showing nary a wrinkle to her ramrod posture and air of command.

Laurel glanced down at the comfortable T-shirt and slacks she had selected as a traveling outfit. The attire that seemed so suitable at home looked out of place and dowdy here. She looked back and caught the full force of an icy blue gaze that swept her from head to toe and left her in no doubt she'd been found wanting.

The woman looked at her companion. "My granddaughter, Laurel Masters," she announced in a flat tone.

Laurel held out her hand in a reflexive gesture. The man took it with a gracious smile and bowed over it. He continued to hold her hand, pressing her fingers between his.

"Allow me to introduce myself," he said in a silky voice. "I'm Everett Keller, a friend of your grandmother's."

Laurel tried not to recoil at the prolonged contact with those soft fingers. She had the absurd feeling her own might start twitching at any moment. To distract herself, she focused on Keller's appearance. His immaculately tailored pale gray suit matched his odd-colored eyes. Silver hair completed the monochromatic effect, offset only by his olive complexion.

She curved her lips in what she hoped looked like a sincere smile and forced herself to meet his gaze. Those gray eyes had a piercing quality that made her feel he could read her thoughts.

"I'm sure you'll enjoy your visit to Capstone, Miss Masters. I know Millicent has been looking forward to your arrival."

"Thank you." She withdrew her hand and tried to mask the relief she felt when Keller let go. "Do you live nearby?"

"Alas, no. I have far too many demands on my time to make more than an occasional visit, much as I wish it were otherwise.

"I'll be on my way now," he said. "I wouldn't want to intrude on such an auspicious occasion. I do hope I'll meet you again during your stay, my dear." He looked over Laurel's shoulder, and she heard the sound of tires crunching on the gravel driveway behind her.

Turning, she saw a white limo pull up. A chauffeur stepped out and opened the door. Before entering the elegant vehicle, Keller bowed over her grandmother's hand and touched his lips to her fingers. "Good-bye for now, dear Millicent. May you and your granddaughter enjoy your reunion."

The three women watched his departure in silence, then Millicent turned to Laurel. "So you're here at last," she said.

"Yes." Laurel tried to reconcile the difference between reality and the picture she'd built up in her mind. So much for the soft-bosomed, grandmotherly embrace she'd looked forward to. There would be no sentimental welcome here.

"You aren't what I expected." Her grandmother echoed her thoughts. "Nevertheless, thank you for accepting my invitation. I'm sure you'd like to get settled." She turned to the woman hovering behind her. "Please show Laurel where she will stay," she said. To Laurel, she added, "This is my niece Avril. Your second cousin."

Laurel smiled with genuine pleasure. "I didn't realize I had a cousin."

The other woman eyed her with a cool expression, then dipped her head in a brief nod. "I'll show you to your room." She led the way inside.

Laurel picked up her suitcases and followed. Her sandals slapped against the flagstone floor, sending an echo bouncing throughout the cavernous room. Her artist's eye noted the contrast between the rugged log walls and the soft southwestern colors that accented the interior.

"This is the gathering room," Avril called over her shoulder without slackening her pace. She pushed open a door in the far right wall and kept on going.

"You could gather quite a crowd in here." Laurel did a quick estimate of the number of couches and easy chairs. The room could seat thirty to forty people without a bit of crowding. *Say good-bye to Grandma's cozy cottage.*

Avril rounded a corner, and Laurel quickened her steps to keep up. Her cousin's ash blond hair swayed gracefully above her slender shoulders—hair only a couple of shades darker than her mother's had been. Laurel bit her lip to fight off the sudden shaft of pain that shot through her. After her mother's death, Pastor Ron counseled her that healing would take time. She only wished she had some way of knowing how far along she'd already come. Just about the time she thought she'd succeeded in taking another step through the grief process, some unexpected connection made her feel like it had begun all over again.

Avril stopped near the end of the hallway and opened the door to a bedroom. "This is where you'll stay," she said in a tone as cool as her blue-eyed gaze. "I hope you'll be comfortable. I'm told the furniture belonged to your mother."

Laurel set her suitcases beside the bed and gasped in delight. The white eyelet comforter on the four-poster bed matched the ruffled curtains that fluttered at the window. Bright throw rugs on the wood floor added splashes of color to the decidedly feminine room. "It's lovely."

She turned in time to see Avril close the door and lean against it, arms crossed. Her cousin eyed her with a speculative air. "Why now?" Avril demanded.

Laurel shook her head and frowned. "Why—what?"

"Why show up now after all these years?" Avril circled her, eyeing her closely like an entomologist studying a new specimen of insect.

"My grandmother invited me here. The timing wasn't my idea."

"Mm." Avril completed her inspection and took up her position at the door again. She tapped her cheek with her forefinger. "I've seen pictures, you know."

"Pictures?" Laurel echoed, feeling more lost by the moment.

"Of your mother." Avril's nostrils flared. "Her hair was blond like mine. She was tall like my mother and Aunt Millicent. . .and me. You don't look a thing like her."

"You're right." Laurel had the satisfaction of seeing a flicker of confusion in Avril's expression. "I take after my father."

Avril's eyes shone with a deep blue fire. Her hand snaked out and encircled Laurel's left wrist. She leaned so close that Laurel could feel the warmth of her breath. "Who are you really?"

Chapter 2

Laurel stepped back, but she couldn't break Avril's hold. "What do you mean?"

Avril tightened her grip. "You're good, I'll grant you that. Such wide-eyed innocence!" Her expression hardened. "Who sent you?"

Again Laurel wrenched her arm and pulled free, wincing when Avril's crimson nails raked down her wrist and the back of her hand. "What are you talking about?"

"Do you expect me to believe anyone would just pack up and come here for the summer without a second thought? I want to know who sent you. Who's paying your expenses?"

Laurel fixed her cousin with a steady gaze and folded her arms across her chest to hide her trembling fingers. "I'm an artist. A number of galleries carry my work. Two paintings sold before I left and brought in enough to cover my expenses for the next couple of months."

Avril's confident expression wavered, then she dipped her head in a quick nod. "All right. I'll buy that. . .for now. Maybe you really are Delia's daughter." She stepped back and twisted the doorknob without taking her gaze off Laurel. "And maybe you aren't. Just be assured of one thing, dear cousin: I'll be watching you."

Laurel stood frozen long after the door closed. Her whole body trembled. Avril might have gone, but the sense of menace that entered with her lingered in the room. Laurel blinked her eyes, trying to rid herself of the memory of her cousin's accusing stare.

What was that all about? Her left wrist throbbed. Looking down, she saw four raw streaks, parallel trails left by Avril's fingernails.

She traced her forefinger across the tangible reminders of the ugly scene. Up until a few moments ago, she hadn't even realized Avril existed. What could she have done in that short time to inspire such animosity?

Laurel shrugged the question aside. She had come to visit her grandmother, not Avril. Turning, she lifted the suitcases onto the bed.

She quickly found places for her clothes and shoes in the roomy closet and dresser. She reached into the bottom of her suitcase and drew out the three remaining items: a sketch pad, her mother's Bible, and a silver-framed photograph. She set the sketch pad on the dresser and slid the Bible into the drawer of the nightstand. The photograph weighed heavily in Laurel's hands. She brushed a speck of lint from a corner of the frame and stared at the two faces pictured there, one fair, one dark. Her parents smiled back at her, caught in a moment of unguarded happiness.

Laurel settled the photo on the nightstand, next to the

ornate wooden lamp. She started to zip her suitcase shut but as she did, she gave the lamp a second glance. Nostalgia flooded over her. It was almost—no, exactly—like the one that served as her mother's favorite reading lamp for years.

Laurel ran her fingers along the familiar lines of the lamp, remembering the day her mother brought its twin home from a shopping foray in Granbury. Now she could understand her mother's joy in acquiring what Laurel had seen as just another lamp. It must have seemed like a touch from the past for her mother to come across a replica of one from her childhood home.

Puzzlement creased Laurel's forehead. But surely such delight in owning a reminder of earlier years argued for good memories, some desire to maintain a connection with the past. So why all the secrecy surrounding her mother's life before her marriage? It was one more piece in a puzzle Laurel feared she might never solve.

With a quick shrug, she put the questions out of her mind. She couldn't change the past, only deal with the present. And the present was waiting right outside her door. She went to the closet and glanced through her wardrobe. A quick survey told her that if she wanted to dress according to Millicent Reed's standards, she'd need some new clothes. Perhaps she could borrow a car and make a quick shopping run into town in the morning.

Laurel stepped into the adjoining bathroom to touch up her makeup and pull her thick brunette hair back into a clip. She retraced her steps toward the gathering room, scolding herself when she realized she was bracing herself against another appearance by Avril. *It doesn't matter what she thinks, cousin or not. Your whole purpose in coming here is to get to know your grandmother. It's time to make up for all those lost years.*

Her steps quickened, anticipating the discoveries the summer would hold. In this isolated spot, surely there would be ample time for long walks and talks. She would ask questions, learn the answers to the questions that puzzled her, and listen to her grandmother reminisce about her mother's life before she left home.

Another fragment of memory floated to the surface. Herself at age ten: "The whole fifth grade is putting together a collage of pictures of our parents when they were our age. I found some of Daddy, but I don't see any of you."

Her mother's tight smile and reply: "I don't have any from that time, I'm afraid. I always felt like my life started when I married your father."

The vague reply always struck Laurel as odd, but perhaps now she could fill in the gaps in her knowledge. She pushed open the door at the end of the hallway, once more taken aback by the sheer size of the gathering room. In the far corner, Garrett and Avril stood locked in conversation. Garrett looked up when Laurel entered and smiled a greeting. Laurel waved and started toward them. Avril glanced over her shoulder, following the line of Garrett's gaze. The look she directed Laurel's way could have curdled milk.

Laurel's feet faltered and she pulled up short. Obviously, Avril wasn't plagued by second thoughts about extending a warmer greeting to her long-lost cousin.

Now what? Laurel shifted direction and picked up a lavishly illustrated book someone had left on the nearest couch, trying to look like it had been her intended destination all along. She made a show of thumbing through the volume, all the while peering around to get a better picture of her surroundings.

Once again, she was struck by the contrast between the cozy cottage of her imagination and this massive building on its lonely hilltop. *The Capstone Center for Spiritual Studies. Who'd have thought?* She had never expected to find her grandmother living at some kind of learning facility. Looking around with new eyes, she saw similarities between Capstone and retreat centers she had visited. Yes, the huge central fireplace of lichen-covered rock would certainly fit that setting, as would the floor-to-ceiling bookshelves that lined a nearby wall.

Capstone was a much smaller campus, of course. It would never hold hundreds of conferees like the one she attended in the Smoky Mountains a few years before. Still, it had its charm. Laurel wondered when the next session would start. Perhaps she could sit in on some of the workshops. A thrill of anticipation shot through her. Why hadn't her mother ever told her she'd grown up in a place with such a dramatic setting and filled with opportunities for spiritual growth?

A door in the opposite wall swung open, and her grand-mother appeared, accompanied by a man who threw Laurel's memory back to high school and her sophomore English class, when they studied Washington Irving's *The Legend of Sleepy Hollow*. If ever a person had been created in the image of Ichabod Crane, this one fit the bill, from his tall, loose-knit frame to his spindly neck and broad feet. Laurel pressed her lips together to suppress an adolescent urge to giggle.

"Ah, there you are." Millicent beckoned Laurel toward her with a regal gesture. "I want you to meet Arthur Lyddon, our resident instructor. He lives in a suite of rooms at the end of the guest wing." She indicated the door through which they had just come. "Arthur, my granddaughter, Laurel Masters."

Ichabod's double smiled with a warmth that dispelled any similarity to Irving's character. "It's a pleasure to meet you. Millicent didn't tell me how long you intend-to stay, but I hope you'll be able to join us for a seminar or two while you're here. Our next session won't start for several weeks, but it would be a delight to discuss some of the topics with you in the meantime."

"I'd like that," Laurel said, pleased by the invitation. "Maybe we can talk more over dinner this evening."

Arthur shot a quick glance at Millicent, who cleared her throat and reclaimed control of the conversation. "I'm afraid not. Arthur and I have a meeting scheduled. We'll be working through the dinner hour." She started to walk away, then paused and added, "I'll have a tray sent to your room. I'm sure you're tired after your flight."

"No, really. I'd rather—" Laurel broke off when she realized she stood talking to a closed door.

She darted a quick look around, wondering if anyone had witnessed her abrupt dismissal. Garrett and Avril must have slipped out while she had her attention focused on her grand-mother. *Good.* She moved toward the towering front doors, suddenly anxious for a breath of fresh air.

"That didn't go too well, did it?" Avril stepped out from behind the shelter of the fireplace. "Can't you see you're wasting your time here? Maybe you ought to catch the next flight back to wherever it is you came from."

Laurel swallowed hard and willed her heart to go back down into her chest. "I came here to get to know my grandmother. I intend to do just that."

Avril's lips curled in a feline smile. "Not tonight. It looks like you're on your own."

Head down, arms folded across her chest, Laurel scuffed along the flagstone walk that fronted the wing opposite hers—the guest wing, according to her grandmother's brief mention. *And that's the most conversation I've gotten from her since I arrived. Why invite me here if she doesn't intend to spend any time with me?* Laurel aimed a kick at a lone pebble on the clean-swept walk and sent it skittering across the flagstone and into a border, where it came to rest under a low juniper shrub. One corner of her mouth curved upward in a rueful half smile at her display of temper. Thankfully, no one else had seen her childish behavior.

Or had they? A flutter of movement off to the side caught Laurel's attention. She looked back in time to see the edge of a curtain settle into place across one of the guest wing windows. Laurel blinked. Had she imagined the flash of motion, or did someone stand there observing her?

Who could it have been? Avril, more than likely. Her earlier comment of "I'll be watching you" lingered fresh in Laurel's mind. Laurel brushed away the prickly sensation at the back of her neck and chided herself for her overactive imagination. It was painfully obvious that no one at Capstone had the least interest in what she might be doing.

Up ahead she spotted the long, low building she earlier

identified as the garage and strode toward it, a woman with a purpose. With a garage that size, there ought to be plenty of vehicles. Tomorrow she would borrow one of them and drive into town to buy some new clothes. Spending her first full day in Arizona going from store to store didn't fit her previous picture of a tender reunion, but it beat kicking rocks and wondering when she would be granted an audience with Queen Millicent.

Her conscience stung. *I'm sorry, Lord.* Her grandmother didn't merit that kind of disrespect. After all, she had her hands full running this center. Having a granddaughter she'd never seen before descend on her doorstep. . . *No, wait.* She's *the one who asked me to come.*

Again the question nagged at her: *Why invite a guest and then ignore her? I just don't get it.* She reached the garage and wiggled the doorknob. Locked. She should have known.

"Out for a walk?" a voice boomed behind her.

Laurel did a series of quick skips that would have done Baryshnikov proud and clutched her chest with both hands.

Garrett Harper watched her gyrations with a wide grin splitting his face. "I didn't mean to frighten you."

"Do you always lurk around waiting to scare the daylights out of people?" The words came out sounding more waspish than she intended, but she was too shaken to care. She bent forward and rested her hands on her knees, gasping as though she'd just sprinted the length of a football field.

A deep chuckle rumbled from Garrett's chest. "Not always. Some days I stand right out in the open, some days I lurk. This is one of my lurking days."

Laurel grinned and raised her right hand. "Okay, point taken. I apologize for overreacting."

"No problem. I'll try not to sneak up on you next time. Is there something I can help you with, or are you just getting acquainted with the place?"

"Could you let me into the garage to look at the cars? I'd like to borrow one of them to make a run into town tomorrow."

"Sorry." Garrett spread his arms wide and shook his head. "No one goes on or off the mesa without Millicent's permission, and she doesn't give that easily. I've got the keys for the garage door and all the cars in my cottage, but if I go handing them out without authorization, I'll be out of a job."

"That's ridiculous!" Laurel sputtered.

Garrett held up both his hands. "Don't shoot the messenger, okay? If you can talk your grandmother into it, that's fine with me. I'm just the hired help." He touched his forefinger to the brim of his Stetson. "I've got to check the generator before supper. If Millicent says you can take one of the cars, let me know. I'll have the key off its hook and in your hand in a flash."

Laurel watched him go, feeling even more of an outsider than before. She scuffed across the gravel driveway, not caring whether anyone saw her this time.

Back inside the empty gathering room, she paused to consider the bookshelves. At least she could take advantage of the time at her disposal and select a book or two to peruse back in her room. *Maybe three.* It looked like it was going to be a long evening.

She stepped over to the shelves and ran her finger along

the rows of volumes. Maybe she could find a local history to give her a feel for the area or a guidebook with ideas of attractions to visit. Assuming she ever got off the mesa, that is. Even a nice, juicy mystery would give her something to fill the hours. And from the looks of these titles, she'd found the right section: *Out from the Shadows. Voices of the Ascended Masters.*

"Wait a minute. Are these suspense novels, or. . ." She scanned the spines of the next few books. *Who You Are Now/Who You Were Then: How Your Past Lives Affect Your Present.*

Laurel snatched her finger away as if the shelf were red hot. "Those aren't fiction," she whispered. "What does a retreat center want with books like those?"

She backed away and breathed deeply, trying to collect her ricocheting thoughts. "Don't jump to conclusions," she muttered. An argument could be made that one had to know the flaws in false teachings in order to refute them. Maybe this section held books that demonstrated unbiblical beliefs as a means of educating the center's students. A reference section, nothing more.

A group of books by Arthur Lyddon caught her attention. Eager to gain some insight into the resident teacher's thinking, Laurel pulled the first one off the shelf: *Lifting the Veil: Jesus and the Christ-Consciousness.* Flipping the cover open, she noticed an inscription on the title page: "To Millicent Reed, supporter and disciple." She closed her eyes and clasped her hands together to still their trembling.

The sign over the entry gate flashed into her mind. "The Capstone Center for Spiritual Studies? I never thought to ask what kind of spirit. What have I gotten myself into?" She took a quick step back and banged her calf against a low table. The pain that shot from her ankle to her knee had the unexpected effect of restoring clarity to her thoughts. She examined the bookshelves systematically from top to bottom, side to side. Every shelf was packed with books on self-focused spirituality.

Bile rose in her throat. Laurel pushed through the door to the family wing and fled down the hallway as though the very presence of evil pursued her.

A small table with service for one stood in the corner of her bedroom. A savory aroma emanated from the covered dish atop the linen tablecloth. Half an hour ago the smell would have sent her taste buds into a frenzy of anticipation; now, it turned her stomach.

I've got to get out of here. Laurel dragged her suitcase from beneath the bed and started piling clothes inside, heedless of whether or not they wrinkled. A few creases didn't matter. Getting away from this den of deception did.

Center for Spiritual Studies. Ha! The whole place was steeped in false teaching. Laurel jammed her alarm clock into an empty space beside her blow dryer. The more distance she could put between herself and Capstone, the better.

She shoved a pair of jeans aside to make room for her cosmetic bag. So much for family ties. Her reception here couldn't have been further from what she'd expected. For whatever reason, Avril hated her. And her grandmother. . . Unexpected tears stung Laurel's eyes and she dashed them away, surprised by the ache of disappointment that swept over her. She had managed this long without a maternal grandmother. She could live the rest of her life without one.

First thing in the morning, she would ask, beg, do whatever it took to get Garrett to drive her back to the airport. If she had to wait all day before a flight left for Phoenix, so be it. Anything would be better than staying here.

She took the Bible from the nightstand drawer and clutched it to her chest, remembering the series of sermons Pastor Ron preached on the dangers of dabbling in the occult. "In whom are you putting your faith?" he said. "Understand that we're waging a spiritual battle, and the enemy is very good at camouflaging himself as an angel of light. Christians have no business accepting a counterfeit version of Christ."

A verse he'd used popped into her mind: "Do not be yoked together with unbelievers. For what do righteousness and wickedness have in common? Or what fellowship can light have with darkness?"

Laurel cleared a spot on top of the jumbled clothing in her suitcase and tucked the Bible into the hollow space. "That settles it," she whispered. "This place is filled with darkness. I have no business staying here." The sense of loss assaulted her again, and she squeezed her eyelids shut, feeling hot tears trace a path down her cheeks.

Gritting her teeth against the sobs that threatened, she reached for her sketch pad. Another verse sprang unbidden to her mind: "How, then, can they call on the one they have not believed in? And how can they believe in the one of whom they have not heard? And how can they hear without someone preaching to them?"

Judging from the inscription in Arthur's book, her grandmother fit into the category of those who didn't believe. What would happen to her? What hope did someone caught up in false teaching have of hearing about Jesus if Christians ran from the battle? Millicent Reed might be cold and aloof, but she was the only family Laurel had left. How would she hear the truth about Christ's love without someone to tell her?

"But does it have to be me, Lord?" Laurel picked up her mother's Bible again and thumbed through its well-worn pages, stopping when she spotted an underlined passage: "I am sending you to them to open their eyes and turn them from darkness to light."

Her fingers trembled on the page. How could she abandon her grandmother to the spiritual darkness that engulfed Capstone?

She couldn't. The knowledge swept over her in a tide that was both relief and torment. Much as she shrank from the idea, obedience compelled her to stay.

Laurel sank onto the comforter and laid the Bible open on her lap. "Okay, Lord, if You want me to stay, You'll have to show me what to do." She fluffed her pillows and shoved them behind her back, then pored over passages in both the Old and New Testaments. By the time she reached Isaiah, the words began to blur. She rubbed her eyes with her thumb and forefinger and focused on chapter 43:

"When you pass through the waters, I will be with you; and when you pass through the rivers, they will not sweep over you. When you walk through the fire, you will not be burned; the flames will not set you ablaze."

Laurel stared at the words for a long moment, then read them again, letting their promise of God's presence and protection sink deep into her heart.

Closing the Bible, she set it back in the nightstand drawer, then rubbed her weary eyes again. Her stomach rumbled, reminding her she hadn't eaten anything since the minuscule bag of pretzels on the plane. She swung her legs off the bed and stretched, then went to investigate her dinner. The tantalizing aroma had long since dissipated. Laurel lifted the lid and eyed it hopefully. The sight of congealed trout almandine sent her appetite back into hiding.

Maybe she could try another walk. Some time outside the confines of her room might do her good. A glance at the window put a stop to that idea. The shadows had long since melded into darkness. She walked to the window and peered outside. For the first time, she realized how truly secluded Capstone was. Other than the glow spilling from windows farther along the family wing, not a single light could be seen, save for the stars overhead.

Laurel stared at the myriad pinpoints of light in the sky, taken aback by their number and brightness. Amazing! Even the Milky Way could be clearly seen. *Father, You are truly awesome!* Caught up in reverent wonder, she started to turn away when a flicker of motion captured her attention.

The prayer of thanksgiving stuck in her throat. Had she seen something, or had it only been a product of tired eyes and frayed nerves? She pressed closer to the glass and probed the darkness but saw only shadows.

Another hint of movement arrested her gaze. *There!*

Something darker, more solid than the shadows. Laurel's breath quickened as she watched a dark shape detach itself and fade back into the night. *An animal*, she tried to reassure herself. *Looking for food or a place to sleep.* Then why did she have the distinct impression that someone—or something—had been standing out there in the darkness, watching her?

With a quick move, Laurel yanked the curtains closed. She turned from the window, her hands rubbing at the gooseflesh along her arms.

Chapter 3

Laurel bent over the bathroom sink and splashed water on her face. She patted her cheeks on the towel and stared at her reflection in the mirror. Puffy eyes and a pale complexion gave mute testimony to her sleepless night. A quick touch-up with concealer and blush covered most of the outward effects, but nothing could take away the jumpiness she felt after the unsettling events of the past twenty-four hours.

She brushed her dark hair back and surveyed her image. *I guess that's as good as it's going to get.* Bracing herself for whatever surprises this day might hold, she headed to the gathering room. Her stomach rumbled and she pressed her hand against her midsection. After nothing more than pretzels as yesterday's main course, she felt ravenous. Today she needed all the fortification she could get to bolster last night's newfound determination to stay.

More than anything, she needed to see her grandmother alone, to find out how much of this nonsense she really believed. With a sense of mission, she pushed through the gathering room door and came nose-to-shirt-button with a sandy-haired man.

Laurel skidded to a halt, feeling a wave of heat flow from her neck to her hairline. She eyed the stranger warily. Another spiritual teacher?

"Good morning." He grinned and took a step backward, seemingly unaffected by their near collision. "Where did you come from?"

The friendly, open smile tugged at Laurel's heart, but she pushed the feeling away. "Dallas," she hedged, looking up into smoky gray eyes.

He laughed. "I meant, it surprised me to see you coming from the family wing. I haven't seen you around here before. I'm Jason Wells."

Laurel responded automatically to his extended hand and gave his fingers a tentative squeeze. "I'm Laurel Masters, Mrs. Reed's granddaughter. I just got in yesterday."

"Are you on your way to breakfast? I'll show you the setup." He guided her through a door at the rear of the gathering room. "There's no set time for breakfast. Just help yourself when you get here."

He led the way to the dining room, where a tempting array was spread out buffet style. Laurel scanned the room, fighting down a pang of disappointment at the sight of empty chairs. She would have to wait to talk to her grandmother. Her stomach growled again and she winced at the sound. Jason bent over the buffet, but from the way the corners of his mouth twitched, Laurel knew he'd heard. *Another wonderful first impression.*

She slid an omelet onto her plate and surrounded it with sliced fruit, then seated herself across the table from Jason and bowed her head for a brief prayer. When she looked up, Jason was just raising his head and opening his eyes. Their gazes met and held, and a flicker of excitement sparked inside her.

"So do you work here, or are you another relative I haven't met yet?"

Jason chuckled. "Neither." His chuckle grew into an outright laugh at her look of confusion. "I'm doing some work for your grandmother, but it's only on a short-term basis. At least, it started out as short-term. I'm a computer systems consultant. She hired me to set up a new network for the center and upgrade the computers she already has in place."

"But you take your meals here?"

"I'm staying in the guest wing. It's easier than driving back and forth from Flagstaff. You may have noticed it's fairly remote."

Laurel propped her elbow on the arm of her chair and rested her chin in her hand. "I've noticed." The amusement that glimmered in Jason's eyes turned the spark of excitement into a warm flame.

He continued, "I'm pleased with the setup, if I do say so myself. It's a state-of-the-art system; your grandmother spared no expense. You can imagine how impossible it is to get a decent cell phone signal out here. With the new satellite phones she installed, you'll be able to send E-mail and use the Internet as easily as you would back in Dallas." His lips quirked up in a proud smile. "Not bad for way out in the boonies, is it?"

Laurel stared into his smoky eyes. *Not bad at all.* She shook herself out of her reverie and sat erect. "That's good to know. I hadn't thought about not being able to get online. I brought my laptop so I could keep in touch with my galleries."

Jason tilted his head and frowned.

, "Where my work is displayed," she explained. "I'm an artist. I need to stay in touch with the gallery owners."

"Then I'm glad the satellite phones were in place in time for your visit. I've just finished installing some new software in the reservations computer. Next on my list is to upgrade the operating systems on all the computers over in the guest wing, and your grandmother says she has some other projects for me once I've finished that." He took a long sip of coffee and sighed. "If I didn't have other customers, I could probably spend the whole summer here on the mesa."

"So you stay here full-time while you're working at Capstone?"

Jason nodded. "It only makes sense, considering how far it is from everything. But Northland Computers—that's me— has clients all over northern Arizona, so I do a lot of traveling. I can't say your grandmother's any too happy about having to share me with my other customers—"

"I can imagine," Laurel put in.

"But she really doesn't have much choice." Jason grinned. "There aren't too many people willing to come out this far for days at a time, even if she does pay top dollar."

Laurel nibbled an orange slice, mulling over what she'd just learned. A top-of-the-line computer system and extensive upgrades, satellite phones, and what amounted to live-in con-tract labor. She made a mental estimate of the cost and gulped. Her grandmother must have a substantial amount of money available, to be able to spend so freely. *I wonder if Avril sees me as a threat. Maybe that's why she was acting so territorial.*

Jason polished off the last of his breakfast. "But I don't mean to sound like I'm complaining. This account has been a real blessing for my business."

A blessing? Laurel laced her fingers together and cleared her throat. "This may sound odd, but I need to ask you something. Are you a believer?"

Jason fixed her with a steady gaze. "There are lots of beliefs floating around. . .especially at Capstone. But if you're asking if I'm a believer in Christ, the answer is yes."

A wave of relief washed over Laurel. "Then maybe you can tell me something about Capstone from a Christian perspective. I really don't know much about the place. Just exactly what do they teach here?"

A skeptical look crossed Jason's face. "You're Millicent's granddaughter and you don't know?"

"I know it sounds crazy, but believe it or not, I only met my grandmother for the first time yesterday. I looked at some of the books on the shelves out there last night, and if that's any indication of what's going on around here, I feel like I'm in over my head."

Jason pursed his lips and gave a low whistle. "You mean you walked in here without a clue of what this place is like? That must have been a shock."

"That's putting it mildly." Laurel leaned forward and rested her arms on the table. "Don't you feel out of place here? Doesn't it bother you to work in the middle of all this?"

Jason paused before answering. "At first I was ready to give back the retainer Millicent paid me and head out of here without looking back. Then I started wondering where I'd be if no one ever bothered to tell me about Jesus. I felt I had to stick around and try to connect with your grandmother and the other people here." He traced a pattern on his plate with his fork. "I can't say I've made much headway, though."

"Have you talked to my grandmother directly? Explained the difference between what the Bible teaches and the falsehood they dish out here?"

"I've tried. Several times, in fact. I can't say she's been very receptive." Jason's face brightened. "Maybe it'll be a different story with you, since you're a relative."

Laurel thought back to her tepid welcome the day before. "Somehow, I doubt that."

Jason glanced at his watch, then folded his napkin next to his plate and pushed his chair back. "It's time for me to get to work. I hope I'll be seeing more of you. It's nice to have someone around here who understands what I'm talking about." He gave her a smile that sent her heart into overdrive, and left.

Laurel popped a strawberry into her mouth and finished her coffee. A thought rose in her mind: With Jason here, Capstone already had someone in place to shine the light of Christ. Maybe she didn't have to stay, after all.

Remembering the way his warm smile made her insides melt, she realized that leaving didn't seem nearly as appealing as it had an hour before. Maybe it wouldn't hurt to stay around a little longer.

Jason opened the protective envelope that held the new computer processor. *If Millicent wants these computers running at screaming speed, this ought to do it.* Popping the clips loose from the old processor, he pulled it out and blew the dust off the motherboard with a spray can of compressed air.

He stepped back to let the dust settle and thought of Laurel Masters. The excitement he'd felt since breakfast distracted him more than once during the morning. Dealing with delicate computer parts didn't leave room for daydreaming. He forced his attention back to the task at hand, sliding the new processor into place. Next came putting the screw back into the case, something he could do with only half his mind focused on the job. "She's beautiful, Lord. And I don't think she has any idea what a knockout she is. Is connecting with her grandmother the only reason You brought her here, or is there a chance she's the one I've been praying for?"

Avril stepped through the doorway and sent a disgusted look his way. "The computer at reception has locked up. . .again. You must have done something when you installed that new software. It hasn't worked decently since."

Jason held back the comment that sprang to his mind but mentally bet himself the cause would wind up listed on his records under OP: Operator Problem. Avril's lack of concern with following directions had added more than a few service hours to Millicent's bill.

"I'll be there as soon as I've finished putting this back together."

"You'll come now," Avril snapped. "You created the problem; you fix it. It's simple." She pivoted on her heel and disappeared down the hall.

Jason picked up his tools and started for the reception area. *Now there's a woman who knows exactly how good-looking she is. . . at least on the outside.* Laurel's beauty, though, shone from a place deep within her soul.

Chapter 4

After a week at Capstone, Laurel felt ready to rethink her decision. Maybe she had mistaken God's leading. How could it be His will for her to stay and share her faith in Christ with her grandmother if she never got the opportunity to do so? Millicent's time seemed to be filled with daily phone calls to Everett Keller, discussions with Garrett on maintenance and upkeep, and study sessions with Arthur.

Arthur. Laurel felt her skin crawl every time the man came near. Despite his easy manner, she sensed an undercurrent of dislike. She could think of no reason why, but the man seemed to resent her very existence. At least Avril didn't put on a hypo-critical front. Her distaste remained as obvious as it had been since the day Laurel arrived.

Thankfully, she could count on Garrett giving her a friendly greeting whenever their paths crossed, although he remained adamant about adhering to Millicent's orders not to hand out keys to the vehicles. "It would cost me my job," he told her once, when she'd resorted to outright pleading. "That's how strongly your grandmother feels about it. I'm not going to go behind her back and risk getting kicked off the place."

Laurel told herself it didn't matter. Being on the mesa provided a rare opportunity for leisure, and she couldn't take advantage of that if she went driving into town every time she took the notion. But after one straight week of enforced inactivity, she was beginning to think leisure might be an overrated commodity.

If not for Jason's company, she might have given up altogether. Their visits during his afternoon breaks had become the highlight of her days. She took a seat on the front patio just in time to see him come walking up from the direction of the guest wing.

"Hi there." His eyes lit up in the way that never failed to send her heart skittering into high gear. "Enjoying the sunshine?"

Laurel wrinkled her nose. "Do I have anything else better to do? I've spent so much time staring at the view from here, I could sketch every pebble from memory."

Jason squatted down in front of her chair and balanced on the balls of his feet. "So why not try a different view? You've got plenty to choose from. Haven't you gotten away from the buildings to do any exploring?"

Laurel squirmed. "I guess I'm just a city girl at heart. The idea of venturing off into the woods on my own spooks me a little."

"Then it's time you got better acquainted with the great outdoors." Jason rose and pulled her from her chair, then led her past the end of the flagstone walk and threaded his way through a stand of pines, oak, and juniper.

He held back a juniper branch so she could pass. "If you've

been spending all your time hanging around the center, you're missing out. This place is beautiful, especially when you get off on your own. You might come across a squirrel or a cottontail out here, but there isn't anything that could hurt you."

"It's incredible," she agreed, taking in the Indian paint-brush and clumps of baby asters. It did seem harmless out here with Jason. She pushed back thoughts of the shadowy figure she'd seen from her window. That had been at night; surely it was safe in broad daylight. She paused a moment to look back the way they had come. No one lurked behind the bushes. Nothing seemed out of place. Why, then, did she still feel as though her every move was being watched? Maybe she'd nailed it when she told Jason she was a city girl and all her jitters could be chalked up to her unfamiliarity with being face-to-face with nature.

She followed Jason for a quarter mile or so, reveling in the feeling of freedom that increased with every step she put between herself and Capstone. Why hadn't she drummed up the nerve to do this before? This wouldn't be her last time to investigate the hidden corners of the mesa, she promised herself.

The path took a downward turn, and they left the dense pines behind. Before them stood a scattering of oak trees sur-rounding a shallow pool set at the base of a rocky outcropping. Cattails swayed at the far edge, fringing a sweep of vivid green grass that angled up the slope on the other side. A humming-bird swooped down to hover for a moment over the water, then darted away.

Laurel stood wide-eyed at the unexpected glimpse of Eden. "Beautiful, isn't it?" Jason stepped behind her and rested his hands lightly on her shoulders.

"Beautiful," Laurel agreed, not sure whether she meant the captivating view or the tingle that shot through her at Jason's touch.

"I discovered it not long after I got here. It makes a nice place to take a break and refocus. I'm glad you like it."

"I like it very much." Laurel let herself lean back ever so slightly, enjoying Jason's warmth and the connection that seemed so right in this idyllic setting.

"Maybe I can show you some of my other favorite spots when I get back."

"Back?" Had the ground just shifted beneath her feet? Laurel blinked and tried to regain her balance.

"I'm afraid so." Jason gave her shoulders a light squeeze and released her. He stepped up beside her, and she could see the regret in his eyes. "A client in Kingman has a system that keeps crashing. Probably nothing more than a software conflict, but I'll be gone a day or two at least. I didn't want to leave without saying good-bye." He brushed her cheek with the backs of his fingers. "And that's a first. Usually, I can't wait to get out of here. Do you want me to walk you back?"

"I think I'll stay here a while. It's lovely." And it would give her a chance to sort out her feelings without being the target of watchful eyes. Laurel listened until the sound of Jason's footsteps faded into silence. What, if anything, had just passed between them? Surely she wasn't alone in feeling the quiver of electricity when his hands touched her skin. Jason's company had become the one thing she looked forward to each day. Was this turning into a special relationship or simply a case of both of them feeling like square pegs in round holes at Capstone?

Laurel bent to pick up a small, flat stone and sent it skimming across the surface of the pool. "Get a grip," she muttered. "It's like being stranded on a desert island. The only other person there starts looking pretty good after a while. It's a matter of proximity, nothing more." She pressed her fingertips against her cheek where the warmth of Jason's touch still lingered. *Yeah, right.*

❧

Laurel strode briskly from the house, sketch pad in hand and the strap of her digital camera looped over her wrist. Her brief excursion with Jason laid to rest her qualms about venturing into the woods on her own. She walked to the end of the path fronting the guest wing and kept going. Beyond the main buildings lay the promise of beautiful spots just waiting to be discovered, and her fingers itched to capture them on paper. The camera would record the colors for future reference. If she couldn't spend time with her grandmother, she would make sketches to use as the basis for new paintings when she went home.

She sniffed when she passed the garage, reminded of the ridiculous rule about not being able to borrow a car. There had to be a way to persuade her grandmother to let her drive one of the vehicles. Even an old work truck, if her objection stemmed from some fear Laurel would trash one of her more expensive cars.

Laurel circled around the back side of the garage and paused, trying to decide which way to go next. A jay fluttered by in a swirl of blue feathers and landed on the lowest branch of a nearby pine. Laurel watched him, captivated by the bird's bright gaze. She closed her eyes and filled her lungs with the pine-scented air. The center's buildings were filled with a dark, brooding feeling, despite the upscale decor. Outdoors, all was sunwashed brightness.

Filled with a renewed sense of optimism, she set out to the north. A few yards farther along, she spotted a small white-frame building. Laurel hesitated, then continued toward it at a slower pace, her steps crunching softly on the pine-needle carpet. Uncertainty drew her to a halt. More crunching noises sounded behind her.

Laurel gasped and whirled around. No one was there.

She gave a shaky laugh. *So much for braving the wilds alone.* She had to shake off this paranoia!

"Looking for me?" Garrett stepped out from behind a clump of juniper. Laurel yipped and leaped back, sending her sketch pad and pencils flying.

Garrett laughed and bent to help her retrieve her things. "I don't usually have this effect on women."

Heat flooded her cheeks. "And I don't usually jump and squeal like some Gothic heroine."

Garrett shook dirt from the pages of the sketch pad and brushed it off before handing it to her. "You were heading toward my cottage. I thought maybe you were coming for a visit."

Her embarrassment escalated. "I didn't mean to intrude. I was just out walking."

"Are you on your own this afternoon?"

Laurel nodded. "Again."

Garrett shot her a quick glance then smiled. "Would you like to tag along while I take care of the generator? After that I'll be free for a while, if you'd like me to show you around the mesa."

Another guided tour with someone who seemed to enjoy her company? Maybe things were looking up. "Thanks. I'd like that." She matched her pace to Garrett's long stride. It would be good to have someone to talk to...even if it wasn't Jason. *Careful. Don't let yourself get too interested.* No telling how long he'd be gone. With a client base spread across the northern half of the state, he might get another call he'd have to respond to before returning to Capstone. *Better not get too used to having him around.*

Garrett made short work of checking the dipstick and pouring a quart of oil into the oversized generator that provided the center's electrical power. He tossed the empty oil container in a nearby barrel and wiped his hands on a paper towel. "Ready for your tour?" He bowed and offered her his arm.

Laurel stifled a giggle at his courtly behavior. Tucking her sketch pad under her right arm, she placed her left hand in the crook of Garrett's elbow and strolled beside him through mingled pines, oaks, and junipers.

"Watch out for that prickly pear." Garrett steered Laurel clear of the sharp spines. "We may be up in the pines, but this is still Arizona. You'll find plenty of cactus around here."

When the way grew too narrow for them to walk side by side, Garrett stepped ahead to lead the way. The hush of the forest made conversation superfluous, and they went on in silence.

Laurel found it a challenge to keep up with Garrett's easy stride across the increasingly rugged terrain. The quiet suited her mood, giving her the opportunity to concentrate on their surroundings and soak up the atmosphere.

Garrett seemed to sense her pleasure and limited his communication to smiles and frequent appreciative glances.

Laurel caught herself smoothing her hair in response to one of his looks and chuckled at her display of vanity. *I have to admit he's good for my morale. He doesn't make any secret about liking the way I look. And he's here, not off on a job halfway across the state.*

Without warning, they stepped out of the dense growth and into an open area dotted by a sprinkling of scrubby bushes. Garrett gestured with a broad sweep of his arm, as if taking credit for the breathtaking view ahead.

Laurel's lips parted and her heart thudded slowly in her chest. Before them, the mesa came to an end, culminating in an abrupt drop-off. Beyond the ledge of bare rock stretched a broad vista of juniper-studded grassland and hills that seemed to roll on forever. A tangle of dirt roads wound like a maze across the valley below. Laurel turned her head in a slow sweep of the landscape, taking in the panoramic view.

"God really outdid Himself when He put all this together," she whispered.

Garrett moved beside her and nodded. "A man would have to be a fool not to recognize some kind of design in all this."

Laurel only smiled, but inside she shouted for joy. Learning that Jason was a fellow Christian had buoyed her spirits; hearing Garrett's words of affirmation was an unexpected bonus.

Curiosity crinkled her forehead. "How long did you say you've been working for my grandmother? Doesn't it get to be a strain?"

Garrett stared out across the wild, rugged view and shrugged. "It's a job. I do my work, and the pay is good. There's a possibility of advancement soon. I can't complain."

Memories of her deep sense of isolation swirled through her mind. "But don't you ever feel lonely?"

One corner of Garrett's mouth lifted in a crooked grin. "Who could be lonely with a beautiful woman keeping him company?"

Laurel felt a flush stain her cheeks. "That wasn't quite what I meant."

Garrett let her off with a knowing wink. "Come over here. I want you to see the view from the caprock. It's my favorite spot on the mesa." He walked toward the bare rock that rimmed the drop-off.

Laurel followed him but stopped ten feet from the edge. Garrett continued to the lip of the precipice and sat, dangling his feet over the side. The thought of nothing between him and the rocky ground two hundred feet below made Laurel's knees go weak.

Garrett swiveled around and held out his hand. "Come on over. It's safe."

"This is close enough. I don't do well with heights." The understatement of the year. Already her legs wobbled and her breath came in quick gasps.

"Take my hand," he insisted. "It won't be so bad if you're holding on to me."

Laurel summoned up all her courage and stretched her fingers out to touch his. To her surprise, the physical contact did help. Clinging to Garrett's hand, she inched her way onto the massive slab of granite until she crouched just behind him. She was still alive. So far, so good.

She sought for something to say to take her mind off the unobstructed distance between her and the valley floor. "What did you call this? The caprock?"

"Right. This thick layer of stone caps the top of this section of the mesa. So. . .it's called the caprock. I suspect that's where your grandmother got the idea for calling this place Capstone."

"And you're sure it's safe to be out on the edge like this?"

"On a day like today it is." At Laurel's questioning glance, he went on. "The granite gets slick when it's wet after a rain. Your feet will slip right out from under you, you don't want that to happen here. . .it's a long way down."

Laurel dared to lower her gaze and trace the sheer drop from their vantage point to the rocks below. A fall like that. . .well, the results didn't bear thinking about. With Garrett's muscular arm steadying her, she began to relax. The light breeze ruffled her hair, giving her the feeling of standing on the prow of a mighty ship, surveying a vast sea. Or maybe it was more like looking over the very edge of the world. In that moment, exhilaration overcame her fear. Laurel knew she would visit this spot again and again.

She looked over her shoulder, wanting to remember the route they took to get to this magical spot. To her surprise, she could see the driveway some distance away through the branches of the trees to her right. Beyond, the center's ornate front doors were clearly visible.

She glanced back at Garrett. "How did we wind up so close to the center? It seemed like we walked a lot farther than that."

"We crossed behind the main building and circled." Garrett traced a wide arc with his hand. "We did put in a lot of walking, but it's a lot more scenic to do it that way than to cut straight across."

Laurel nodded and breathed deep of the clear, pure air. She turned her back on the buildings and looked out across the broad vista. If she focused ahead on the magnificent view spread out at her feet, it was as if the center and all it represented didn't exist. For the first time since her arrival at Capstone, she felt free of the sensation that someone lurked in the shadows, watching her every move. Oh yes, she would definitely come to the caprock again.

✥

Bright afternoon sun glinted off the fallen log at the center of the scene Laurel was sketching and dazzled her eyes. She set her sketch pad to one side and stretched her arms overhead to ease the strain from her muscles. The sun's rays kissed her bare shoulders, flooding her with a wave of contentment. Laurel crossed her legs and shifted to a more comfortable position on the flat rock she had adopted as her seat at the caprock. Set back a comfortable distance from the drop-off point, the large slab of sandstone afforded her a clear view across the rolling hills. *In a fairy tale, this could be a throne. Here I sit, queen of all I survey.* She chuckled at her flight of fancy.

June in Dallas typically found her darting from air-conditioned house to air-conditioned car to air-conditioned building. Here, the higher elevation subdued the summer sun's heat. *But not its intensity.* She pressed her fingertip against her shoulder and winced at the contrast between the

white print her finger left and the bright pink skin sur-
rounding it. She reached into the tote bag beside her for a
bottle of sunscreen and slathered the soothing liquid over her
exposed skin.

Rubbing the last of the lotion into her hands, Laurel stood
and stared across the hills. The view affected her now as
strongly as the first time she'd seen it. If the sketches filling her
pad were any indication, she would have enough ideas to keep
her busy at her easel for a long time to come.

She bent at the waist and stretched her hands toward the
ground to ease the muscles in her back, then settled back on
her perch. She dug in the tote bag again, this time pulling out
her laptop. She turned the computer on and opened her mail
program. If she didn't check in soon with her galleries, she
might miss out on a potential sale. Thanks to a decent battery,
she could compose the messages now and send them later
when she'd hooked her laptop up to the satellite phone. Her
fingers tapped out a quick rhythm on the keyboard.

Footsteps rustled through the undergrowth. Laurel looked
up to see Jason striding out from the trees. A broad grin spread
across her face before she could stop herself. "Hi there," she
called. *You're not getting involved with him, remember? Wipe that
smile off your face.* Her lips refused to comply, widening even
more when Jason returned her greeting with a smile of his own.

He settled on the rock beside her. His nearness sent a
warm glow coursing through her. "Setting up your office out
here?" he quipped.

"Just catching up on a few E-mails. I'll send them once I get
online back inside." Laurel combed her fingers through her

bangs and shot a sideways glance at Jason. "I thought you were coming back two days ago." She winced the instant the words left her mouth. *Watch it. That sounded downright possessive.*

"I got another call while I was in Kingman from one of the concessionaires up at the Grand Canyon, and I had to take care of that." He flashed a smile. "I'd like to think it's the last call I'll have for a while, but computers have a way of going down during the height of tourist season. How have things been around here while I was gone?"

"Creepy."

Jason's eyes widened and Laurel hurried to explain. "I'm not sure how to describe it. Sometimes I get the feeling I'm being followed. . . ." Her words trailed off into an embarrassed chuckle. "I really don't know how to put it into words. Maybe the place is just getting to me." *Or maybe it's Avril who's getting to me. Or Arthur and his weird ideas. Or knowing that my grandmother is financing some kind of occult training center.* She waited for Jason to laugh off her uneasiness.

Instead, his expression became somber. "I knew you felt uncomfortable here. I've been concerned." He reached out to tuck a loose strand of hair behind her ear. Laurel's breath caught in her throat at the tender gesture.

Who are you kidding? Garrett might be fun to talk to, but his company didn't begin to bring her the joy Jason's did. With Jason, she felt relaxed and at peace. And he'd been thinking about her while he was gone. She stared into his smoky eyes, wondering at the intensity she saw there.

"Have you had a chance to talk to your grandmother? I've been praying for you."

Praying, too? Laurel swallowed hard before she could speak past the tightness in her throat. "I've only talked to her once or twice. Now that she knows it's a topic I want to discuss, she heads it off as soon as she sees it coming. I don't know how to reach her. I feel so inadequate." She looked up at Jason through a film of tears. "Any ideas?"

He shook his head slowly. "I'm afraid I'm fresh out. I've tried everything I can think of." He paused. "You know how, in football, a team will drop back and punt in order to gain some distance before they lose possession of the ball? Maybe what we need to do now is drop back and pray. So often, people look at that as a do-nothing cop-out, when it's really the most effective thing we can do. Maybe this is a time we need to stand back and let God work."

He pointed to her laptop. "Why not E-mail your pastor back home and see if he has any advice?" He glanced at his watch and pushed himself up off the rock. "I'm back on your grandmother's clock, so I'd better get moving. I just wanted to see you before I got caught up in work." He tapped the tip of her nose and strode off through the pines.

Laurel followed him with her gaze, not bothering to squelch the warm, fuzzy feeling that enveloped her. He'd stopped to see her even before he reported back for work. And he'd been praying. . .for her.

She picked up her laptop and opened a new message screen, wondering whether Garrett would have thought about praying for her. Doubtful, since he'd hedged every time she brought up a spiritual topic after their talk at the caprock.

Then again, her own behavior didn't always mirror her

commitment to the Lord. Who was she to judge?

She typed a brief message to her pastor, outlining the situation at Capstone and asking for suggestions. She would send it, along with her messages to the galleries, as soon as she could hook up her computer to the phone inside.

Feeling lighter knowing she could expect his response, she put the laptop back in her tote bag and flipped open the sketch pad. Her first thoughts of painting the view from the caprock had grown into a bigger plan. This vista was too big for one landscape to do it justice. She would break the setting down into smaller components and do a whole series of studies: the pines and broken rocks close at hand, the sweeping panorama to the north, maybe several views of the caprock itself.

She picked up her pencil with renewed enthusiasm, feeling more at peace than she had in a long time.

Chapter 5

Laurel pushed back the eyelet curtains to let the sunlight flood her bedroom. Filtered light this time, since a bank of clouds had rolled in from the west to screen the sky. Flopping down across the comforter, she propped her chin on one hand and opened her sketch pad to review the drawings she'd been working on. She flipped from one page to another, excitement mounting as she envisioned the series of paintings. Maybe the summer wouldn't turn out to be a total loss after all.

The cloud cover thickened, dimming the light further. Laurel reached out to pull the lamp closer and switched it on. She traced its surface with her fingers, drawing comfort from the familiar contours. It might not be the same lamp Delia had kept in their living room, but its shape evoked a sense of connection with her mother. The same curves, the same smooth grain. . .

Laurel's hand stilled and she probed the irregularity her fingers had just encountered. She scooted around so her back rested against the headboard and drew the lamp into her lap for a closer examination.

The lamps weren't identical after all. She ran her fingertips over the crack hidden in the design of the carved wooden base. *Maybe the wood dried and split?* No, the fracture was too regular for that. She turned the lamp on its side and peered at the rectangle formed by the thin fissure more closely. It might be a spot where the lamp had broken and been repaired. Or. . .

Laurel wedged her fingernails into the crevice and tugged gently. Nothing changed as far as she could see, but she thought she felt a slight give. Thoroughly intrigued, she bounded from the bed to dig through her cosmetic bag and returned with a sturdy metal fingernail file. She inserted it into the crack and pulled against the wood, giving the file a slight twist at the same time. A panel slid to one side, revealing a rectangular opening.

Laurel blinked. Why would anyone want to hollow out a lamp? On impulse, she reached inside the narrow space. Her heart quickened when her fingers touched a solid form. Tightening her grasp on the object, she drew it out.

A small leather-bound book lay in her hand. Laurel turned it over. No title appeared on the cover or the spine. *Odd.*

The book wasn't new. She could tell that at a glance. But neither did it have the appearance of great age. If she had to guess, she'd place it somewhere between twenty-five and thirty years old, which would make it. . . *No, it couldn't be.* Still, if the furnishings once belonged to her mother. . . With the feeling she stood on the brink of discovery, she opened the cover.

Delia Reed's Diary.

Laurel stared at the words, her emotions rioting at the sight of her mother's girlish handwriting. How long did her mother keep the diary? Did this small book hold the key that would unlock the questions that plagued her? With trembling fingers, she turned the first page.

Laurel looked at the starting date and calculated. Her mother would have been twelve years old when she began this. Laurel tried to conjure up a mental picture of her mother at that age. Blond, of course, probably going into a preadolescent growth spurt that would result in her becoming the tall, graceful woman Laurel remembered. She smiled at the image her mind produced: a coltish figure, all knobby knees and gangly limbs.

Laurel bunched the pillows behind her back and began to read the youthful musings on first crushes and slumber parties. To all appearances, Delia had experienced the roller coaster of emotions typical of a young girl's life.

She continued through the pages—rhapsodies over an A in history, frantic worry over her mother's reaction to a C in algebra. Laurel thought back to her own efforts at keeping a journal. Her mother showed significantly more ability to stick with it than she had at that age. A few entries later, she came to a series of blank pages and smiled. Apparently even Delia's tenacity had its limits.

She reached out to set the little volume on the nightstand, but it slipped from her grasp and landed on the floor. When she reached to retrieve it, the diary lay open to a later page covered with writing. Laurel picked up the book and scrutinized this new find. From the more mature appearance of the penmanship, Laurel guessed several years had elapsed between the first set of entries and this one. Why had her mother taken up her journal again after abandoning it for so long? She plumped the pillows into a more comfortable shape and bent over the pages again.

> *Here I am again, my old friend. I set you aside long ago, thinking I'd grown too old for girlish confidences. Now I find myself in need of a friend once more. I found you waiting in my trunk, faithful as ever after all these years. There is no one else around here I can trust. Sometimes I look behind me, feeling as though someone watches every move I make. To be sure what I write stays just between us, I have made a new home for you in my bedside lamp. I'll tuck you away for now and write more tomorrow.*

A chill teased its way up the back of Laurel's neck. It was as though her mother described the very feelings she'd experienced ever since coming to Capstone. She turned the page and read on.

> *Mother pushes me away more with each passing day.*

Laurel blinked. So much for the notion she'd gotten a cold shoulder because she didn't resemble her mother. Apparently Delia herself hadn't fared much better.

> *It all seemed to start when she started reading those weird books and attending spiritual seminars. I can't put my finger on anything wrong with them, but they don't hold the same fascination for me. The wall between us seems to grow higher and stronger all the time.*

"I know just how you feel." Laurel swallowed hard. Not since her mother died had she felt such an intense bond.

Mother is talking about adding on to our house and turning it into some kind of center—a "learning facility" she calls it—where people can come to renew their minds and spirits. I ought to be pleased, I guess, since it makes her happy. But if it brings in more of the same type of people she's had staying around the place lately, with all their new ideas. . .

Laurel lifted her gaze and stared at a point on the opposite wall. So her mother felt uncomfortable about the center from the start. Was that the reason for the rift between her and Millicent?

It's official. Our home is going to be transformed into the Capstone Center for Spiritual Studies. The contractor comes tomorrow to finalize the plans for the new addition and supervise the project. I wish I could be as thrilled as Mother. Maybe she's right and I'm being selfish.

"No, Mom. Just smart." Laurel skimmed the following pages, surprised when the next few entries took on a lighter tone.

The contractor arrived last Friday, and what a surprise he turned out to be! I expected someone with a middle-aged paunch and wearing a hard hat. Well, the hard hat is there, but he isn't middle-aged and there's

*certainly no paunch. He looks like he's more used to working
out than reading blueprints. But he knows his business.
Mother seems to approve of Ray Masters, and I know I do.*

Laurel read the last line again, slowly. Ray Masters. *Dad
was the contractor?* So that was how her parents met! Another
piece in the puzzle of her family's past slipped into place.

She bent over the pages again, anxious to soak up every
drop of new information. She held her breath when her
mother described the thrill she felt when her gaze met that of
the young contractor, and the electric tingle that ran between
them the first time their hands touched.

"The same way I feel when Jason is around." Laurel leaned
her head back against the pillow and pondered the parallels.
Her parents met at Capstone; she met Jason at Capstone.
Coincidence or precedent? Laurel reined in her wandering
imagination. The future would have to see to itself. Right now
her attention was absorbed by the past.

I went out to the caprock today,

the journal continued. Laurel felt yet another link. It was one
thing to know her mother spent years of her life at Capstone,
quite another to know she also visited the place that held such
a fascination for Laurel.

*When I got there, I found Ray sitting in my favorite
spot, reading. He looked so comfortable, I didn't want to
disturb him. But he heard me and asked me to come sit*

with him. Of all things, it turned out he was reading a Bible. I've never known anybody who looked at one outside of a church. He told me what he'd been reading, and he made it sound like he was talking about people he knew. Mother's seminar leaders talk about spirituality all the time, but Ray brings God to a personal level. When he talks about Jesus, it's like he's talking about his best friend. I want to hear more, and I want him to talk to Mother. She needs to hear about Jesus, too. I could listen to Ray talk forever. What do you think, my friend? Could I be falling in love?

A loud knock rattled the door, and Laurel jumped, knocking the book askew. Before she could say anything, Avril opened the door and stuck her head inside the room.

Avril's mouth puckered as though she'd been sucking on a persimmon. "Aunt Millicent wants to see you."

Laurel scrambled to her feet. "Right now?"

"More like five minutes ago. If I were you, I'd freshen up and get out there in a hurry. Aunt Millicent doesn't like to be kept waiting." She withdrew her head and pulled the door closed with a loud *thud*.

Irritation welled up. After all the time she'd been there, *now* her grandmother wanted to see her. *Take it easy. This journal has been waiting to share its secrets for years. A few minutes more won't make any difference.*

She started to set the journal on the nightstand, then she glanced at the lamp. She didn't like the idea of leaving the diary lying out in the open where prying eyes might spot it. *Prying eyes? Oh, brother. Maybe I am being paranoid.*

But Avril hadn't hesitated about pushing the door open when she knew Laurel was in her room. What would she—or any of them—do if they knew the room was unoccupied?

She slid the little book back into its spot in the lamp's base. The panel slid shut with a reassuring *click*.

⤜⊹⤛

"You wanted to see me?"

Her grandmother looked up from behind her ornate desk and waved Laurel to a nearby chair. "I've just been on the phone with Everett Keller. You seem to have made quite an impression on him." The look she gave Laurel gave clear indication that for the life of her, she couldn't understand why. "Everett feels you have great potential. He is willing to hold a study here, just for the three of us."

A stirring of unease danced along Laurel's spine. "What would we be studying?"

"Everett has gained some unique insights into the Bible and wants to share them with us. It's a rare opportunity, one I'm sure you won't want to miss."

"A Bible study?" Laurel spirits rose. "That would be wonderful. I had no idea Mr. Keller was a Bible teacher."

Her grandmother sniffed. "Don't make him sound like some backward pulpit pounder. Everett is far more enlightened than that. He is a highly sought-after lecturer and endorses a few select learning centers. Capstone is proud to be among them."

Help, Lord, another wacko! "Grandmother," she said gently, "I would love to study the Bible with you." She flinched at the flicker of triumph in the older woman's eyes. "But I'd like it to be just the two of us."

60

Her grandmother drew herself erect. "You dare to compare your knowledge to that of one of the most renowned experts in spiritual matters?"

"The Bible is God's love letter to man. It's meant to be studied by all people, not just a select few." Laurel's passion for God's Word gave her the courage to ask, "How much of the Bible have you actually read yourself? You might find more within its covers than you'd ever expect."

Her grandmother stared at her for a long moment. "I'll tell Everett he needn't bother to come. You're obviously too closed minded to benefit from his teaching." She waved her hand in a dismissive gesture.

Back in her room, Laurel went straight to her nightstand and pried open the panel in the lamp. She couldn't ignore the parallels between her mother's time at Capstone and the events unfolding now. More than ever, she wanted to know the rest of her mother's story.

She pulled the small book from its place of concealment and riffled through the pages. Finding the place where she left off, she skimmed the pages quickly. The chemistry between the young couple fairly leaped off the pages, even after the interval of years. Laurel blushed along with her mother when she wrote of her growing attraction to the handsome contractor and wanted to cheer when Ray's sharing of his faith bore fruit and Delia Reed turned her life over to Christ.

That elation quickly turned to despair when Delia related her attempts to share her newfound faith with her mother.

I asked Ray to talk to Mother today, and I prayed the whole time they were together. Prayed that she would see the truth instead of the lies the others have been feeding her.

Laurel caught herself praying right along with the young Delia and laughed in spite of her growing tension. Obviously her grandmother hadn't been swayed by her father's words, but what did happen? She continued reading.

What happened next was so ugly I can hardly bear to write about it. Mother listened politely. . .up until Ray pointed out the verse that says Jesus is the only way to heaven. She argued that there are many paths to God, but Ray stood his ground. For the first time I can remember, Mother lost control. Her whole body shook. Even her voice trembled. She pointed her finger right in Ray's face and said, "I won't have a common laborer filling my head with that kind of narrow-minded negativity. Keep those poisonous thoughts to yourself, or I'll find another contractor."

I couldn't stand it anymore. I got between them and told her she was wrong. You should have seen her face! I don't think anyone ever told her that before—certainly not her daughter. I begged her to listen to Ray again and told her how I'd come to know the truth, that I belong to Jesus now, and all because of Ray. Then she started screaming. She told Ray she would have no more of his tainting influence, that he was fired as of that minute.

Ray didn't argue. I was beside myself. "If he goes, I go," I told her. "I love him, Mother."

Her face twisted when she turned to look at me. "No daughter of mine is going to align herself with such small-minded bigotry. If you leave the mesa, don't plan on coming back."

A droplet fell on the page and Laurel realized she had been sobbing without knowing it. Her mother's anguished state of mind lay evident in the handwriting on the next page, where jagged scrawls slashed across the paper instead of her usual neat script.

I'm leaving tonight with Ray. We'll go after everyone has gone to bed to keep from having to endure another scene. The hardest part is knowing I can never come back here. Mother made that clear enough. She hates Ray and she wants no part of Christ. And I can't give up either one.

I must pack now so I can grab my things quickly when the time comes. I'll put you back in your hiding place, dear friend, but I'll come back to take you with me when I leave. You are all I'll have left of childhood memories.

The rest of the pages were blank. Laurel closed the book slowly and held it against her chest, trying to picture her mother's hurried flight back to her room to gather her belongings. Had she been elated, or terrified, or both?

Apparently, she had been too rushed to retrieve her cherished diary. What could have happened during those last fleeting moments before she left the mesa forever? Laurel squeezed her eyelids shut and felt a warm tear course down her cheek. She would never know.

She cradled the diary in her arms and rocked back and forth as if comforting a child. After a moment, she set the diary aside and picked up the photo of her parents. She stared at her mother's image. "So that's why you kept me from her all these years," she whispered. "I understand now, Mom. I understand."

She saw the difference between her mother's upbringing and her own with poignant clarity. All her life her parents showered her with love and acceptance. No matter what she did, her mother would never have turned her away. Laurel wept, grieving for the young Delia and the choice thrust upon her. What a price she'd been forced to pay!

A price paid by everyone involved. Unexpected sympathy for her grandmother welled up inside Laurel. What would it be like to live with the knowledge that your words had driven your only child away forever? Laurel could only imagine what her grandmother must have endured through all those lonely years, wondering where Delia had gone, what she was doing, whether they would ever see each other again. What a shock it must have been to finally discover Delia's whereabouts, only to learn that her daughter had died.

"No wonder she sent for me." Laurel voiced the thought aloud. "It was her chance to reconnect and make amends."

No, that wouldn't work. There had been plenty of opportunities for them to mend that breach, and her grandmother had avoided them all. Laurel's throat tightened. Her grandmother had hardened her heart once years ago. Was it too hardened now to respond to the gospel?

"Don't let that be the case, Lord. I'll try harder. I'm the only link she has left between the past and the present."

Chapter 6

After breakfast the next morning, Laurel followed her grandmother into the gathering room. "Do you have a minute? I'd like to talk to you."

Her grandmother hesitated, then lowered herself onto one of the chairs.

"I have something for you." Laurel reached into her canvas tote and pulled out her mother's Bible. "I thought you might need a Bible of your own to read. This belonged to my mother. I think she'd want you to have it." She pressed it into her grandmother's hands, praying the connection with the daughter she'd lost would help begin to heal old wounds.

Her grandmother rubbed her fingers across the leather binding and lowered her gaze. Laurel covered one of the blue-veined hands with her own. "I can't imagine what it was like for you after she left. It must have been so hard, not knowing where she was all that time." Emotion thickened in her throat. "And then when you did find out, and realized she was gone. . ."

"But I did know."

Laurel blinked. "You what?"

Her grandmother raised her head and faced Laurel with a steely gaze. "I knew where she was. Where all of you were. Do you think I would just let her slip away? I knew every move she made from the moment she left."

Laurel wagged her head from side to side, trying to make sense of what she'd just heard. "You mean you knew when my parents got married, and when I was born?"

"October 14, three years after their wedding." The answer came without hesitation. "At least I didn't have to wonder whether they eloped because she was pregnant."

Laurel dragged air into her lungs. "All those years, you knew I existed. And you never so much as sent me a birthday card? You knew when I graduated, and when I went to college? And when my father died?"

Another thought struck her. Laurel felt her throat constrict even further, sending her voice to a reedy pitch. "You knew about my mother's illness? That she and I were going through that horrible time. . .all alone?" She choked back a sob. "And you never bothered to tell her good-bye?"

Millicent compressed her lips into a thin line. "Your mother abandoned me. I made it my business to know where she was. I wanted to be prepared if she ever decided to come crawling back." High color suffused her cheeks, and she jabbed a trembling finger at Laurel. "Never forget that she is the one who walked out, the one who made the decision to sneak off in the dark of night despite her so-called Christian scruples. She abandoned me!"

"How could you—" Bitter thoughts cartwheeled through Laurel's mind, but she couldn't allow them past her lips. She wheeled and bolted toward the family wing door. Behind her, she heard her grandmother calling for Avril.

She collided with her cousin in the doorway. "What's wrong with Aunt Millicent?" Avril demanded. "What did you do to upset her?" Without waiting for an answer, she shoved Laurel aside and ran to the gathering room.

Laurel pushed herself up off the mattress with unsteady arms. The comforter lay on the floor in a twisted heap. Damp splotches dotted the sheet where she sobbed out her grief for the past hour. But all the tears in the world wouldn't assuage her pain. She needed wise counsel; she needed Jason.

She ran her fingers through her hair and winced when they caught in the tangled mass. Stumbling to the bathroom, she reached for her hairbrush and moaned when she glanced in the mirror. She couldn't go to Jason now. She couldn't bear for him to see her blotchy cheeks and puffy skin, not to mention the raw pain still written in her eyes.

Back in the bedroom, she reached for her laptop. She could still make contact with the outside world and no one had to witness her disheveled appearance.

She opened a new message file and typed in Pastor Ron's address. He hadn't responded to her first message yet, but she wouldn't worry about that now. More than anything, she needed to share what was going on with someone who would understand and care.

Wait. When was the last time she'd checked her mail? Maybe a message was waiting for her right now. The modem made its familiar high-pitched squeal as it connected with her Internet server.

Sure enough, her inbox showed two new messages. She recognized the first sender's address as one of the galleries she'd written to. She opened the message.

> *Congratulations! We sold two more of your landscapes. You can expect payment within the week.*

Laurel typed out a quick note of thanks and clicked SEND. She glanced at the second message. Instead of Pastor Ron's name, she saw an unfamiliar address.

Her finger hovered over the DELETE button, but she pulled it back. It might be a query from a potential buyer. She clicked on the message to open it.

> *Life is short. Don't make yours shorter. Stay out of matters that don't concern you.*

Laurel stared at the screen, willing the words to rearrange themselves into a normal, friendly message. An icy wave of dread numbed her body. She sprang up and headed down the hall. Blotchy face or not, she had to find Jason.

"Take it easy." Jason cupped her shoulders and pulled her to him. "Let's step back and look at this from an objective point of view."

Laurel let herself relax in the shelter of his arms. He hadn't commented on her bedraggled appearance when she burst into the office where he was working and started babbling about death threats. She drew a deep breath and let her tension float out in a long sigh, enjoying the softness of his shirt against her cheek. Somehow, the danger that threatened seemed to dissipate when Jason was around.

"You really don't think there's any reason to worry?"

He stroked her hair and cradled her head against his chest. "I think you've had a bad time of it ever since you got here. You've been rebuffed, ignored, and treated like a non-person. Plus, you've had those feelings of being watched. No wonder something like this spooked you."

Laurel pulled away far enough to look into his face. "It sounded serious enough to me."

Jason's eyes glowed with sympathy. "That's understandable. But I suspect it's just someone's sick idea of a joke. That doesn't mean it's from anyone who knows you. More than likely, somebody picked you at random, or sent out a mass mailing to a number of addresses, hoping to create a stir."

"Like an anonymous poison pen letter?" Laurel turned the thought over in her mind, finding comfort in the idea. So much easier to deal with that than think she might have been targeted deliberately. Jason must be right. Who in her circle of acquaintances would do such a thing? No one back home, but. . .

"Could it be from somebody here at Capstone?"

He pursed his lips. "It could be. But then, it could have come from anywhere on the planet. How about if I try to track down the sender? No guarantees, but if I can, it'll give you some peace of mind. I'll get the sender's address from your laptop when I'm finished here."

"Thank you. That would be a huge relief." Laurel stepped

back, feeling the weight of worry lift from her shoulders. "I'll let you get back to work now. Sorry for making a mountain out of a molehill."

The comfort of Jason's protectiveness lingered with her. With him she felt safe, special. She wondered if this was the way her mother felt when she fell in love with her father. And whether Jason could possibly return her feelings.

Jason tried to keep his mind focused on directing a spray of compressed air inside the computer he was working on rather than dwelling on how it felt to hold Laurel in his arms. The memory of the silky touch of her hair under his fingers made him long to have her lean against him again. He caught himself spraying air on the monitor screen instead of blowing dust out of the computer's insides. *Better keep your mind on what you're doing.* Had she come because she trusted him, or because she was scared? Would anyone else have filled the bill equally well. . .Garrett Harper perhaps? The thought set his teeth on edge.

His fingers checked connections automatically while his thoughts raced ahead, working out possible steps to identify who sent that E-mail. Regardless of how he'd minimized his concern to allay Laurel's fears, he didn't like the situation one bit.

Laurel logged on to her E-mail account to check for Pastor Ron's reply one more time. She tried to laugh off her squeamishness at touching the laptop.

You want to know if he answered, don't you? There's only one way to find out.

A dialogue box popped open: *Receiving 1 of 2 messages.* The new messages appeared at the bottom of her inbox.

Laurel's fingers froze on the keyboard. The address on both was the same as the threatening note from before. "It's a random prank," she whispered. "Random, not personal." She clicked on the first message to open it.

> *So you've sold another painting. Congratulations.*
> *Now you have enough money to go back home.*

"That isn't random." Mind reeling, she pressed the NEXT button to open the second message.

> *Where is Pastor Ron when you need him? You want*
> *advice? Let me give you some: Pack your bags and leave.*
> *The sooner the better.*

Laurel felt the blood drain from her face, and the screen blurred before her eyes. "He read my mail. How could he do that?" Thoroughly unnerved, she tucked the laptop under her arm and rushed to find Jason again.

Jason slid the last screwdriver back into its slot in his tool case. He snapped the case shut at the same moment the door slammed open and Laurel burst in, wide eyed. She held out her laptop and thrust it toward him.

He caught the computer before she could drop it. "Whoa, what's going on? I was going to check for that address later."

"He knows me. He knows who I am!" White ringed the

irises of Laurel's eyes like a frightened filly's.

"What makes you— You mean you got another one?"

Laurel bobbed her head, her breath coming in frantic gasps. "I checked my mail again. Just now, to see if there was a message from my pastor. There were two more from the same person. They talked about an E-mail I received and another one I sent. Don't you see? He had to have read my messages somehow. He knows who I am!"

Worry settled over Jason like a dark cloud. He took Laurel by the shoulders and pulled her to him for the second time that day. *What's going on here, Lord?* He slid his hands up and down her arms, trying to rub warmth back into her trembling body.

He felt, rather than heard, her tiny whimper and fought to keep her sense of panic from infecting him.

"Okay, settle down." He cupped his fingers under Laurel's chin and tilted her head up to face him. The pleading in her eyes made him ready to take on any foe. "It looks like somebody's playing at a higher level than I thought, but that's no reason to panic yet. He's managed to get access to your computer, but that may be nothing more than the kind of prank kids pull when they pick a name at random from a phone book. They make a few harassing calls, then move on to someone else. Chances are this person—whoever it is—will do the same."

The fear in Laurel's eyes faded, to be replaced by a gleam of anger. "This is more than a prank!"

Thanks, Lord. Anger is better than fear. He brushed his lips against her forehead. "Let me see what I can find. I won't stop until we figure out who this is or find a way to stop him, I promise."

Laurel probed his gaze with hers and then nodded. "How long do you think it will take? Will you know something by tomorrow?"

Uh-oh. Jason had hoped he wouldn't have to drop that little bomb just yet. He gave her shoulders a quick squeeze. "There's something I need to tell you. I got another call from my customer at the Grand Canyon. I have to leave right after lunch, but I expect to be back tomorrow afternoon." He saw panic well up in her eyes again and took both her hands in his. "Remember, this guy operates through E-mail. He could be anywhere from Texas to Thailand. It isn't like it's someone within arm's reach who could do you physical harm. You'll be okay."

Reaching for his wallet, he pulled out a business card and scribbled a number on the back. "Here's the number for my cell phone. If anything else happens, if you feel uneasy in any way, call me. And try not to worry. We'll get to the bottom of this."

Laurel hugged her laptop to her chest all the way back to her room. Halfway there, she paused and turned. She could go back right now and ask Jason to take her with him. Her feet took two steps in that direction, then she stopped and turned back toward the family wing. She wasn't a child. Besides, where would she go once she got off the mesa? She could hardly expect to tag along with Jason while he worked.

I could go back to Dallas. The thought stopped her in her tracks. All she needed to do was get to Pulliam Airport. From there, it would simply be a matter of catching the next flight to Phoenix, and then home. The thought tantalized her. But leaving Capstone meant leaving Jason, and that idea left her feeling as desolate as a desert landscape.

Brace up. You'll see him again tomorrow.

In the meantime, she could pray about leaving and bring that possibility up when Jason got back. . .if she decided to bring it up at all.

Chapter 7

He's gone. Laurel sorted through her drawings, re-grouping them to find the best combination for the series of paintings she planned, all the while trying to ignore the fact that Jason's absence left a void in her heart the size of the Grand Canyon.

Why hadn't she gone with him? She'd asked herself the same question repeatedly in the hours since he left. But she knew the answer. Since discovering her mother's journal, she recognized the similarities between their situations. Once again, her life seemed to be playing out in parallel with her mother's story. With her grandmother still so bitter about Delia's supposed abandonment, wouldn't she see Laurel's sudden departure in the same light?

She had to stick it out. Staying here might make a differ-ence in her grandmother's life—an eternal difference.

She tried to reassure herself that the sender could be some-one across the country or on the other side of the world, but to no avail. Despite Jason's belief that the messages came from someone who didn't know her personally, she wondered if her cyberstalker could be someone at Capstone. The reason for anyone wanting to frighten her in such a nasty way still eluded her, but did a stalker need a reason for what he did?

A stalker. She'd heard the term before, but never realized the implications, the incredibly vulnerable feeling its victim would have, never knowing when she might be under observation. Why, even now. . . *Stop it!*

Her mind turned back to the inhabitants of Capstone. Avril and Arthur both showed signs of enmity. When it came right down to it, even her grandmother's attitude might bear watching. For that matter, how much did she know about Garrett or Jason? Jason undoubtedly had the computer skills to gain access to her E-mail. She had no evidence to point to any of them, she reminded herself. On the other hand, she didn't have reason to exclude any of them from suspicion. The knowledge made her feel even more isolated than before.

She stacked the drawings on her dresser, then headed outdoors, unable to bear being shut up inside the center a moment longer. Taking a shortcut through the trees, she soon found herself at her favorite spot on the caprock. The brisk walk and fresh air cleared her mind and refreshed her spirit. Seating herself on the flat rock, she bowed her head and tried to pray away her confusion.

A twig snapped nearby and she jerked upright, every sense alert. When no one appeared, she chided herself for her jumpiness but found it impossible to relax again. She stared at the dark wall of clouds overhead and started when a spear of lightning streaked across the afternoon sky. *I won't have to worry about a stalker if I get struck by lightning. But that doesn't sound like the best answer, does it, Lord?* The heavens opened, unleashing a driving rain, and Laurel ran for shelter.

She stood dripping on the mat inside the front door, trying to decide how to get to her room without tracking water across the floor. Garrett entered from the guest wing and bit back a chuckle when he saw her.

Laurel glared at him. "I know, I look like a drowned rat. I thought Arizona was supposed to be dry."

Garrett's lips twitched. "It generally is, except for monsoon season."

"Monsoons? I thought those happened in India, or maybe on tropical islands."

He grinned. "And in Arizona. It'll rain every afternoon for a while now, and we're grateful for it. That accounts for most of the moisture we'll get this year." He reached behind the reception counter and pulled out a towel. "Here, that'll soak up enough of the water till you can get back to your room and dry off."

❧

In the privacy of her bathroom, Laurel squeezed the water from her hair and toweled her head dry. Amazing how soggy a person could get in just a few minutes. She tossed her sodden floral print shirt and blue capris across the shower curtain rod and pulled on a fresh outfit. By the time she finished, the storm had passed.

What to do next? The ground outside was too damp for walking, and she had no one to talk to. Laurel glanced at her laptop, curious yet fearful. Would there be another message? Curiosity overrode her trepidation. She downloaded her mail, feeling a leaden weight in the pit of her stomach when the now-familiar address appeared.

> *If you stay here, it'll take more than prayer to keep you safe.*

The top of a photograph stretched across the screen. Laurel scrolled down to bring the whole photo into view. A woman sat outdoors, her head bowed in prayer. The familiar view from the caprock showed clearly in the background. Laurel's hand flew to her mouth. "Oh dear Lord, it's me."

She peered closely at the screen, trying to determine when the picture was taken. She noted the heavy clouds that cast a shadow across the rock where she sat, and her outfit, a floral print shirt and blue capris. A sour taste filled her mouth. The same outfit she'd taken off only moments before. The picture had to have been taken that very afternoon.

She slammed the top of the laptop shut. How could anyone come close enough to photograph her without her knowing? She recounted her movements, remembered sitting on the rock, then bowing her head. . .and the snapping twig she had chalked up to an overactive imagination.

But she hadn't imagined it. She now had tangible proof that someone at Capstone was behind the E-mails. She dashed out her door and down the hall, frantic for someone to talk to. By the time she reached the gathering room, she realized there wasn't a single person in the place she could trust.

"Where is Jason's card?" She hurried back to her room and scrambled through the stack of papers on the dresser until she found it, then picked up the phone and punched in Jason's number.

One ring. Two rings. *Click.* "The customer you are trying to reach is not available at this time. Please leave your message after the tone."

Laurel hesitated, then pressed the OFF button. What she needed to tell Jason was too involved to condense into a recorded message. Still, she needed to let him know what was happening. Wherever he stopped for the night, surely he would check his E-mail. She scooped up her laptop and pressed the ON button. Nothing happened.

She tried again, and again, with no result.

What did I do, Lord? Did I break it, shutting it so hard? She lifted the laptop again and frowned. It seemed a bit lighter than normal. She turned the machine over. The open battery slot stared at her like an empty eye socket.

Laurel set the laptop down and backed away, wishing she could deny the obvious: The stalker had moved out of cyberspace and into her room. *How? When?* Whoever it was had to be watching closely to know when she left her room and took that brief opportunity to remove the battery. Watching where—through her window? From one of the rooms across the hall?

"I've got to get out of here." *But how?* The impossibility of escape struck her like a physical blow.

Think! Was there any way to get access to one of the cars? She discarded the idea as quickly as it popped into her mind. The only keys were in her grandmother's and Garrett's possession. Besides, if she did manage to find a key, she had no idea how to get back to civilization. The tangle of rough dirt roads she'd seen from the caprock threaded across the land-scape and wound off into the distance, with none looking any more well traveled than another. This wasn't like the city. There were no friendly signs to point her way. It would be impossible to tell which route led where.

She couldn't leave, not yet. It was as simple as that. As soon as Jason came back, she would ask him to take her away, that very moment. As for tonight. . .

She put her shoulder against the dresser and shoved. The heavy piece resisted at first, then slid across the polished wood floor in a burst of shrill squeaks until it rested in front of the door.

Now you're really acting like a heroine in a Gothic novel. You do realize that you're going to have to move it again in the morning? It didn't matter. Nothing mattered but establishing a sense of security. No one would be coming in through that door tonight.

What about the window? She whirled and looked at the rest of the furniture. Nothing in the room would be tall enough to block the glass. A weapon. She needed something she could use if she had to defend herself. She ran to the closet and wrenched the rod loose. Her clothing spilled on the floor. She didn't bother to pick it up. It could stay there until morning.

Laurel climbed onto her bed and sat atop the covers with the closet rod at the ready. There would be no sleep for her that night.

Chapter 8

"Are you all finished eating?" Millicent Reed swept the lunch table with a regal gaze. "If so, you may be excused. I'd like to talk to my granddaughter."

The room cleared as if by royal decree. Laurel pushed back her chair and started to rise before she realized her grandmother meant for her to stay. A sleepless night left her brain feeling like it had been stuffed with cotton batting. *Not now. I don't want another confrontation when I can't think straight.*

"Could this wait?" she began.

"It cannot." Her grandmother beckoned her to the head of the table. "I want to make you an offer. Call it a business proposition, if you like." She folded her hands in her lap and leaned forward. "Despite your unwillingness to study under him, Everett feels you have great spiritual potential, and I agree. I would like you to consider making Capstone your home."

Laurel stared, unable to form an answer.

"I realize we have had our differences, but knowing your upbringing, I am willing to overlook a great deal. I have high aspirations for this center and I don't have enough time left to see them all fulfilled. If you will stay and agree to run the center after I'm gone, I will leave all my estate to you."

"But I—"

Her grandmother pushed back her chair and rose. "I will give you until tomorrow to make up your mind. This means you will have to become more tolerant of views other than your own, but I am sure you can overcome your prejudices, given the right incentive." She exited the room with stately grace.

Laurel gaped at the closing door. In her wildest dreams, she had never considered anything as bizarre as this. Did her grandmother honestly think the promise of wealth could entice her to compromise her faith?

She started toward the opposite door and heard footsteps scuttling away. Who had been listening this time? It didn't matter. She was thoroughly sick of all of them. As soon as Jason got back, she would shake the dust of Capstone off her feet.

As soon as Jason got back. . . Unable to sit and wait, Laurel paced the flagstone walkway until she thought she would wear a groove in the pavement. Another round of rain drove her back inside, where she prowled the gathering room and the hallways.

Rain poured down upon the roof and spattered against the windows. At any other time, Laurel would have welcomed its steady rhythm; today the sound grated on her nerves until they felt like a raw mass. The bright spot that marked the sun's location behind the curtain of clouds sank lower in the west, and a deepening gloom settled over the mesa. And still no Jason.

By the time the rain stopped and shadows began to lengthen, Laurel resigned herself to the fact that Jason wouldn't be arriving that night. Dejected, she retreated to the sanctuary of her room. Her mind was too on edge to let her sleep, but her body felt on the verge of collapse. She could at least lie down and give herself a chance to rest.

With a weary sigh, she pulled back the comforter and a scream caught in her throat.

Atop the pillowcase lay another photo. Laurel picked it up gingerly and held it closer, staring at the image of herself standing on the sheltered front porch looking out into the rain. She glanced at the picture, then down at herself where she saw the same dark jeans and T-shirt, the sleeves of the same navy sweatshirt tied around her waist. The picture couldn't have been taken more than an hour ago.

Hot bile scalded the back of her throat. Whoever took and printed out the photo had also taken time to draw a bright red *X* across her face.

"That's it. I'm leaving now." Jason or no Jason, she couldn't stay a moment longer. Praying she hadn't stayed too long already, she fumbled for the phone and punched in Jason's number. *Please, God, please let him answer.* One ring. Two. Three. Laurel's grip tightened on the handset when she heard Jason's voice.

Panic sent her voice an octave higher than normal. "Jason, it's me—"

"I'm not available right now, but I'll get back to you as quickly as possible."

Laurel placed her thumb on the OFF button, then held back. At this point, the details didn't matter. "Jason, it's Laurel. Things have gotten really bad. Whoever's sending those E-mails is here on the mesa. . .and I think they want to kill me. I'm leaving now.

I'll call you as soon as I get to another phone. Pray I make it out of here." After pressing the OFF button, she continued to hold the phone like a lifeline, her mind in a whirl.

The time for waiting was past. She had to act now. Laurel glanced outside and pulled the navy sweatshirt over her head. With that and her dark jeans, she would blend fairly well into the shadows. She cast a longing glance at her sketches but left them where they lay.

Is this how you felt the night you left, Mom? How many things besides your journal did you have to leave behind?

She crept down the hallway and pushed the door to the gathering room open a mere crack. Seeing no one, she slipped across to the front door and out into the gathering dusk.

Which way? Garrett's cottage, she decided. He would be making his evening rounds now. If she could get inside and find the key to a vehicle, she would take it and flee without looking back. Even if she got lost once off the mesa, she would be free of this place and the nightmare that went with it.

She rounded the corner of the main building and made her way toward the cottage, flitting from shadow to shadow. Only a few more yards. . .

Oh, no. She felt it again, that prickle on the back of her neck as though someone watched her from behind. She froze and listened, every muscle tense.

She heard it then. Footsteps, coming from somewhere behind her. Without hesitation, Laurel left the path and took cover in a clump of young oaks. She held her breath, waiting for the person to pass by.

Instead of striding past, the footsteps slowed, and then

turned in her direction. Laurel edged behind the oaks and slipped away, thankful for the damp oak leaves that deadened the sound of her flight. To her horror, the footsteps followed.

Running now, Laurel stumbled through the increasing dimness, slapping at the branches that tore at her clothes. *What's that up ahead?* She sobbed with relief when she recognized the dark shape as a huge fallen log. Like a hare pursued by hounds, she dove behind its bulk, curled up into a tiny ball, and settled down to wait.

Where is he? She strained to listen for the footsteps, but heard only water dripping off the trees. Long minutes passed. *I must have lost whoever it was.* She gave it a few moments more to be sure, then drew a deep breath and rose up from behind the log. Her cramping muscles screamed in pain.

Something whizzed by her head and thunked against a tree behind her. Instantly, Laurel plunged into the shadows and took shelter behind some brush.

Above the harsh rasp of her own breathing, she could hear the crunch of tires on gravel. A car door slammed. Laurel strained to see through the trees and could just make out the front of the center. The porch light outlined Jason's form as he pushed through the massive front doors and hurried into the house.

Relief flooded her, to be replaced by an agony of frustration. Only seventy yards closer, and she could be held in his protective arms. With every fiber of her being, she longed to call out but didn't dare give away her position.

The front door flew open and Jason rushed back outside, calling her name. His presence pulled at her like a magnet.

Jason meant safety, a way out of this madness. Hoping his voice would cover the sound of her movements, Laurel eased out of her hiding place and circled toward the house.

She heard a step behind her and whirled around.

"Hi there," said a familiar voice.

"Garrett!" She could just make out his shape against the trees. Her pent-up breath whooshed out of her lungs and she took a step toward him.

Garrett raised his arm and the moonlight glinted off the large rock in his fist.

"Nooo!" She spun around and raced away, heedless now of any sound she made. Ragged sobs tore from her lungs.

The trees and brush thinned and her feet pounded on dirt, then bare rock, and Laurel knew she had reached the caprock. Her sneakers splashed through shallow puddles on the granite.

She glanced back and saw Garrett's shadow approaching, then spun around to run again. Without warning, her feet slipped out from under her. Her body slammed against the unyielding rock ledge. Laurel knew the sickening loss of control as she started sliding downward. An instant later, her legs met thin air, and she plunged over the edge of the caprock.

Dear God, no! Her mind screamed the prayer while her hands scrabbled for something to grasp. Her fingers slipped into a crevice and she latched on to the handhold with all her strength. She hung by her fingertips, desperately scrambling for a foothold on the slick, broken face and trying not to make a sound that would let Garrett know where she was.

"Laurel, where are you?" Jason's voice boomed out, nearer now. She wanted desperately to answer but didn't dare with

Garrett only yards away. Gravel crumbled from the crevice and she felt her fingers slip.

"Laurel!" Jason shouted again.

Her fingers slipped another fraction of an inch. If she called out, Garrett would find her. If she didn't get help, she would lose her grip and plummet to the bottom of the cliff. She would be dead either way. Summoning her last reserves of strength, she screamed Jason's name.

Heavy steps crashed through the brush. Nearer to hand, steady footfalls advanced. Laurel looked up to see Garrett looking down at her and smiling. He raised his foot, ready to smash the heel of his cowboy boot down on her fingers. Laurel moaned and braced herself for the blow.

"Get away from there!" Jason yelled.

Garrett pivoted to face the threat behind him. He stumbled, and Laurel watched his boots slide on the wet rock. Arms flailing, Garrett let out a hoarse scream and toppled slowly over edge.

Laurel felt the brush of air as he plunged past her, as though it wanted to pull her down, as well. She dug her fingernails into the rock in a final attempt to hang on. Then a pair of hands gripped her wrists and held them fast. Laurel jerked her head up and saw Jason reaching over the edge.

With a mighty heave, he dragged her back over the lip of the rock and pulled her into an embrace that squeezed the last of the air from her lungs. Pulling her back to firmer footing, he lifted her and carried her back to the center.

❧

Alternating red and blue lights splashed across the gathering room walls. Laurel watched them from her cocoon of blankets on one of the couches. Muted voices conversed at a point just outside her range of vision, bringing her out of the fog she had been in ever since Jason scooped her up and carried her away from the nightmarish scene on the caprock.

"Have you found him yet?" Her grandmother's voice lacked its customary tone of command.

"Not yet." Laurel rolled over to see a uniformed deputy talking to Jason and her grandmother. "We've called in Search and Rescue, but I wouldn't give you much for his chances. By the way, we turned up something interesting in his cottage." The deputy held out a sheaf of papers. "It seems your employee was corresponding with an Everett Keller. Is that name familiar?"

A bit of color returned to her grandmother's cheeks. "Yes, he's a very dear friend of mine."

The deputy raised one eyebrow. "Your dear friend seemed to think he stood to inherit this place one day. He paid Garrett Harper handsomely to be his spy and watch out for his interests. When your granddaughter showed up, he got nervous and plotted with Harper to scare her off."

Laurel found her voice. "Garrett was sending me those E-mails?"

"Not only that, but he informed Keller you'd decided to stay on permanently. That's when Keller ordered him to get you out of the way by whatever means necessary."

Her grandmother slumped, and Jason hurried to ease her into a chair. "That isn't possible. Everett is a deeply spiritual man."

"Not according to these E-mails I printed out. Keller's whole focus has been on getting his hands on this place, at any cost." The deputy nodded at Laurel. "Glad to see you're look-ing better. I'll be back in the morning to see if you have any-thing to add to your statement." He strode out the front door, and Laurel's grandmother bowed her head, covering her face with her hands.

"How could either one of them do this? I trusted them."

Jason knelt before her and took her hands in his. "That's why it's important to know where to put your trust. People may fail you, but the God of the Bible will always keep His promises."

She raised her head and looked straight at Laurel. "That's what your mother said. She told me I ought to trust the Bible, not the teachings of men." She breathed out a sigh. "You and your mother—so alike in so many ways."

Her tender tone sent a flutter of hope through Laurel. "About the Bible. . . ," she began.

"I've been reading the one you gave me," her grandmother cut in, smiling at Laurel's quick gasp. "Do you remember the part where Agrippa asked Paul, 'Do you think that in such a short time you can persuade me to be a Christian?' Much to my surprise, in my case the answer is almost a yes."

Jason smiled and squeezed her hands. "Get past the 'almost' and you'll have it, Millicent. We'll both be praying for you."

"Thank you. I believe I'll go to bed now. It's been a long, trying day." She pushed herself out of her chair and turned to Laurel. "Good night, my dear. Perhaps we can start over on a new footing tomorrow."

Jason helped her to the door, then returned to sit on the

edge of Laurel's couch. "When God moves, He moves fast, doesn't He?" His smoky gray eyes stared into hers, and Laurel felt like she was about to step off a cliff of a different kind.

Gently, he tucked her hair behind her ears and cradled her face in his hands. "When I got your message, I broke every speed limit along the way to get here. And then, when I couldn't find you and no one seemed to know where you'd gone, I thought I might have lost you forever." He stroked his palm across her hair in a gesture that sent ripples of delight along her nerve endings.

"God is working in your grandmother's life, and I believe He's doing something between us, as well. Would you be willing to stay on so we can discover what He has in mind?" Jason's eyes glowed with an intensity that set her heart racing. His breath caressed her cheek as he lowered his face and pressed his lips to hers. He pulled away slightly and one corner of his lips tugged upward. "Arizona has some beautiful scenery. You ought to be able to find some views worth capturing right around here."

Laurel framed his face with her hands. "I'm sure I can." She smiled. "In fact, I'm staring at one of them right now."

CAROL COX

Carol makes her home in northern Arizona. She and her pastor-husband minister in two churches, so boredom is never a problem. Family activities with her husband, college-age son, and young daughter also keep her busy, but she still manages to find time to write. She considers writing a joy and a calling. Since her first book was published in 1998, she has seven novels and nine novellas to her credit, with more currently in progress. Fiction has always been her first love. Fascinated by the history of the Southwest, she has traveled extensively throughout the region and uses it as the setting for many of her stories. Carol loves to hear from her readers! You can send E-mail to her at: carolcoxbooks@yahoo.com.

Then Came Darkness

by Gail Gaymer Martin

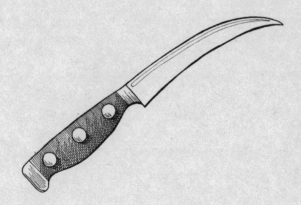

When I looked for good, then evil came unto me:
and when I waited for light, there came darkness.
JOB 30:26 KJV

Everyone who does evil hates the light,
and will not come into the light
for fear that his deeds will be exposed.
But whoever lives by the truth comes into the light,
so that it may be seen plainly.
JOHN 3: 20–21 NIV

Chapter 1

The sprawling mansion stood before her like a weight pressing on her spirit.

Gerri Ward paused in the shadow of a towering oak and studied the brooding building. Like the ivy clinging to the gray stone, the dark secret had choked the life from those who lived inside. That's what she had heard from her father over the years.

Strangled by fear, Gerri pulled at the neck of her sweater. If her purpose had not driven her forward, she would never have come to Emory Estates—to a house that she prayed could clear her deceased grandfather of murder.

She stepped to the back of her sedan, opened the trunk, and pulled out two pieces of luggage. Gripping the vinyl handles, she willed her feet to climb the concrete steps, moved across the broad portico, and paused at the impressive front door. She lowered her suitcases to the drab cement and, with a trembling finger, pushed the doorbell. A deep, dolorous chime echoed through the closed door.

Waiting, she pivoted her head as her gaze traveled the

length of the porch. Paint, yellowed with age, peeled from the window trim, doorframes, and porch roof. The building was blemished with disrepair—like a beautiful woman whose powder and adornment could no longer hide her age. But Gerri perceived more than that. A sense of misery. . .deep sorrow blanketed the surroundings as if the sun could not penetrate the encircling gloom.

A sound filtered through the wide door, and Gerri focused her attention. She watched the brass knob turn and the door inch open.

"May I help you?" Only a shadow identified the speaker.

Gerri squinted her eyes to see through the screen door. "I'm Gerri Ward. The agency sent me over. I'm your new housekeeper."

For a lengthy moment, the silhouette did not move or speak.

Gerri held her breath, wishing he would send her away, then fearing he would. Since she'd made her plans, her emotions wavered daily. But she forged ahead, sensing that God was the director of her path.

When the door swung open, Gerri eyed the gaunt, sallow-faced man who peered back at her.

"Come inside," he said.

Drawing in a deep breath of morning freshness, Gerri gripped the handles of her baggage and stepped across the threshold. The fresh air dissipated, replaced by the dank odor of decay. Her gaze swept the grand foyer. Though once elegant, the walls had grayed with years, and the bright carpet had faded with use. Soap, water, and lemon polish could not dispel the sense of foreboding that crept through Gerri's body and pressed against her heart.

Though the man hadn't introduced himself, Gerri suspected he was the estate owner, Blayne Emory. From what her family told her, she knew him not to be more than thirty-five, but he appeared older, his countenance and posture weighted by years of misery.

Without a word, he motioned toward the stairway, then grasped the nearest of her cases from her hand and strode toward the staircase. She followed, awed at the grandeur that must have been. Just as she had read in books, the staircase was lined with portraits—glowering faces of men and women in rigid poses. She caught her breath as one portrait looked down from above and met her gaze. Though only paint and canvas, dark, evil eyes seemed to stalk her ascent. Victor Emory, Blayne's grandfather, she felt certain. A brass plaque validated her guess as she passed.

Ahead of her, Blayne opened a door and climbed another set of stairs. No longer elegant, the narrow wooden steps, unadorned with carpet, rose between plain walls, once white, but now browned with age.

At the top, he opened another door and motioned her inside. "This is your room. It should be adequate." He dropped her suitcase on the floor.

This time Gerri remained silent while her gaze moved across the barren decor lit by a single ceiling bulb. A small bed, one ladder-back chair, a pine dresser, and a library table pushed against the wall. Not a picture, rug, or lamp in sight. "This will do just fine." Though she said the words out of courtesy, she knew her response was far from the truth.

"Good." He shifted his suit jacket sleeve and looked at his watch. "I'll be leaving in a few moments. Before you unpack, I can show you the kitchen and supplies."

"Yes, sir," Gerri said, placing her suitcase on the bed.

The man turned and headed down the stairs.

Gerri gave the room one more sweeping look and followed him to the first floor, her skin prickling in gooseflesh when she passed the sullen painting of Victor Emory.

With as few words as possible, the man gestured to the rooms as they passed, outlining her duties, and by the time they had reached the kitchen, his instructions jumbled in her head. She calmed herself and viewed the facilities—modernized, at least.

"You'll find the pantry and refrigerator well stocked, and I've left a list of weekly duties on the table," he said with another glance at the time. "I trust you can find your way through the house and calculate what needs to be done."

What needed to be done? Her thoughts flew to all she'd seen and all God had directed her to do. The task could take forever.

"I'll return around seven this evening and would like dinner ready," Blayne said, turning on his heel and leaving her alone in the kitchen.

Pausing to orient herself to her task, she opened cupboards and doors, finding a storage closet with cleaning supplies, then a butler's pantry filled with china. When she moved to the center of the room, she heard the outside door close. Her shoulders relaxed, and she clasped her fingers together in a silent prayer. She'd made it this far, undetected, and if God were truly on her side, His protection would keep her safe, despite her fearful task.

Retracing her steps, Gerri opened her bedroom door and stood on the threshold surveying the small, unappealing room. She'd look later for an unused scatter rug. . .or two to cover the bare floor, and perhaps somewhere she might find a lamp to soften the glare of the overhead bulb.

Sunlight filtered through the window curtains, and Gerri headed for the brightness. She pushed back the cotton damask and pressed her forehead against the pane. Pleasure circled through her chest, seeing the trimmed shrubs and flower garden below where the beds held summer blossoms. A bit of brightness in her gloomy world.

Longing to complete her work and go outside to enjoy the sunlight, she unpacked with speed. She changed into her work clothes, tied back her long, straight hair with a rubber band, then returned to the floors below to organize her tasks.

Gerri wanted to make a good impression on her new employer. Fortified by God's grace, she'd applied for the position and shortened her last name to Ward, fearing detection. Yet, she'd never been a housekeeper in her life. What would she do if he dismissed her for incompetence before she had time to complete her mission?

Perhaps her hope was foolish. Possibly no clues remained in the Emory mansion to exonerate her grandfather, but Gerri believed if God led her to the estate, He would also provide what she needed. . .in time. God's time, not hers.

At noon, Gerri paused in the kitchen. Her appetite had vanished when she entered the mansion, but she knew she needed energy for the work ahead. She opened the refrigerator and found an apple in a crisper drawer. She took a bite, remembering the adage that an apple keeps the doctor away. She wondered if it worked on fear.

Leaning against the kitchen counter, Gerri thought about Westfield, a small town filled with Victorian buildings and gingerbread houses that had been the home of her grandfather, Arthur Seward. Her father had been born here, too, but the family moved away when her grandfather was falsely imprisoned for murder.

Pushing away her thoughts, Gerri hurried through the rooms as she dusted and vacuumed, passing family heirlooms, leather-bound books, and a display of antique weapons in a locked case. When she could bear the gloom no more, she made a piece of toast, covered it with jelly, and stepped onto the back porch. A rusted metal chair sat in the shadow, and she pulled it forward into the sunlight's warmth.

A few clouds dappled the blue sky, and for the first time that day, peace slowed her galloping pulse. She bit into the jam-covered bread and closed her eyes.

"Taking a break?"

A man's voice caused her to jump. Her eyes flew open and her gaze settled on a grinning face with pale blue eyes.

"Hi," he said, smoothing back his scruffy hair with no success. Wisps poked upward, choosing their own direction, and giving him a boyish look. "I'm the groundskeeper, Rich Drake."

"Gerri Ward," she said, accepting his handshake and marveling at the warmth that traveled up her arm. "I'm the housekeeper. I started today."

He nodded as if he'd figured that out on his own. He stepped back and rested his hip against the porch railing. "You have your job cut out for you. Most of the housekeepers don't stay long."

"I'll stay." *As long as I must*, she added in thought.

His grin widened. "Good for you." He folded his arms across his chest and gazed at her.

His prodding look set her on edge. . .not that she didn't like his company or his appearance, but his inspection embarrassed her. "Why are you staring at me?" Though her question was blunt, it matched the directness of his gaze.

"No reason. Well. . .I'm wondering why an attractive woman like you wants to lock yourself up in this dungeon."

"You work here."

"My job is outside mostly." He uncrossed his arms and gestured toward the door. "When I go inside for repairs, I'm relieved when I'm finished. No matter how many windows are open, that house is dark."

She understood, but she wasn't sure how much she wanted to say. . .or admit.

"It's not just gloomy," he said. "When I go inside the house for repairs, joy seems to vanish. The atmosphere presses against my spirit."

Instinctively, she nodded her head. "Mine, too. I've only been here a few hours and felt it when I walked inside."

"I think it's the past," he said, drawing his fingers through his hair again with no success at discouraging his wayward tresses. "Sin works its way into the woodwork—like it does with an evil person. A God-fearing person senses it."

"You're a Christian?"

"Raised knowing Jesus from my toddlerhood. You?"

His question triggered a moment of guilt. "The same. Born and raised in a Christian home." But she'd not always been devoted to her faith. . .not until she felt God's gentle nudge that had brought her to her senses.

The knowledge wrapped a sense of security over Gerri. Since she'd decided to accept the housekeeper position, she'd felt alone. She'd avoided telling her family, knowing they would not approve of her plan and demand she forget the family's sorrow. Her father's voice rose in her mind. *Let God be the judge, Gerri. He'll take away our pain and sorrow in heaven. Your grandfather's with the Lord. He's been freed from it all. Our turn will come.*

But she couldn't wait, and as if God gave her a hand, doors opened, and she'd found herself driving the eighty miles from the Detroit suburbs to Westfield, resting on the banks of the Raison River.

"You're not from Westfield, are you?" His voice cut through her deep thought.

Jolting her, she refocused. "No. I'm from Clawson. It's in the northwest suburbs of Detroit."

"What brings you here?"

"A job."

He shook his head. "I realize that, but why a job. . .like this? Why here in this small town?"

She longed to tell him, but she couldn't for fear he'd give her away. "Curiosity." Though evasive, the answer was true.

"Curiosity? You mean seeing what life's like in a small town?"

"Sort of." She shrugged, getting closer to the truth. "I felt as though God led me here."

"Really." His response wasn't a question. A look of acceptance covered his face. "Interesting." He looked away from her for the first time, in the direction of the estate property, and stretched his arms back, as if to relieve tension. "Would you like to see the property?"

She glanced at her watch. "I have to start dinner in a half hour or so. . .but I'd like to look around."

Rich watched the young woman rise and brush crumbs from her brown slacks. She wore a lilac-colored knit top and, with her straw-colored hair, she reminded him of an Easter basket filled with surprises.

"Do you live on the grounds?" Gerri asked, reaching up to remove something that bound her hair. Her tresses tumbled down around her shoulders and fluttered in the breeze.

"No." He gave her a quick, admiring smile. "I live in town not too far from my mother."

"That's nice. You're close to your family."

Rich liked her expression when she responded and guessed she was a woman with strong family ties, too. In honesty, he liked more than her expression. She'd intrigued him from the moment he saw her sitting on the porch and holding a piece of toast. From the way she nibbled her toast, she looked pensive. He could see the crumbs dropping to the floor and onto her clothing when she sat in the old rusty chair. Later he would look in the shed and see if he could find a chair in better condition.

He pulled his thoughts back to his task. . .giving her a tour of the estate. "The outbuildings aren't used much anymore. Only to store the riding mower and garden tools. The barn is empty. My mom tells me years ago they had horses here. This house has been in the Emory family for years, but a bad experience years ago. . ."

An interested look jumped to her face, but he faltered, not wanting to relate town gossip. "I understand the family's finances dwindled away, so the place is in bad repair."

"If that's the case, how can Mr. Emory afford a housekeeper and you working on the grounds?" Her voice edged with challenge.

He shrugged. "Sorry. That's the scuttlebutt you hear in town. You know, small town, big mouths."

Her serious expression softened with a smile. "People do gossip about their neighbors, I guess."

"Not everyone keeps God's commandments." He said the words and reprimanded himself for doing the same. He thanked the Lord for stopping him from flapping his mouth any further with hearsay.

Changing the subject to safeguard his errant thoughts, he led her across the meadow to the estate's stream and over a small wooden bridge toward the woods. She expressed interest and asked questions, and when they turned back, she commented on the time.

"Mr. Emory said he expected dinner by seven. If I don't run, the meal will be late. Not a good impression for a first day, I don't think."

He quickened his steps, but noticed she had trouble keeping up with him. Though she took long strides, her shorter legs were a hindrance even though she swung her arms to keep her momentum while her silken hair billowed behind her on the wind.

When they reached the mansion, the warmth had vanished and gloom seemed to permeate the surroundings.

"Thanks so much for the tour," Gerri said, her arms folded across her chest and her hands massaging her bare skin. "I'd better get inside."

Surprised at his feelings, Rich longed to warm her in his arms—to cover her in his protecting embrace. *Protecting her from what?* The question disturbed his thoughts. "Nice meeting you, Gerri. If you need anything, just let me know."

"I will," she said as she trudged up the porch stairs. Though she smiled over her shoulder, her eyes had filled with fear.

Chapter 2

Gerri wiped the last dish and slipped it onto the cabinet shelf. Through the window, the morning sun burned her tired eyes. She hadn't slept well in the strange surroundings. Night sounds had made her jumpy, and thoughts had fluttered through her mind like moths around a light bulb, keeping her from sleep.

Since Blayne Emory would be gone for much of the day, Gerri looked forward to quiet time to adjust to her new environment. She left the kitchen and gathered the cleaning supplies from the closet. Earlier she'd studied her duty list and devised a plan of dividing the house into daily tasks. Today she'd decided to clean the parlors. Dust rose from the dark walnut furniture as she wandered from table to table, woodwork to woodwork, and when she finished, the French-pane windows glistened, and the brass hardware shone, yet disappointment hovered over her. She'd seen nothing out of the ordinary—nothing that triggered a hint of scandal or a clue to the trial years ago. For that matter, Gerri had no idea what she was looking for. What did she want to find? Her thoughts were void.

During lunch, Gerri envisioned her empty room and longed to do something to make it homier. She needed a solace from the drab environment surrounding her. Even the rooms filled with antiques seemed weighted with somber purpose.

When she'd finished her meal, she headed to her quarters on the third floor. Along the narrow corridor, other doors stood closed, and curious, she turned the knob on the next one. It opened, but inside the room held even more gloom than her own. One narrow bed and a straight-backed chair occupied the narrow space.

She closed the door and tried the next. Locked. She turned the next knob, and it opened to an empty room. Puzzled, she returned to the earlier door, hoping it was only jammed. When she tried again, she knew it was locked, but why?

Gerri's mind began to crank out possibilities. If the door were locked, then something behind it was important. It only made sense. She pondered the thought as she returned to her room. She sat on the edge of the bed, wondering about the locked room and where she might find a lamp and perhaps a rug. Although she could ask her employer, she questioned the wisdom. A low profile is what she wanted, and asking for more would only draw attention to her.

Enjoying the sunlight coming through the lone window, Gerri's focus drifted to the library table. If the table were beneath the sill, she would at least benefit from the outdoor light if she wanted to read in the early evening. She rose and scooted the piece away from the wall, then lugged it to the window. When she set it down, Gerri noticed a small drawer that had been hidden against the wall.

A drawer meant something might be inside, and she slid it open, her heart in throat. To her disappointment, it was empty, but the sunlight did spread its rays across the pine top. She would benefit from that. As she lifted her gaze, she saw Rich working by the shed, and her heart lifted. Though she barely knew him, his presence was a breath of fresh air against the dank aura of the house.

Wondering if he might have some ideas about locating a key to the upper rooms, Gerri skipped down the stairs and into the warm sunshine. Her arms prickled with awareness. Like night and day, the brooding house overshadowed the summer sun.

"Good morning," she said, approaching Rich.

He looked up and gave her a wave. "How was your first evening? Did you sleep well?"

She shook her head. "I never do in a new environment."

"It's natural," he said, plucking dead stems from the plants.

Gerri bent down and pulled up a large weed, then dropped it into his trash container. "I thought maybe you could help me."

His head lifted, and his eyes held concern. "If I can."

She told him about the locked rooms and asked her question about the key.

"If I were you, I'd stay out of locked rooms. They're locked for a reason. I just do what I'm told and keep out of his way."

She longed to tell him the truth of her search, yet Gerri didn't know if she could really trust him. "All I want is a lamp and a rug. Anything to brighten my quarters. Have you seen anything like that around?"

"I don't get inside often. Maybe the basement."

"That's locked, too. I tried the door yesterday."

"Did Mr. Emory give you a key to your room? It's probably a skeleton lock. That's what opens those old doors, but I still think you should steer clear if you want to keep your job."

Gerri had to bite back the words that flew to her tongue. She longed for his advice, and she sensed he would be on her side, but wisdom prodded her to only nod. "I suppose I better go back inside. I don't want him coming home while I'm chatting with you out here."

"Wait a minute," he said, lifting his index finger as he walked away.

She watched his movements until he vanished behind the shed, and soon he returned carrying a colorful bouquet of flowers.

"Zinnias," he said, handing her the blossoms. "I planted some seeds and look how they grew."

She clutched the colorful display to her chest. "Thanks. This will be a bright spot in my otherwise dull room."

"The room would never be dull with you inside," he said, giving her a gentle smile.

His words settled over her as heat rose from beneath her neckline and traveled to her cheeks. Gerri had never learned to handle compliments well. Finally, she repeated her thank-you, then turned and hurried back inside.

Unable to locate a vase, Gerri found a tall tumbler in the pantry and carried it to her room. She filled it with water from her bathroom tap and arranged the flowers, then set the glass on the corner of her table. The sunlight highlighted the colorful display and, for the first time, added cheer to the room.

Gerri returned to the first floor with thoughts of preparing the evening meal while keeping her eyes open for a skeleton key. The kitchen drawers seemed a likely spot, but after searching, she gave up and started dinner.

When the meal was nearly ready, tires crunched against the stone-covered driveway, and Gerri's back prickled, knowing her employer would be opening the front door. She heard the sound and braced herself to cover her fear.

"Dinner's nearly ready," she said as he came through the kitchen archway.

"Good. I'll be going out after dinner." He carried the evening paper and walked past her to the dining room.

Gerri filled the tray with a salad bowl and a platter of veal cutlets with oven browned potatoes and carrots. She included a basket of fresh dinner rolls. Later she would bring in coffee and dessert.

When she came through the doorway, he glanced at her, then returned his gaze to the newspaper. Gerri laid out the dishes and stepped back. Her mouth worked around the words waiting to be spoken before she found courage. "I wondered if I could have a key to my room."

His head flew upward, and he stared at her with narrowed eyes. "Why? No one is in the house but you and me."

"I—I would like to ensure my privacy. I'd. . .uh. . .feel more comfortable if—"

"I will not enter your room, Miss Ward. You can be assured."

"Yes, but—"

He sent her another dark look, and she backed away, knowing that her request had been useless. Her own privacy was not her concern, but if she had the key, maybe— She

110

wiped away the thought. He'd never relinquish a key and unless she could find one or buy one. . .

The thought brightened her spirit. Tomorrow she would go into town. Perhaps a hardware store would have such a key.

❧

"You went to town," Rich said, more a question than a statement.

Gerri clutched her paper sacks, afraid to tell him she'd purchased a skeleton key while she was out. She patted a bag and nodded. "Just a few groceries. Mr. Emory has an account at the store."

"Did you find a key?" he asked.

He'd caught her unaware, and she felt a flush rise to her face. "Nothing in the house," she said, hoping to avoid the subject further. "I asked for a key to my room, but he said I didn't need one."

"I figured." His eyes searched hers, but he didn't probe further.

"The flowers look lovely in my room. Thanks again." He made her nervous today, probably because she'd been evasive, and Gerri wasn't good at that. She almost felt as if she were lying, and that's something she didn't do.

"Speaking of your room," he said, "I found a lamp for you."

"You did?"

She watched him turn and head for his car. At the trunk, he dug into his pocket and pulled out a key, then turned it in the lock. He lifted the lid and pulled out a table lamp, nothing elegant, but very practical. He closed the lid and brought it to her. "I figured you could use this one. Nothing fancy, but it works."

"Thank you. It's perfect, and it'll save me hunting through the rooms."

"That's what I'm trying to save you from doing," he said. His words sent her a deeper message, and she wondered whose side he was on.

"I'll carry it inside for you," he said.

He followed her as she carried the groceries onto the back porch and into the kitchen. After she set the packages on the counter, she turned and accepted the lamp. "I really appreciate this." She set it near the hallway door then returned to him. "Would you like some lemonade?"

"Sure," he said, sending her a smile that made her catch her breath.

Gerri distracted herself by pulling out a glass and filling it with the tangy drink. "By the way, could you check the pantry door, please? It seems to stick."

Without her direction, Rich walked to the pantry door and gave it a push. It dragged across the floor in its stiff manner. "Swollen from humidity. I'll bring a plane tomorrow and shave off a little."

"Thanks," she said, handing him the drink.

He took a lengthy swallow and wiped the excess with the back of his hand. "I was more thirsty than I realized."

"Would you like some more?" she asked. Though she loved his company, today she longed for him to leave so she could test the new key.

"No, this is fine," he said, draining the glass and returning it to her. "Thanks. I need to finish up here. I have another job to do this afternoon." He gave her a wave and retreated out the back door.

Gerri hurried to put the groceries away and checked the

112

time. She needed to start dinner before Mr. Emory returned home, but anxiety nudged her to ascend the stairs and test the key. With apprehension, Gerri darted up the stairs and headed for the locked door. Her hand trembled as she pulled the skeleton key from her pocket and slid it into the lock. Before turning it, she closed her eyes and sent up a quick prayer. *Father, be with me and protect me. You know my purpose, and I ask Your blessing in Jesus' sweet name.*

Drawing in a quaking breath, Gerri turned the key and felt the pressure of the bolt. She used both hands to add strength, and finally, the lock gave way. Her heart hammered as she grasped the knob and gave it a turn. The door opened, and she stood on the threshold, peering into the room.

Disappointment flooded through her, but as she let her eyes traverse the enclosure, her hope returned. A small antique secretary and a chest of drawers sat across the room. Perhaps something was inside. She bounded across the room and lowered the lid to the desk. She withdrew yellowed papers from the pigeonholes and fingered through the envelopes, waiting for something to catch her eye. Bill receipts, flyers, a postcard from a traveler—nothing that made any sense, but she needed time to search. Maybe one small, innocent-looking paper would hold a clue.

A distant *thud* resounded up the staircase, and Gerri's heart flew to her throat. Was her employer home already? Her pulse beating against her temple, she raced to the doorway and listened. Yes, he was home. She stepped into the hallway to close the door, then remembered she'd left the secretary desk open. Darting back, she shut the lid, then closed the door as quietly

113

as possible and locked the door with shaking fingers.

When she turned, Mr. Emory's voice sailed up the staircase.

Gerri dropped the key into her pocket and hurried to the head of the stairs. "I'm sorry," she said as she made her way down. "I came up for an aspirin."

He gave her a dour look, and she bounded past him and down the second set of stairs to the kitchen. He didn't follow, and her stomach knotted as she heard him take the set of stairs to the third floor. He was checking on her, she was certain.

❖

"Come in," Gerri said the next morning when Rich knocked on her door.

He entered carrying the plane and a small bouquet of roses. "From my mother's garden," he said.

This time the bouquet included a small vase, and Gerri was taken aback by his kindness. She uttered her surprise and set the vase on the kitchen counter. "You'll make that drab room sunny and bright with your kindness."

He only smiled and went about his work.

Gerri checked the cinnamon pastries she was making to see if they had risen as Rich pulled the pins on the six-paneled door and stretched it across two chair backs. He set out with the plane, making quick work of shaving off the bottom while she sprinkled in the pecans and twisted the dough into a long spiral.

"What are you making?" he asked. "It smells good already."

"Cinnamon buns." She lifted the pan, slid the dough into the oven, and set the timer.

After he finished the planing, Rich smoothed the surface

114

with sandpaper, then lifted the door from its housing and placed it back onto the hinges and set the pins. He gave the door a push and it swung smoothly back and forth without a catch.

"Thank you," Gerri said, smiling at his ability. He'd made the job look easy. "In a few more minutes, you can have a bun if you'd like."

He grinned as if he'd hoped she would invite him.

She gestured toward the chair, but he sought out the broom and swept away the debris before joining her at the table.

Gerri poured him a cup of coffee, and the luscious scent filled the room.

"Are you happy here?" Rich asked.

Gerri turned to him in surprise at his pointed question. "Are you?" she asked, hoping to waylay her need to answer.

He smiled. "It's an income."

"Same here," she said, "until something better comes along."

"This job doesn't suit you," he said.

"You don't think I can cook and clean?"

"No, I think you're more than capable. You make me curious."

Her heart gave a kick. "You arouse my curiosity, too. Is handyman your life goal?"

He chuckled. "I'm working on my master's degree. This is good summer employment for me."

"I'm on a hiatus myself," she said.

"But why here?" He gave her a bewildered look. "Is this for a college thesis or a study of some kind?"

"You could call it that. It's temporary, but please don't let Mr. Emory know," she said, wishing she'd kept her mouth closed.

He put his finger to his lips with a *shh*. "My lips are sealed."

"Thank you," she said, turning to pull the rolls from the oven.

The aroma filled the room as she poured a thin glaze over the buns, then moved two of them to plates and set them on the kitchen table. She poured coffee for herself and refreshed Rich's before joining him.

They were quiet a moment while each dug into the delectable rolls.

"Delicious," he said after the first bite.

"Thanks," she said, licking the glaze from her fingers. She grabbed a paper napkin and wiped away the rest of the goo, then leaned back in the chair. "Tell me about yourself, Rich."

❧

Rich ran his tongue over the cinnamon that clung to his lips and studied Gerri. She was an attractive young woman, and no matter what she said, he sensed she had a greater purpose being in Westfield. "Not much to tell. I attend a university in Toledo, Ohio, not too far over the river. I'm working on a degree in community and urban planning."

"And now you're doing garden planning." She grinned.

"That and planing doors."

She chuckled. "Do you live in Westfield?"

"My mom lives here. I have an apartment nearby, but I'm still a homeboy. I like to go there for meals. I'll get a house once I finish my degree." He'd answered enough. Now it was her turn. "How about you?"

"I had my own apartment until recently. I gave it up to move here."

She looked at him with a stoic expression. Unable to read her face, he tried to probe, but Gerri put a damper on his attempts.

"I'm a private person," she said. "Very boring."

He knew better than that. After a final bite of the cinnamon bun, he drained his coffee cup and wiped his fingers with the napkin. She'd piqued his interest, and Rich wasn't ready to give up. "Do you know anything about this family?"

"Not much," she said. "Mr. Emory needed a housekeeper. Then I came along."

"He doesn't keep them long," Rich said, hating to gossip, but figuring she should know the truth.

"He has a dour attitude. I've seen that. He could scare the ears off a rabbit."

"Good thing you're not a bunny."

She gave him a shy smile. "Something about this house doesn't set well with me. It's gloomy, and not the kind of darkness that is dispelled by light. It's something inner."

"The family's had problems. They've always had a shroud of malevolence hanging over them. What they touch seems to shrivel. It's always been that way."

From her expression, he realized he'd caught Gerri's interest.

"Are you trying to scare me?" she asked.

"No, but I've warned you to be careful. The family's reputation is riddled with rumors."

"What kind of rumors?" Her eyes widened as she searched his face.

"They're only rumors, Gerri. I don't like to spread them, but I want you to be careful." Rich was sorry he'd said anything, but his heart told him to warn her. He didn't spread gossip. He was

117

a Christian, but he'd always suspected some truth to what he'd heard about the family. Despite her pleading look, he couldn't let himself say any more.

She gripped his arm with the power of a vice. "Do you know something? If you do, please tell me."

He only shook his head and turned toward the back door.

Chapter 3

Gerri had spent a week shuffling through papers she'd found in the desk of the locked bedroom. She found nothing significant in the dresser. The closet held only old clothes, and she'd even dug into the pockets and felt the hems. Nothing came to light, and she wondered why that door had been locked. It didn't make sense to her.

She'd felt angry at Rich for not providing her with what gossip he'd heard, but the more she thought about it, she realized he was following his Christian principles. She so easily bypassed the Lord's expectations of Christian behavior. Even prayer was sporadic in Gerri's life, and she knew that only with God's help would her mission at the Emory estate be accomplished. The Lord had to be in charge.

After dinner, Gerri wandered into the library. As she entered, the large glassed-in display of weapons—rifles, guns, knives, bow and arrows—sent chills down Gerri's back. Though they were for hunting, she never liked weaponry of any kind. Instead of looking in that direction, she pulled her gaze away from the case and focused on the shelves of books. Gerri needed something to do during the long evenings alone. As she studied the titles, hoping to find something that would catch her interest, the telephone rang. Gerri moved toward the doorway to answer, but the ringing stopped, and she assumed Mr. Emory had taken the call from his second-floor study above the library.

Gerri shifted her focus from one bookcase to the next, but when she reached the wall, she halted. Her employer's distant voice reached her through the furnace grate. She looked over her shoulder, feeling guilty for eavesdropping, but his angry voice captured her attention, and she stood still, caught up in his words.

"I must do something," he said, his voice ringing with frustration through the grate. "I have the housekeeper and a part-time handyman. I can't trim anymore. The family home needs too much upkeep for my dwindling income."

Gerri leaned closer to the wall but heard only silence.

"That won't help," Emory said, finally. "I need to sell some of the family antiques or the estate itself. My healthy inheritance seems to be fading. If you can think of something better, you let me know."

The telephone hit the receiver with a *clang*, and Gerri jumped away from the wall and hurried from the room. In the kitchen, she grabbed a soda, then returned to her bedroom and closed the door.

She sank into the ladder-back chair by the desk and looked out the window at the setting sun, her fears growing as fervently as the brilliant colors that spread across the sky. If her employer sold the furnishings or the estate before she had a chance to continue her search, she would never learn the truth—never clear her grandfather's name.

Her head throbbed with concern, and she lowered her face in her hands. *Lord, be my Guide. My quest may seem foolish to many people, but to me, it's a tribute to my grandfather who suffered for a crime he didn't commit. Perhaps it's pride, but Father, I believe it's more than clearing the family name. I believe it would bring honor to Your name, too. My granddad was a Christian man, and I know he was innocent.*

When she lifted her eyes, a shaft of golden sunlight cut through the orange and mauve clouds like a heavenly promise. Gerri knew God was light, and evil was darkness. A verse came to mind, and she reached for her Bible resting on the corner of the table. She opened the pages and searched the book of John. Finally the words came into focus. "Everyone who does evil hates the light, and will not come into the light for fear that his deeds will be exposed. But whoever lives by the truth comes into the light, so that it may be seen plainly." This house was heavy with gloom and shadows. Gerri wanted to live by the light. She longed for the truth, yet sometimes she felt like Job who looked for light and only found darkness.

Forgive me, Lord. She pushed the black thoughts aside. *God is my refuge. My help in trouble. Whom shall I fear?* The thoughts gave her strength. Though her surroundings were steeped in darkness, Gerri had to keep her eye on the light.

❧

Gerri stood in the church parking lot and watched families head toward the doorway. She disliked visiting a new church, never knowing what to expect and not knowing a soul, but she'd felt driven to find a church home in Westfield.

Since she'd arrived at the Emory mansion two weeks earlier, she'd felt weighted by her mission, and even Rich's bright bouquet had soon withered and faded like her spirit. She tried to focus on the positive, yet she felt guilty of hiding her true identity and prayed God understood her purpose and would forgive her.

Music sounded through the doorway, and Gerry hurried up the steps and slipped into a pew near the back of the sanctuary. Her eyes adjusted to the dim lighting, and her heart lifted when she noticed Rich ahead of her. He leaned over and spoke to an elderly woman sitting beside him whom Gerri guessed was his mother. Seeing him filled her with comfort.

The songs and message brightened her spirits, but the Bible reading from First Chronicles touched her heart the most, for it was what she needed to hear. "Do not be afraid or discouraged, for the Lord God, my God, is with you."

Gerri wrapped those words around her heart. Since she'd entered the Emory residence she'd felt overcome by despondency, but God was with her. She lifted her gaze again to Rich. He'd heard the same message and sang the same hymns. If he were truly a Christian man, perhaps she could trust him.

She'd been troubled by her employer's conversation about selling the estate. Wisdom told her that selling property took time, but how much time? She'd longed for someone to talk with, and Rich could be the one. Today Gerri hoped their faith could bond them together as friends. She raised her eyes to the cross and asked Jesus the question. *Can I trust him, Lord?*

When she glanced toward Rich, he turned, and his eyes

sparked with recognition, as did his smile. His look soothed her, and she truly believed God had sent her an answer to her question. The congregation rose with the final hymn, and when the song ended and people moved into the aisles, Gerri waited in the pew.

❦

A warm sensation rolled down Rich's spine when he saw Gerri behind him. He slipped into the aisle and waited for his mother, then made his way toward Gerri, pleased that she'd found her way to his church since he'd never told her where he attended. Sometimes Rich sensed that God led him in unexpected directions. He wondered if Gerri was part of the Lord's plans for him.

He liked her, liked her character and personality, as well as her outward charm. Rich sent her a smile, and she gave one back, sending his pulse throbbing up his arm. He'd never had a woman affect him like Gerri had. He wondered if it was her vulnerability or that special aura that surrounded her as if she were on a secret mission. She intrigued him, as well as caused him concern.

"Good morning," he said, reaching her.

She greeted him while her gaze drifted to his mother.

"Gerri, this is my mom, Carolyn Drake. Mom," he said, turning to the woman at his side, "this is Gerri Ward who works at Emory Estates."

He watched his mother's eyebrows lift as she greeted Gerri. "You must have a great deal of fortitude to work in that gloomy place."

Gerri's face flickered with question until she grinned. "It's a job. I don't have great expectations."

His mother's face softened into a smile. "Rich has mentioned you. I give you credit."

"Thanks," Gerri said. "It's not that bad."

"You're new in town?"

"Yes, I have an old friend nearby, a woman who works for the employment agency. That's how I found the job. She knew I was looking. Other than that, I know Mr. Emory and Rich."

"If you have time today, please join us for lunch," his mother said, surprising, yet pleasing, Rich.

"Great idea. Can you?" he asked.

Gerri looked from him to his mother as if she weren't sure if the invitation was real. "That would be wonderful, if I'm not putting you out."

"Never. We'd love to have you." She shifted her attention to a woman passing by. "Could I catch a ride with you?" his mother asked the lady. The woman welcomed her, and she waved good-bye as she headed through the church doors.

"We walked to church this morning," Rich said, "but I suppose now that Mom has a guest for lunch, she wants to hurry home to get things ready."

"I'm glad we're alone," Gerri said. "I'd like to talk with you."

Concern filled her eyes, and Rich slipped his arm around her shoulders and steered her toward the exit. When they stepped outside, the bright summer sun caused Rich to squint as they bounced down the steps to the ground. His mind jogged, too, with curiosity. "Is something wrong?" he asked, once they reached the sidewalk.

She gave a slight shrug, her eyes averting his.

Rich let his arm slip from her shoulders and walked beside her, their hands brushing with each step. He longed to weave his fingers through hers, to comfort her uneasiness that seemed so evident. He didn't push but waited for her to be ready to tell him what was troubling her.

"I've deceived you," Gerri said, finally.

Her words struck him in the chest. "What do you mean?"

"My name isn't Gerri Ward. It's Gerri Seward." She looked at him, her face pinched with dread. "I don't know if that name means anything to you."

It didn't, but her serious expression filled him with apprehension.

"I'm not a housekeeper as you suspected. I took the job to get into the Emory mansion for a personal reason."

He faltered. "I don't understand."

"My grandfather died in prison for a murder I know he didn't commit. My parents have suspected that the Emory family was involved in that crime, and I've taken it as a mission to vindicate my grandfather's name."

Her words startled him. "No. You can't do that."

"But I am."

Her look nailed him to the spot. "But it could be dangerous, Gerri."

"I'll take my chances. I know many years have passed since the crime, but my family has suffered with the deepest wounds. If you knew my grandfather, you'd understand. He was a kind man. It was circumstantial evidence, but he was nobody, and the Emorys were a wealthy, well-known family. Granddad didn't have a chance."

"Your grandfather died, you said."

"Yes, but that doesn't clear his name. That isn't justice."

Rich's stomach tightened at the news. He'd heard rumors about the Emory family who'd been on the fringe of many scandals. "I'm too young to remember all that, and so are you."

"That's true, but my family remembers, and God is on my side, Rich. He knows the truth, and I'm here to learn what happened."

"Why was your grandfather convicted?" he asked, not knowing the story.

"Grandpa was in desperate need of money from what I understand. He'd had some serious financial losses and had been laid off, too. My dad was young then, and he barely remembers, but Granddad had sent my grandmother and the kids away to visit relatives until he could find a job. Apparently he talked to the Westfield bank president about a loan, but the man refused him even though he knew my grandfather was good for his word. They had words that were heard by bank employees and customers."

"That was the circumstantial evidence?"

"Yes, and when the bank president was found murdered that evening, my granddad had no alibi."

Rich's chest tightened. "None?"

"The confrontation had riled him, and when he got home, he had an epileptic seizure due to the stress. He stayed in bed for the rest of the evening but couldn't prove it. He had no witnesses.

"What makes you think the Emorys were involved?" Rich asked.

"My dad remembers my grandfather wasn't the only suspect. Some of the employees were interrogated, too, for one, Blayne Emory's grandfather, Victor, who was an employee, as was Blayne's father, Jack Emory. Dad said they all had alibis."

Rich's heart went out to her as he listened to the story unfold. Her voice trembled with the telling, and her face had blanched with stress. He wanted to believe her, and if she were right, her family had been dealt an unfair blow years earlier. "Maybe my mom can help you. She might remember something."

"Do you think?" Gerri asked.

"She's never added to the town's gossip—it's not her way—but she might be able to help you."

Gerri yawned as she finished cleaning the kitchen. She'd been unable to sleep well the night before after talking with Rich and his mother. Carolyn Drake had remembered the story of the murder, and she recalled the name Arthur Seward, but she had little to add.

Though she'd made no progress, Gerri wasn't ready to give up. Questions still prodded her on. Why was the empty bedroom locked, and what was in her employer's office desk and in the parlor's small locked secretary? It could be nothing, yet it could be the answer she'd been looking for. Somewhere in that house, she sensed she would find the proof she needed.

Through the window, she heard Rich's truck pull into the driveway. Anxious to see him, Gerri went to the door and greeted him as he came into the backyard.

"You look tired," he said.

"I didn't sleep well."

"Why?"

"Thinking."

He narrowed his eyes, and his face filled with apprehension. "Thinking about what? Don't do anything foolish, Gerri."

"About the locked desks. I know where Mr. Emory keeps the keys."

His face paled as he measured her words. He shook his head. "You're not planning to—"

"Yes, I am. I want to find out why the doors are locked."

Rich stepped forward and clasped her shoulders. "Locked desk drawers are common, Gerri. People keep their financial information inside. Private letters. When they have housekeepers or servants, they lock drawers. It's not necessarily something sinister."

"But it might be. How will I know?"

A look of fear and frustration washed over his face.

"I know you're thinking of my good, but I overheard Mr. Emory talking on the telephone. He's having financial problems and might sell some of the antiques. He said he might sell the estate. I don't have time to wait until he makes a move and then my chance is lost. I've waited too long for this opportunity to get into the house, Rich. You don't understand. This mission has gnawed at me for a long time before the right circumstance came along. It finally happened when my friend saw Blayne Emory was looking for a housekeeper."

"Oh, Gerri." His hands slid farther around her shoulders and drew her closer. "Be careful, please. In the short time I've known you, I've begun to care about you very much. I couldn't bear seeing you hurt. Blayne Emory might go to any length if he suspects you're trying to drag that crime out of hiding."

"I already told you, I must take the chance."

He drew her closer to his chest while his hand slid to her cheek, and Gerri breathed in his clean scent mixed with the summer air.

"You're brave, and I admire your determination," Rich said, "but I can't stand back and let you endanger your. . .your life." He tilted her chin upward and looked into her eyes. "Promise me you won't do anything foolish."

"I can't promise you anything, Rich. I'm here on a mission. God is on my side. I have to trust Him."

Chapter 4

That evening, Gerri closed her Bible and flipped open her journal. She'd begun to keep a notebook of her thoughts since she'd made the decision to vindicate her grandfather. Her journal captured her thoughts and dreams, her fears and sorrows, her joys and longings. Tonight she wrote about Rich and his gentle ways. She knew he was concerned about her, but she'd made the decision, and God had given her the courage to move ahead. She believed her employment at the Emory estate had been with the Lord's blessing.

Gerri lifted her pen and wrote about a new sensation that had rolled over her in the afternoon when Rich had taken her in his arms. So often during the past years, she'd felt alone. At twenty-six, she'd found no man who'd captured her interest, and thoughts of marriage and a family had escaped her. But today in Rich's arms, she'd felt protected and treasured for the first time since she was an adult.

Rich's intentions were noble. He worried about her, but he didn't understand the driving need she felt. It was a feeling she couldn't explain. Gerri placed her pen on the table and closed the journal. Perhaps she was careless to write her thoughts in the book. Though Mr. Emory had stated he would never enter her room, could she trust him? Instead of leaving the journal on the desk beneath her Bible, Gerri opened the small center drawer of the library table and pushed the journal inside. She tried to close the drawer but felt resistance.

Curious, she shifted the journal and its contents, then closed the drawer again, but it didn't slide in smoothly as usual. Determined to shut it properly, Gerri rose, pulled the drawer from its tracks, and set it on the table. She bent down and looked into the dark crevice, then shoved her hand inside to find what was obstructing the drawer's closure. Her hand touched papers.

She'd been careless with her belongings, she guessed, and drew the items forward. She recognized a list of her household duties, a form from the employment agency, and a checklist of tasks she hoped to accomplish. As she sorted the papers, a yellowed envelope slipped from her fingers and dropped to the floor. Seeing it, Gerri's pulse skipped. She bent to retrieve it and saw it was addressed to Victor Emory. She pulled the aged letter, written in a flourished hand, from its housing and scanned the contents.

Her skin prickled as the words flooded over her. Dated 1947, the letter had been signed by Beatrice Emory, Victor's wife and her employer's grandmother. Gerri trembled as the contents registered in her mind. The letter was a good-bye from Beatrice to her husband.

I am ashamed that I have given you an alibi and allowed an innocent man to suffer. I will not betray you,

*but I can no longer live under your roof knowing what
I know. The children and I will be fine, and you will
survive without us. Do not beg me to return. If you do,
I will find it necessary to admit what I know.*

Gerri gasped for breath. Her lungs ached, and she crumpled to the chair while her head spun with the news. Though Beatrice did not admit her husband's guilt, the letter left no other possibility in Gerri's mind.

"Thank You, Lord," she whispered, aware that the letter gave her assurance that her mission was worthy. With God on her side, Gerri knew she would succeed. Unwilling to wait until tomorrow, Gerri took a chance of being detected. She lifted the telephone and dialed Rich's phone number. He'd insisted she take his phone number after they'd talked the evening before.

When Rich answered the phone, he sounded surprised to hear her voice.

"Could you meet me in town?" Gerri asked.

"Now? It's after nine."

"I know, but this can't wait."

"How about Zoe's Diner?" Rich asked.

"I'll be there."

Rich hung up, but Gerri froze, sensing the line was still open. She waited breathlessly for a *click*, but heard none. Finally she hung up. Fear was a horrible monster.

Gerri tucked the yellowed envelope into her handbag and tiptoed down the stairs, then out the back door. Her gaze was riveted to the windows, wondering if her employer had heard her leave. She saw nothing, but Gerri didn't turn on her head-lights until she'd pulled away from the house.

Her hands trembled against the steering wheel, and lights from oncoming cars blinded her tear-filled eyes until she turned onto the main street of downtown lighted with street lamps. She found a space at Zoe's Diner and hurried inside. Rich beckoned to her when she entered, and she wasted no time sliding into the seat.

Gerri dug into her purse and handed him the envelope.

He eyed the date and the handwriting, then opened the letter. She watched his face shift from curiosity to shock. When he finished, he folded the paper closed and slid it back into the envelope. "What are you going to do?" he asked.

The waitress appeared and set a cup of coffee in front of her. Gerri nodded her thanks, her attention locked on Rich.

"I don't know. A jury could say this could mean anything, but I know what it means. He was guilty, and all I need is one more piece of evidence to corroborate this letter. Then I can take it to the authorities."

"I worry about you, Gerri," Rich said, lifting his cup without taking a drink. "My mom remembered something this evening. I planned to tell you tomorrow, but now it's not news. She recalled Beatrice Emory left her husband and didn't return to the estate until Victor died. He must have left the estate to her or Blayne." He took a swallow of coffee and set down the cup.

"I feel I'm on the right track, " Gerri said. "I have to go on." She looked into his concerned eyes. "You do understand, don't you?"

He captured her hand and gave it a squeeze. "I understand,

but I'm not happy about this. If I could take your place, I would."

"But you can't."

"I know." His defeated look grew tender, and he slid his other hand over hers with a caress. "Gerri, do you think this has been God's plan, bringing us together?"

Her heart thumped against her chest, and she was afraid to speak.

"I mean," he said, drawing her hand more deeply into his, "you've become so important to me. You're always on my mind, and I worry about you. I don't know if Blayne Emory is dangerous or not, but I can't bear to take the chance."

"You have no choice. If you care about me, then understand. I must do this. It's not for me. My grandfather's been gone a long time, but it's for his memory. It's for him that I want to clear his name. If he's found innocent, the people of Westfield will know he was telling the truth and think of him as the honest Christian man he was."

Rich lowered his gaze and didn't speak. "I'll pray for you, then. That's all I can do."

"And that's all you have to do, Rich. . .that, and be my friend."

"You can count on that," he said.

Rich didn't sleep well, worrying about Gerri. How could he convince her to give up on her plight? Logic said Blayne Emory was not a dangerous man, but the other part wasn't so sure. Spreading rumors and gossiping had never been part of his family's life, but the letter Gerri had showed him gave truth to the rumors he'd heard.

He'd cautioned himself about his feelings that seemed to be growing into a deeper interest in this woman. His mother had commented, and her words made him realize, that what he thought was mere curiosity had become far more. He was attracted to Gerri and truly admired her strong family allegiance, as well as her undaunted courage.

Yet, mixed within her bravery was Rich's own concern that Gerri was taking chances and endangering her well-being. If murder to protect the family name was part of the genetic factor in the Emory family, then Gerri's life could be in danger. What would Blayne Emory do to cover the family shame? Could he be so desperate for money that he would do anything to protect what he still owned?

Rich feared the worst.

He'd dragged himself out of bed with the night's quandaries still pressing against his spirit. Today he needed to visit his other customer's property and not allow himself to spend all his time at the Emory residence. Though that estate was his main income, Rich had picked up other work to supplement. He'd been able to fit those jobs in with no problem until Gerri came into his life. Now he wanted to spend all his time at the mansion, both to see her and to look out for her safety.

Today he'd give way to wisdom and stay away from the Emory property.

⌘

Gerri waited to make sure her employer had gone for the day before she began her search. Though she didn't have the key for the desk, she still had the skeleton key, and she guessed it would open the cellar door. Since it was locked, she assumed Blayne Emory had a reason to keep people out, and Gerri wanted to know what that reason was.

She pulled the key from her pocket and inserted it, then held her breath and gave a turn. The lock didn't budge. She used all her strength, twisting the key, and finally she heard the *click* as it gave way. Gerri's pulse escalated as she turned the knob. She paused to drop the key into her pocket, then took her first step downward. She closed the door behind her and, fearing detection if she turned on the light, descended into the gloom.

Along the staircase, webs straggled across her face, and she brushed them away with her hand. At the bottom, she peered into the dusky cellar lit only by four gritty windows. When her eyes adjusted, she viewed storage boxes, some antique furniture, and old porter trunks. Gerri wished she'd, at least, brought along a flashlight. Perhaps next time—if there were a next time.

With halting steps, she moved across the room to the boxes. She opened the first and began to explore. Nothing captured her interest. She shifted to the next, then the next, keeping an eye on the fleeting time, and fearing her employer might return if she dallied too long. Being afraid she'd miss something important, she searched with care. The process took precious time.

Finding no clues in the first room, Gerri made her way through a doorway and found herself in a wine cellar. Bottles lined the walls—some dark with red wines, some clear with amber-colored contents. All were covered with dust and draped with cobwebs. She feared touching the flagons, lest she leave fingerprints that her employer might notice. She peered between the bottles and saw nothing out of the ordinary.

Disappointment slithered over her, and she retraced her steps, then made her way into a narrow alcove and another enclosure. The plank door creaked open and inside the cold, marble-like walls she observed empty shelves and open barrels. She'd heard about root cellars but had never seen one from the inside. She remembered seeing a trapdoor on the side of the house when she'd been talking to Rich. The room was barren, except for three steps against the wall, leading upward.

She returned to the larger storage room and opened the last door. Inside, a round-bellied furnace faced her in the crowded, soot-coated room. With only a small coal chute opening to let in a crevice of light, the dark room left her eyes needing time to adjust. She peered into the empty coal bin and walked around the furnace. As she retreated to the doorway, Blayne Emory's voice called to her down the basement stairs.

Gerri's heart flew to her throat. What could she say to him? She panicked, fearing the worst. Instead of answering, she inched closed the alcove door and squeezed her narrow frame behind the furnace, gasping with fear.

She heard him coming nearer—the kick of boxes, doors opening and closing. His calls sounded nearer.

She heard him outside her hideout. When hazy light struck the furnace room wall, Gerri closed her eyes and held her breath. His footsteps grated on the dirty concrete floor. She could hear him breathing while her heart hammered against her chest with such force she feared he could hear it.

He muttered an oath before slamming the door.

Gerri listened to his steps retreating with the distant

thudding up the steps to the first floor. She shifted forward and made her way toward the staircase. Hiding below the shadow of the stairs, she heard the key turn in the lock.

He'd locked her in the cellar.

Gerri's heart stood still. How could she get out of her prison? How could she explain her absence from the house? Fearing detection, Gerri moved away from the basement stairs and shifted closer to the furnace room.

Tears filled Gerri's eyes. Why had she allowed herself to get into this predicament? She settled on an old trunk and bowed her head. *Lord, help me. Give me the answers I need. You know, Father, I'm doing this for a worthy purpose. I praise You.*

Her silent *amen* left her as she raised her head and stared into the gloom. While her mind whirred with confusion, a tiny thought injected itself. She tiptoed around the boxes and trunks back to the root cellar where she'd noticed the stairs.

She crept inside the alcove. A small crevice of daylight slivered through the trapdoor. Her pulse raced as she climbed the steps and pushed against the barricade. The door didn't budge. She used her shoulder and pushed again. Useless. She remembered seeing the heavy metal hasp and bolt that held the doors closed.

Locked.

Gerri crumpled to the floor as panic swept over her.

Oh, Rich, I need you. If only. . .

Chapter 5

R ich dragged the filled trash bag to his truck and heaved it into the bed. He'd weeded and pruned the Garrisons' backyard, and now with time to spare, he'd decided to head for the Barnetts'. Yet something knotted in his stomach, and a voice inside his head repeated a fearful message over and over. Gerri needed him.

The morning had been fine. He'd enjoyed the sunshiny day away from the gloom that seemed to hang over the Emory Estates. The sun's rays heated the earth, and the scent of flowering shrubs and rich soil surrounded him. He'd eaten a quick sandwich, sitting in the wooden swing in the Garrisons' backyard and watched the butterflies play among the phlox, lantana, and coneflowers, sensing the joy of being alive and of knowing Gerri.

Then something happened. A strange sensation rolled over him, a feeling of emptiness and despair, while his mind filled with Gerri's cries for help. He tried to tell himself he was being ridiculous, but the urgency persisted.

As he packed up his tools, he knew what he had to do. The

Barnetts would have to wait until tomorrow. Today he had to drive to the Emory residence and make sure his fears were groundless.

Rich loaded the truck bed, then headed his vehicle toward the mansion. The closer he drew, the more the voice echoed in his thoughts, and the more fear prickled against his skin. *Are You directing me, Lord?* he asked, thinking he'd gone off the deep end with his fearful thoughts.

When Rich reached the mansion, he noticed Blayne's car parked in the driveway. He hesitated and kept his foot from moving to the brake. He drove past the house, telling himself he would cause more problems by stopping. Then his senses returned. He worked for Blayne Emory. He might have returned for any reason, perhaps to water the new plants or to retrieve a tool he'd forgotten.

He turned around and headed back to the estate, filled with determination. After easing his truck around Blayne's car in the wide driveway, Rich pulled into the back and climbed out. He decided to water the plants. That would take more time and give him a chance to move around the yard. He headed for the hose attached to the back of the house while his gaze drifted to the draped windows, wondering if Gerri were inside watching him. Perhaps she would find a reason to come outside and waylay his fears.

He uncoiled the hose and turned on the spigot, then moved from bed to bed, his mind working through his fears and deciding what to do next. He recalled Gerri saying her room was on the side of the house and he wondered if she were there. If so, he could, perhaps, capture her attention.

He dragged the hose around to the side, then turned on the water again, his gaze raking across the third-story windows, praying Gerri would see him and wave or give him some kind of sign that she was safe and secure. He saw nothing.

As he stepped past the trapdoor to the cellar, Rich paused. Something caught his eye. The door seemed to jiggle. He tightened the spigot and dropped the hose, then made his way to the cellar door. He checked the hasp. The bolt was in place, but a sound behind the door sent his pulse skittering. Gerri had never ventured into the locked basement. So who was there? He glanced again toward the windows, seeing no sign of Gerri.

Rich knelt and stealthily pulled out the bolt, then lifted the hasp and swung open the trapdoor. "Hello," he said, leaning over to look into the narrow access. His pulse coursed like wildfire when a form moved into view.

"Gerri!"

Her tear-stained face shifted into the sunlight. "Oh, Rich," she said, her eyes filled with fear. "I'm so glad you came."

"What happened?" he whispered, afraid that Blayne Emory would hear them.

She hurried up the stairs, her blouse draped with cobwebs, and her arm covered with sooty smudges.

He opened his arms, and she fell into them, telling him quickly how she'd gotten locked in the cellar.

Rich brushed the strands from her blouse. "What will you tell Mr. Emory?"

"I'll just go in as if I was on a walk or I had gone into town. All I can do is pray he doesn't ask. I don't want to lie, and if

I must, I'll have to pray the Lord's forgiveness."

Rich turned on the spigot while Gerri washed her hands and the soot smear on her arm. Though she protested, he lifted his shirt and dried her. "Gerri, please get away from this place. Use the letter you found and be content with that. You're not safe here."

"Don't ask me the impossible," she said, her voice regaining its composure and her face recovering its determination. "I'm staying until I find what I need. Please, don't ask otherwise. Just pray for me, Rich."

He nodded, knowing she would never stop. "I'll stay here, at least, until you signal me that you're okay."

"I'll do that," she said. She stood back and turned in a circle. "Do I look okay?"

He wanted to tell her she looked beautiful. "You look fine. Your flush will give you the appearance of a long walk in the sun."

"Thank you," she said, leaning toward him quickly and kissing his cheek. She pivoted and hurried around the house.

Rich stood still, calming his own unsettled nerves and feeling the pressure of her lips on his cheek. She'd surprised him with the kiss, and he could only wish it were under other circumstances.

He checked his watch, then waited, his pulse skipping faster with every passing minute. Rich looked from window to window. Finally he raised his gaze to the third floor and relief washed over him. Gerri stood in the window, giving him a thumbs-up to let him know she had passed her boss's scrutiny without a problem.

Now he could only pray Gerri's feeling of safety didn't backlash after he was gone.

❧

Gerri dropped her search for a few days. She feared Mr. Emory would come home early again and surprise her, especially if he were suspicious. He'd said little about her being missing or about the unlocked cellar. Perhaps he thought he'd accidentally left it unlocked himself.

Every time Gerri's thoughts drifted to Rich, her heart skittered. He'd come to her rescue, and his concern for her touched her deeply. He was a true Christian who seemed to understand her plight, even though he didn't approve of it for fear she'd be harmed. Gerri knew the Lord was with her. God would not let her be harmed when her mission involved her family's reputation. Gerri loved the Lord, even though she'd challenged Him to explain why He had turned His back on her grandfather.

Still, Gerri knew all things happened for a purpose. The Father had given Jesus as a sacrifice for the world's sin. God did not take that cup from His only begotten Son, and in the same way, He never promised His children a life of roses and sunshine, but He did promise to be by their sides in all things. Gerri knew she was not alone.

Today, she gathered her courage again. With the skeleton key she'd purchased, she returned to the empty bedroom. This time, she pulled out the drawers and reached inside the opening, but still the drawers were empty of clues. She studied the plank flooring and searched for loose boards, felt along the woodwork, and in the hems of the draperies. All purposeless.

She opened the closet and stared at the clothing hanging inside. She'd already searched the pockets and felt the hems. She studied the floor planks there, and this time found something. Molding was missing from a section of the flooring, and when she shifted the clothes aside, she found a door hidden behind the garments. Her heart rose to her throat. She turned the almost unnoticeable knob and the door pushed back. She squeezed behind the clothes and stepped into a storage section of the attic. Gloom shrouded her. She felt the wall for a light switch but found nothing. Gerri glanced over her shoulder before moving deeper into the shadows. To her right, a small window let in a parcel of muted light that spread an octagonal pattern on the wide plank floor, but the brightness dissipated as she shifted to the far side of the small area. Ahead of her she noticed valises, trunks, and a large wooden wardrobe.

She glanced inside the chifforobe. It appeared empty, but she looked through the drawers and inside the compartments and found nothing. A trunk seemed most likely, and she tackled that next. Inside, she found a stack of old linen, a candy box filled with dried flowers that had once been corsages, a soccer trophy, tax forms from the '40s and '50s. A quick scan turned up no clues.

Closer to the bottom of the trunk beneath some textbooks, Gerri saw old copies of the *Westfield Gazette*—newspapers dated 1947. The date flashed through her mind. That was about the time her grandfather had been tried for the bank president's murder. The paper was yellowed and brittle to the touch. Crisp flakes broke from the edges and drifted to the floor as she scanned the pages. Finally, a headline caught her eye. She spotted the date, then piled the newspapers in order of dates and began to read the news story of the murder.

Her pulse raced as she gathered more information. She read the list of suspects, among them a bank manager, who'd had a confrontation with the president a few days earlier; a well-known Westfield businessman, who'd been negotiating a large loan; her grandfather, Arthur Seward; and Victor Emory. Gerri learned the bank officer had died from stab wounds with a parrot-beak-like instrument, but the weapon was never found.

Gerri folded the paper and picked up one from two days later in September 1947. She engulfed herself with the details but learned nothing new that she'd not already known. Finally, she found the story that corroborated the letter she'd found. Victor Emory's wife provided his alibi. She said he'd been home the evening of the murder. No one could prove otherwise. The next articles focused on her grandfather's arrest.

Keeping note of the time, Gerri sat on the floor and fingered through more newspapers as she searched for tidbits of information. Articles had now moved from the front page to unnoticeable, short items deeper in the paper, telling of her grandfather's trial, but as she searched for news, something else caught her eye in an early November issue. A front-page story told of a new finding at the Westfield Bank. Over one hundred thousand dollars had been embezzled and pointed to an inside job. Among the list of those being questioned, Gerri read Victor Emory's name. Had embezzling been a motive for the murder? Perhaps there was no connection at all, but the information settled in Gerri's bewildered thoughts.

With trembling fingers, she folded the newspaper and added it on the pile. Time had passed, and she needed to head to the kitchen for dinner, but she longed to take the newspapers with her. As she gathered them in her arms, she had second thoughts and returned them to the trunk. She knew where they were when she needed them, and leaving them would be less chance her employer would find them among her belongings.

Gerri shifted on tiptoe to the hidden door, slipped into the closet, and checked the room before exiting. She made her way to the bedroom door, looked into the hallway, then closed the door and locked it. Her hands trembled as she slipped the key into her pocket and made her way down to the first floor.

As soon as she could, she would tell Rich what she'd learned. On the first floor as Gerri passed the library, her thoughts also flew to the weapons display. As much as she detested rifles and knives, she wanted to look inside and search for the possible murder weapon—a parrot-beak knife. She hurried to the window to check for her employer. His car wasn't in the driveway, and she darted into the library and to the display case. The glass door was locked and the weapons were in sheathes. She needed to get inside, but how?

The pieces of the puzzle had begun to fall together, and Gerri headed for the telephone, longing to tell Rich, but something stopped her. If her employer was at all concerned about her, if she'd left him with questions the day she'd gotten locked in the cellar, then how could she be certain he hadn't tapped the telephone? She would have to wait until after church tomorrow.

One place Gerri felt safe was in church. Blayne Emory didn't attend worship as far as Gerri knew, and he certainly didn't attend Westfield Community Church. She stood outside the building enjoying the balmy August morning sun. Her thoughts shifted to Rich, and she warmed even more, knowing that he would be beside her in the pew.

As she came through the wide double doors, Rich waited for her.

"Mom's already seated," he said, motioning for her to go ahead of him.

She stepped into the aisle and made her way to where his mother sat. Mrs. Drake sent her an amiable smile and patted the seat beside her. Gerri slipped in, and Rich followed. Gerri opened the pew Bible and scanned the verses until the service began, looking for something to quell her anxiety. She needed to put the clues together, to report what she'd found and leave the gloom of Emory Estates. The longer she stayed the more depressed she felt. She needed the key to the weapons cabinet. Yet she had no idea where it might be, and she was certain Blayne Emory didn't leave it out in the open.

The service began, and as she sat listening to the pastor's message, Rich slid his hand over hers and gave it a reassuring pat. She felt anxious to tell him all that had happened, but she forced her mind to stay focused on God's Word.

"Listen to the words from Psalms," the pastor said, "and take it to heart. Sitting here today are people who are struggling with life's problems and people who are under deep duress. Don't think that God is not with you. The Lord is on your side. His promise is sure, as His Word says: 'Be still before the Lord and wait patiently for him; do not fret when men succeed in their ways, when they carry out their wicked schemes.' "

Gerri's chest tightened as she heard the words from Psalms that summarized all she'd been thinking the past days. She turned her attention to scripture.

" 'But the Lord laughs at the wicked, for he knows their day is coming,' " the pastor said. "We are assured of God's faithfulness."

Gerri knew the Lord was faithful. He'd given her courage and strength through the weeks when she first came to Emory Estates. He'd lifted her morale and kept her focused no matter what happened. Nothing had held her back, because she knew the Lord was with her.

"I leave you with these words from First Chronicles," the pastor said. " 'Do not be afraid or discouraged, for the Lord God, my God, is with you.' "

Rich must have sensed Gerri's thoughts, because she felt his hand press against hers in reassurance, and she gave him a nod to let him know she understood.

The last hymn sounded, and they rose and sang, their voices resounding from the high ceilings. When the service ended, Gerri whispered her need to talk. Mrs. Drake invited her to lunch again, and Rich accepted for her, then told his mother he and Gerri would meet her at home. She seemed to understand and gave them a wave as she went on ahead.

Outside, Rich slipped his arm around Gerri's shoulders as they ambled along the sidewalk toward his mother's house. Gerri told him what she'd learned. "What do you think?" she asked Rich.

He shook his head. "The two crimes could be connected, if that's what you're thinking."

"I've given it thought. Maybe the president was becoming suspicious of an employee."

"He suspected money was missing," Rich added. "Maybe he *knew* money had been embezzled."

"If the embezzler had been confronted by the bank president, perhaps he killed him rather than face arrest."

Rich drew her shoulder closer to his. "That makes sense, but it's all still speculative, isn't it?"

"But I know my grandfather didn't embezzle money. He had no way to do it even if he wanted to. He'd have to work at the bank." Gerri looked at him, hoping he'd affirm her thought.

"He could have had an accomplice, Gerri. You can't dismiss the whole idea without considering that."

Her heart sank, hearing his words. "You don't know my granddad. He was a good Christian. Would I rob a bank?"

"No. I don't think you would," Rich said, "but we're not talking about you."

"We're talking about my flesh and blood—my grandfather. You have to believe me."

Rich halted and turned her to face him. "I believe you, Gerri. I was playing devil's advocate. That's what the police would do. That's what a defense attorney would do. You don't have to convince me. You have to convince them."

His words unsettled her. She bent her head forward and rested it on his chest in defeat.

Chapter 6

Rich felt sorry he'd said anything. He'd known before he'd opened his mouth that Gerri wouldn't listen. He had never met such a determined woman in his life, and now he'd upset her again—made her cry, he feared.

"Are you all right?" he asked, tilting her head upward so he could look into her eyes.

She nodded, but he saw the mist that clung to her lashes. "I know I have to convince the police, Rich, and that's why I must find the murder weapon."

"Do you really think a killer would keep that around?" Rich asked. "It was probably destroyed years ago." She looked agitated, and he realized he'd erred again.

"No. It can't be. I need to find it. The estate has a weaponry display, but the knives are sheathed. I want to get inside. If I find the murder weapon, that's all I need."

He remained quiet, wanting to caution her again, but he decided to give up.

When they arrived at his house, Rich steered her inside. His mother welcomed her with a warm smile, as he suspected she would, and they sat down to a lunch of salad and meats with bread. When he said the blessing, he allowed the prayer to touch on Gerri's concerns, but with his mother present, he feared saying too much. He would ask Gerri to pray with him later.

After lunch, he invited her into the garden. The effort he'd put into the garden showed. The colorful flowers flourished in the summer sun—a blend of daisies intermingled with cone-flowers; tall, stately larkspur beside the runaway blossoms of purple and yellow yarrow; and shorter displays of snapdragons and periwinkle.

Gerri headed toward the roses and bent to draw in the sweet scent. "Did you do this, or is this all your mother's hand?"

"Mostly mine," he said.

"It's lovely. I like a man who can drive a truck and tote wheelbarrows but still plant a host of lovely flowers."

He drew in a deep breath to garner courage so he could speak his heart. "But none's as lovely as you are, Gerri."

She lifted her head and gazed at him as if not sure what he'd said.

"I mean it. You're beautiful from head to toe, and inside, too."

"Thank you, Rich." She studied his face, as if still uncertain as to his purpose. "You're a handsome man yourself. I'm sure you know that."

Her statement surprised him. He'd never thought of himself as handsome. He had always been too rough-and-tumble to be handsome. "Beauty is in the eye of the beholder, I suppose."

"It works both ways," she said.

He realized her meaning and wanted to defend his comments about her charm. Instead, he took her hand and led her to the bench beneath the trees. "We need to talk," he said, having so many things he wanted to say.

She gave him a curious look but settled beside him without question.

The breeze drifted beneath the tree and ruffled the strands of her long, golden hair. She truly was lovely with a sprinkling of freckles brought out by the summer's rays and the deepest blue eyes like a Caribbean lagoon.

"What's this about?" she asked.

He suspected she thought he wanted to talk about her search, but that wasn't part of his concern today. "I want to talk about us."

Surprise filled her face. "Us?"

"You and me, and where this will lead."

Her eyes searched his as if she hadn't given the topic thought, and her look filled him with disappointment. He'd hoped, as he had done, she'd thought about them as a couple and had given consideration to the future.

"When this is over, Gerri, what are your plans? Would you be willing to stay in Westfield?"

"Westfield?" She tilted her head as a frown settled on her face. "I haven't thought of the future. I'm sorry."

"I should have guessed. You're so tangled in the past." He knew the disappointment echoed in his voice.

"But I will think about it, if you want." She reached over and rested her hand on his.

She'd caught him off guard with the gesture. "You'll think about us?"

She nodded. "I have nothing to keep me in Clawson. I gave up my apartment, and I can always visit my folks. Clawson is only an hour and a half away."

"Then you'd really stay in Westfield and give us a chance to. . ." He ran out of words. To what? He knew what he wanted, but did she?

"To get to know each other," she said. "To see where this will go."

"Exactly." She did understand, and his spirit lifted. "I really care about you, Gerri. If I'm honest, I want you to know that I can see you in my future. Not just a friend, but a partner, a—"

"A wife?"

He nodded. "Can you see that at all?"

"You'd make a wonderful husband and father for someone, Rich. You're a strong Christian."

Her comment came as a jolt. "You're strong, too, Gerri."

"Not like you. I can too easily fall by the wayside."

"I don't think so. You've been so preoccupied with the past, I think you've just kept the door to your heart closed too tightly. I think the door is opening, and I'm waiting on the other side. So is the Lord. I know you have one solid foot inside."

"I do," she said. "I've changed, especially since I've come here. I realized what I'd missed by not calling on Jesus for help and comfort. Forgiveness, too. I need a lot of that."

"We all do," he said, shifting closer and slipping his arm around her back.

He raised his hand and turned her chin toward him, his gaze settling on her sweet mouth. The urge arose to kiss her, and instead of fighting it, he lowered his lips to hers. The kiss was gentle and swift, and when he pulled back, he saw a look of pleasure in Gerri's eyes, then she smiled, and his heart filled with thanksgiving to the Lord. He prayed his fears weren't warranted. Maybe she could see him as a husband.

They sat for a while in silence, drinking in the gentle breeze that rustled through the leaves above their heads. Rich wanted again to sway her to leave her project, to use the evidence she'd already found, but he bit back his words. Gerri had to do it her way. If God was leading her, Rich didn't want to be the one to misdirect her.

"Could we pray together?" Rich asked, breaking the silence.

"Please," Gerri said, slipping both her hands into his.

"Father, You are the guide. You know Gerri's purpose and You know the outcome. Protect her, lead her, and give her wisdom to follow Your will. We praise You for all the evidence that she's found, and we ask You to watch over her until her mission is complete. We thank You for the friendship we've found in each other, and Father, if it is Your will, we ask You to bless our relationship as it grows into something deeper."

"Amen," Gerri whispered.

Hearing her agreement lifted Rich's spirit.

Monday evening, the telephone rang as Gerri's employer came through the doorway. She answered and called him to the telephone. He dropped his keys on the table and took the call in his study upstairs.

As Gerri prepared dinner, her employer's voice traveled down the staircase.

"A buyer for the antique weapons?" Emory asked. "How much?"

Gerri's heart thundered, hearing the news.

She heard her employer's intake of breath. "That much? Yes, they've been in the family for years, but I'd be happy to let him take a look. I need the money. You know that."

Gerri sank into the chair and lowered her face to her hands. She needed to act now. She needed God to open another door for her—in this case, the door to the display case. That was her only hope, and time appeared to be running out.

She pulled herself together enough to set out dinner for Blayne when he returned to the dining room. After he'd eaten, he excused himself, and she cleared the kitchen quickly and went to her room to the sound of thunder rolling through the sky. She had suspected as much earlier. The house had been humid and she'd opened windows throughout the house to take advantage of the growing breeze.

Gerri lay on her bed wondering what she could do. Her body trembled with emotion and nervous tension as the growing storm bombarded the night sky. Rain thundered against the roof so close above her, and the shingles seemed to flap with the growing wind.

Hearing the sound, Gerri sat up and remembered the open windows on the first floor. She grabbed her robe and tiptoed down the two sets of stairs, heading for the living room. As she reached the bottom, a bolt of lightning zipped across the sky and brightened the room. In the sudden flash, Gerri's focus settled on the foyer table and her employer's keys. Her heart rose to her throat.

She turned her gaze to heaven. "Lord," she whispered, "he's never left his keys unattended. Have You provided this opportunity?" A boom of thunder resounded, and she sensed God's voice in the reverberating din.

Gerri recalled when Mr. Emory had arrived home. The telephone call had distracted him, and she remembered him dropping the keys on the table. With his preoccupation from the call, he'd apparently forgotten—a first for him.

Glancing up the staircase and seeing only flashes of lightning across the sky from the landing window, Gerri dashed to the table and grabbed the key ring. She scooted into the library and, with shaking fingers, inserted the smallest key into the lock. She forced the key to turn, but it did nothing. Her spirit sank. Quaking with disappointment and fear, she withdrew the key. What now?

The desk shot through her mind. As she stepped into the foyer, she cringed as a roll of thunder and bolt of lightning ripped across the sky. She bounded into the parlor and made her way with the flashes of light to the secretary desk. The key fit, and the lock turned. With no time to waste, Gerri shuffled through the papers and trinkets inside the desk. When she opened a small pigeonhole drawer, she felt a small key. She dropped it into her pocket, then locked the desk with the first key she'd found.

As she turned, a zap of lightning filled the room while a long shadow fell at her feet. She lifted her gaze and saw her employer standing in the doorway, his face obscured by darkness.

"What are you doing?" he asked, his voice raspy with concern. "I thought you were a burglar."

"I'm sorry, sir," she said, clamping the key ring inside her hand. "I remembered I'd left the windows open in the parlor. I didn't mean to disturb you."

"Don't be so careless," he said, a snarl in his voice. He moved forward into the room.

"Please, go back to bed," she said. "I'll close them. It'll only take a minute."

"How can anyone sleep with this storm?" he asked as he proceeded across the room to the farthest window.

The keys pressed against Gerri's flesh, and with a prayer rising to heaven, she darted through the doorway and dropped the keys on the foyer table before returning to close the nearest window. Her arms trembled uncontrollably as she reached to lower the sash. By the time she'd finished, Mr. Emory had closed the other windows and had already returned to the staircase. In the brightness of the lightning, he paused at the table and grasped his keys. The sound jingled with each *thud* of his footsteps as he trekked back up the stairs.

Gerri stood at the bottom, catching her breath. Her gaze shifted to the library, but tonight, she could take no more chances. Tomorrow, she would ask Rich to be her lookout when she tried the new key in the weaponry case.

The storm had damaged a number of trees on the Barnetts' property, and Rich was awakened to a call from the owners. He agreed to go to their house immediately after breakfast. He'd wanted to head for the Emory estate first, wondering how

Gerri had made out in the storm. Instead he decided to call, but she didn't answer. Fear prickled up his neck, and he prayed she was in the shower or somehow hadn't heard the telephone.

The Barnetts' tree damage was more than he could handle, and Rich contacted a tree service for them. They seemed to understand and were grateful for his efforts. He pulled out his cell phone and tried Gerri's number one more time.

She answered on the second ring.

He told her he'd called earlier, and as he suspected, she was in the shower. "Did you fare all right in the storm?"

"Yes, but I need to talk with you."

Her voice sounded edgy. "Is something wrong?"

"No, but I'm not comfortable talking on the telephone. You never know. . ."

Her voice faded, and he understood her fear that perhaps the line was tapped. "I'll get there soon. Are you sure you're okay?"

"I'm fine. Just hurry."

If someone had been listening, she would already be in trouble, he feared. Her tone was filled with urgency, and her cryptic comments would have left little for Blayne Emory's imagination if he were suspicious.

Though he'd wanted to make a courtesy call to the Garrisons', he decided to forego the trip. If they needed him, they would surely call. Instead, he headed directly for the Emory estate. No car stood in the driveway, so he assumed Gerri was alone. He pulled into the back of the drive and climbed out of the truck.

A few dead limbs spread out on the ground, and his work

ethic told him to begin removing them, but his heart told him to go to the door first. When he knocked, Gerri opened the door immediately.

"I have it," she said, her voice catching in her throat.

"Have what?"

"The key."

"To the weapons display?" he asked.

"I think so. I haven't tried it yet because I'm afraid he'll come home." She told him about her scare the night before, and her voice caught in her throat as she relived the event.

Rich stepped into the back hallway and took Gerri in his arms. "This is enough," he said, holding her close while her body trembled against him. "You're scared to death."

"I know, but I have the key—a key, but I'm sure it's it—and then I'll have the proof."

"Don't be so sure. I already warned you that the weapon might have been destroyed long ago."

"But I'll know in a minute. I want you to be my lookout. I'm so frightened now."

Rich slid his hands to her shoulders and held her out in front of him. "Listen to me, Gerri. You have to promise that if you don't find the weapon in the cabinet that you're finished. We'll take what information you have and go to the police. It's circumstantial, but there's enough information to place serious doubt about Victor's alibi."

She averted her gaze, then lowered her head without answering.

"Do you promise me? Please. You can't go on like this. I'm sure he's getting suspicious. Too many suspect things have happened involving you. He'll begin to put two and two together."

Finally she raised her head and nodded. "I promise. God's given me this final chance. The knife has to be there. It has to."

"Thank you," he said, drawing her back into his arms. His lips pressed against her heated cheek, and his chest ached feeling her tremble. He eased back. "Let's get it over with."

"If you watch out the front window, you can call if he comes down the road."

"Okay," Rich said, following her down the hallway. When she paused at the library door, he hurried past and went to the front window.

⁓

Gerri listened for Rich's all clear from the front parlor, then hurried into the library. She dug into her pocket and pulled out the key. Her hand trembled as she pinched it between her fingers and aimed it for the keyhole. The key slid in, and with no effort, it turned in the lock. Her pulse escalated.

Without withdrawing the key, Gerri pulled open the door and grasped the knife deepest in the cabinet. She pulled off the sheath. The blade had a slight curve, but no beak. When she returned it, she grasped the next and pulled it from its housing. Disappointment rolled through her. Her hand trembled as she returned the blade into the case and picked up the next.

She withdrew the blade from the sheath, and her heart stopped. She gaped at the shining wooden handle that held a thick knife blade, at least eight inches long, with a hook at the end, like a parrot's beak, she thought. She opened her mouth to call out, but her voice caught in her throat.

She moved to the library door, the knife clutched in her shaking hand. "Rich. I have it."

"What?"

She heard his footsteps pound toward her. He darted through the doorway and stopped when he saw the knife. "That's it?"

"I think so. It has a hook at the end, like a parrot's beak."

"It's a gut-hook blade," Rich said, "with a drop point. They're not uncommon."

"But it might have blood on it. Today we have DNA tests."

"Yes, that's true." He pointed to the cabinet. "Put it away, Gerri. Don't take any more chances."

She did as he said. She slid the knife into the sheath, replaced it on the shelf, and locked the door. When she withdrew the key, she stared at it, her mind boggled with a new predicament. "How am I going to get this key back into the desk?"

"I don't know," he said, his face filled with frustration. "You've pushed yourself beyond the limit, and you'll have to solve that problem since I can't."

"I know," she said, her thoughts still clicking away at possibilities.

"I can do one thing for you, Gerri. If you give me the letter and the newspapers, I'll go to the police for you. We know where the knife is, and that's all you need."

"You'd do that for me?" she asked.

He moved to her side and embraced her. "I'd do anything for you. I want you out of here, out of this mess where you'll be safe."

"Thank you," she said. She nestled her cheek against his and drew in his clean scent, and with the deep hope-filled breath, reality washed over her. She'd met her goal. God had been on her side and guided her with His loving care. She'd been safe so far. She could hardly believe it was almost over. She couldn't wait to get out of the gloom of this house, to be free again.

Chapter 7

Gerri paced the kitchen, wondering why her employer had not arrived home. She'd kept the dinner warm, but it was drying out, and she didn't know what to do. She longed for Rich to be at her side. Since she'd found the knife, she'd been on edge. Tonight she'd had an uncomfortable feeling, as if something were about to happen. She didn't like the sensation, but she didn't know what to do about it.

Her masquerade was drawing to a close. Soon, she would be free to leave the Emory mansion and make a life for herself. Rich had opened his arms and heart to her, and the event still bewildered her. She'd come to Westfield on a mission, and God had set up a mission of His own. Without looking, she'd found the man of her dreams. Still, she and Rich needed time. Neither wanted to make a mistake, so they would move slowly; but she felt confident with all they'd gone through that God had been in charge all along.

Earlier in the day, Gerri had given Rich the letter from Beatrice Emory to her husband and had handed him the stack of newspapers that held the details about the murder, the trial, and the embezzlement. Rich had promised to take it to the police for her. Gerri had no idea if they would believe him, and even if they did, how long it would take for them to act. Every day she feared that someone would arrive at the mansion to buy the antiques, including the weapons. Her evidence would vanish through the door, and she would have no way to stop it.

Gerri checked the time again, then looked at her dried-out roast. When her frustration had risen to a peak, she heard a sound in the driveway. Within moments, Blayne Emory bounded through the front door and skidded to a halt in the foyer when he noticed Gerri at the hallway door.

"I'm expecting someone," he said. "I've already eaten." He tossed his suit jacket on a chair and dug into his pocket with breakneck speed, as if he were being sought by bloodhounds.

Already irked, she wanted to say thanks for letting her know about dinner. Instead, she muttered a "thanks" for telling her and returned to the kitchen to put the food away. Yet her mind was no longer on the worthless meal she'd prepared or her employer's lateness, but the visitor whom he was expecting.

Wondering why he was so jumpy and why his haste, Gerri found herself wandering back to the hallway door. From where she stood, she watched him pull the key ring from his pocket. He strode into the parlor, appearing purpose driven, and she shifted so she could see what he was doing. Her stomach tumbled to her toes as he unlocked the secretary desk. He lifted the lid and reached inside, but the telephone's ring halted him. Gerri hurried across the hallway to answer the parlor phone, but her employer reached for it. "The buyer," he mumbled as he grasped the receiver and turned away from her as he spoke.

Buyer. Apprehension charged through Gerri. A buyer for what? The house? The weapons? She reached into her pocket and felt the small key she'd used to open the cabinet, then shifted her gaze to the unlocked desk. She had to get the key back into the desk.

While Emory spoke into the telephone, Gerri backed up and when she was close enough, she reached behind her, slid open the small drawer, and dropped in the key while her heart hammered against her chest. As her employer spoke with his back to her, she pivoted and left the room. Though she longed to know the topic of the conversation, her greatest desire was to get out of the room and away from Blayne Emory. The Lord had given her the opportunity to replace the cabinet key, and she'd done it successfully. At least, she hoped he hadn't noticed.

In moments, she heard his voice grow silent, then his footsteps echoed across the foyer tiles. Gerri wrapped the uneaten dinner and slid it into the refrigerator, trying to make herself invisible. Fear rose like a vulture picking away at her confidence. If her employer would notice anything amiss, she feared it would be now.

"Gerri!" His voice crashed through the silence.

She froze to the spot. What had she done wrong? She put the knife back exactly where she'd found it. She'd locked the door. She'd been very careful. Her ears hummed, and the room blurred. *I can't faint,* she said to herself, gripping the kitchen table for support.

"Gerri! Come here."

She pulled herself together, praying his frantic call had

nothing to do with the knife. Perhaps he wanted her to pre-pare something for his guest. Mr. Emory never spoke in a kindly voice, so his gruffness was not unusual.

She moved one foot in front of the other, forcing herself to look confident. Her knees buckled as she stepped into the foyer, and she grasped the wall to keep herself from falling. *Rich, I need you*, her mind cried out. Forcing herself to breathe, she stepped into the library and stopped inside the door. "May I help you?"

Her employer swung his gaze toward her, his eyes narrowed, and his brow knit with anger. She could see the glint of evil in his eyes, and fear pressed against her lungs, taking away her breath.

"Is something wrong?" she asked.

"Who's been in the cabinet?"

"What do you mean?" she asked, hoping to avoid a lie.

"Someone's been inside the display."

"Are you sure?" She willed herself to move closer and looked through the glass, trying to see what he had seen.

"Look." He pointed to the knife.

She saw the evidence. Dust had settled around the weapons, and where she had moved the knife, she'd disturbed the dusty outline and left a clean spot outlining where the sheath had laid for so long. Her mind tumbled with words. What could she say? How could she avoid responding?

"You were in here," he said, pointing his finger at her, then the cabinet.

"I–I. . ." Panic locked her voice inside her throat, and she only stared at him. The heat of discovery that had overwhelmed her now became icy fear.

Emory grabbed her arms and pushed his face into hers. "You were nosing around. You have been all along. I knew something was wrong, but I hoped I'd made a mistake."

The pressure of his fingers pressed into her flesh as he squeezed her arms.

"I should have fired you. Who are you? What are you doing here?"

Fear gripped her heart, and she froze in place.

"I demand you tell me." His voice bellowed in her ear.

Gerri feared for her life, just as Rich had warned her. Harnessing her panic, she sent a prayer to God for protection. She lowered her head to collect her thoughts while his fingers dug more deeply into her tender skin. "You're hurting me."

"I'll do more than hurt you. Who are you?"

"I'm Gerri Seward."

He gasped as his grip relaxed. "Seward?"

"Yes. Arthur Seward was my grandfather."

He staggered backward, his mouth gaping. "Why are you here?"

"To prove my grandfather's innocence. He died years ago in prison, and I waited all these years until I had the opportunity to prove his innocence."

Emory must have regained his confidence. His shoulders rose, and an arrogant look settled on his face. "And how did you plan to prove that?"

"By finding something in this house that would validate what I believe." Gerri's spirit lifted. She had truth on her side, and this man could not hurt her anymore.

He snorted a laugh. "You failed miserably. You have no proof."

"But I do, and it's with the police." She prayed Rich had taken it there tonight, though she hadn't heard from him since he left.

"The police?" He sneered at her. "I'm sure they'll want to drag out an old case that's been solved for nearly sixty years."

"I think they will, because an innocent man paid for someone else's guilt."

He rubbed his temple, and his hand slid to the nape of his neck. "You found nothing."

Though he said the words, his voice had softened as if he'd lost his conviction. Gerri seized the moment of weakness and used it to her advantage. "But I have found proof, Mr. Emory. I found a letter from your grandmother." She told him what Beatrice had said so many years ago. "And I found the newspapers, all the details of the investigation and the embezzlement. My grandfather had nothing to do with stealing money, but I think that yours did, and that's why the bank president was murdered. You've suffered all these years, trying to hide the sins of your family. My heart breaks for you."

Blayne's angry gaze shriveled to despair, and instead of striking out, his head drooped into his outspread hands. A deep moan rolled from his throat that tore at Gerri's soul. She'd never heard such desperation, such hopelessness. She moved toward him, but Blayne staggered backward and crumpled into a chair with a tormented cry.

Gerri grasped for strength, and God met her need. Words filled her mind and heart, words of forgiveness and of hope.

"Mr. Emory, you've suffered so long for your family's sins. I don't know if you're a man of faith now or if you ever were, but God speaks to us about that in many scriptures. Don't you know that the sins of the father don't rest on the children. A son doesn't bear guilt for his father or his grandfather. Each person dies for their own sins."

"You have no idea," he whispered.

"No, I've never been in your shoes, but I lived in my grandfather's shoes for too long. He was a sweet man, a Christian man who fell on bad times, and instead of solving his problems with a short-term loan, he paid the price for a murder he didn't commit. He's in heaven now and free from all of this, but you're not."

"I've known since I was a child about my grandfather," he said into his hands. "My parents tried to cover it, but we lived on tainted money for years. Money embezzled and well hidden, but money that nearly strangled my parents and then me. This house has been a millstone around my neck," Emory muttered. "I've drowned in the memories until I can't breathe."

"And with no cause." Gerri knelt by his side, amazed that the Lord had given her the strength to speak civilly to this man who'd caused her family so much grief. "You should have confessed this years ago and been able to live again. Murder wasn't your sin, only the avoidance of justice. That's been your torment. I feel pity for you."

He seemed a broken man. The fight had left him, and Gerri prayed at his feet, asking God to forgive him and to heal his darkened heart. Her prayer was interrupted by sounds from outside, and she rose as Rich darted through the doorway and

169

came to a halt, his face reflecting his shock at the sight of Blayne Emory, a defeated man.

The police followed Rich through the doorway, and Blayne did not put up a fight. He'd lost the battle, crushed, it seemed, by the reality of his wasted life. While one officer followed Gerri's instruction and took the knife from the display case as evidence, another led Blayne Emory away for questioning.

"I'll come to the station tomorrow," Gerri said to the officer who held the confiscated weapon. "Would that be okay?"

The young man agreed and followed the other officer into the night with Blayne Emory.

The dramatic event washed over Gerri like a torrent, and she caved into Rich's arms with sobs of relief and sorrow. "Thank You, Lord," she said as she clung to Rich.

Rich held her close, murmuring words to soothe her, and finally she pulled herself together and told him what had happened. "It was pitiful. He's a broken man."

"Blayne Emory has been a broken man from childhood," Rich said. "If he'd listened to God's Word, he would have saved himself from a useless life. He didn't know of God's mercy and forgiveness."

The truth struck Gerri like lightning. "But I forgave him, Rich. I can't believe how easy it was. I prayed for him."

He tilted her chin upward and kissed her on the end of the nose. "That's because you have God in your heart. I'm proud of you, Gerri. You amaze me."

"I amazed myself," she said, sending him a faint smile that surprised her.

Rich released her but kept her hand in his. "I know you're

safe now, but you're not staying here tonight."

"I'll be fine, Rich."

"But I won't be. While you pack, I'll call my mom. I know she'd love to have an overnight guest."

"It's not a problem, really."

"Listen to me, Gerri. If I'm going to be the man of the house, give me some credence."

Gerri laughed for the first time in weeks as joy filled her heart. "Is that what I think it means?" she asked.

"In time, it is."

"I can't wait," she said.

He gave her a playful push. "Get ready, and I'll make the call."

Gerri gave him a questioning look, then acquiesced, and started up the staircase. Halfway up, she paused and looked at the dour painting of Victor Emory. Evil shot from his eyes, and Gerri rejoiced she'd never have to see that portrait again. Instead, she could look into Rich's loving eyes and feel safe.

Chapter 8

Gerri sat at Carolyn Drake's kitchen table and read the morning headlines. Her heart lifted, knowing her mission had been accomplished and her grandfather's name would be vindicated for a murder he didn't commit. She also rejoiced for Blayne Emory who could now live in the light, no longer shrouded by the darkness of his grandfather's evil. She prayed the Holy Spirit would enter the man's heart and give him peace.

"Did you sleep well?" Rich's mother asked.

"Very well," Gerri said. "The best sleep I've had since I came to Westfield."

"I can imagine," Carolyn said. "That house seemed to be brooding."

"But no more," Gerri said. "I hope someone can buy the place and the light will return. It's a lovely house. The only thing that brightened it while I lived there was Rich."

"He's a good son," Carolyn said.

"Who is?"

Gerri swiveled in the chair, hearing Rich's voice behind her.

"You are," she said. "You brought me bouquets of flowers. That brightened my days in that somber room."

"And I'm not planning to stop now," he said. He pulled his arm from behind his back and handed her a mixed bouquet of summer flowers. "To my new best friend."

"Thank you," she said with tears in her eyes. "Thanks for the flowers and for being there when I needed you."

"I couldn't have been anywhere else." He settled beside her at the kitchen table and clasped her hands.

"I suppose I should let you two alone," his mother said, backing toward the doorway.

"No, Mom. Stay." He motioned to the bouquet. "In fact, you could put those flowers in water while Gerri and I go for a walk."

"Good idea," Carolyn said, gathering the flowers from Gerri's arms and heading toward the kitchen sink.

Rich stretched both of his arms toward Gerri and hoisted her up from the chair. She chuckled as he lifted her. For the first time in months, she felt buoyant, as if the weight of the world had lifted from her shoulders.

She fell into his welcoming arms, and Rich gave her a hug, then grasped her hand and drew her toward the back door. "We'll be back in a while," Rich said to his mother.

"Have fun," she said, giving them a wave and a huge smile.

They stepped outside, and Gerri breathed in the summer morning air. Her heart felt as joyful as the birds that twittered in the treetops. The past evening had left her drained but confident that God had taken charge, and now this morning, she felt free from the burden and ready for something new. Her pulse skipped, feeling Rich's strong hand holding hers.

"What will happen to him?" Gerri asked.

Rich gave her a sidelong glance. "Emory, you mean?" He shrugged. "Other than hiding a family secret, I don't know if he did anything unlawful. His crime was against God more than man, I suppose. He was only a child when all that happened. He had been no more to blame for his grandfather's actions than you would have been of yours."

"But I couldn't have lived with the sin if my grandfather had committed it. You saw how driven I was to prove my grandfather's innocence. I'm afraid I would have been as determined to admit his crime if he'd been at fault. It's what God expects."

Rich reached toward her with his free hand and tousled her hair. "That's because you're a powerhouse Christian. Not everyone is like you, Gerri. You're a unique human being."

"You would have been truthful," she said.

"Probably," he agreed, "but we never know until we're caught up in the dilemma."

"Anyway," Gerri said, "I've continued to pray for Mr. Emory."

"I'm sure you have." He gave her a tender smile as he guided her into the park.

"And I have to go to the police station this morning. I promised."

"You did," he said, "but right now, let's talk about us, okay?"

Her chest tightened, hearing his words. "Okay," she said, longing to know what he would say.

He drew her into a wooded glade where shrubs and tall flowers created a private arbor. "You know I care about you."

She nodded.

"And I hope you feel the same."

She couldn't cover her grin. "I do. You piqued my interest from the day I met you, and now, we've shared so much."

"We have. I've thanked God every day for bringing you into my life. Without God's direction, I fear you would have been in danger. I don't think you realized that."

"Perhaps, but I knew I was under the Lord's wing. I felt very sure about that. I surprised myself. I was afraid but confident."

"You're human." He stopped and turned her toward him. "God guided us to each other, too. I believe that."

"So do I." She lifted her hand and brushed his cheek. "You were the friend I needed, and soon you were the dream that kept me sane."

He raised his hand and captured hers against his cheek. "I'm falling in love with you, Gerri. I know it's been a short time, but when people are under stress, their true character comes out. I love what I saw, and I can picture living with you for the rest of my life."

Her heart leaped with joy. "I picture the same, Rich. Your mother's a wonderful woman, and you're a true gentleman and a strong Christian. I'd love to be part of your family. You're what I always wanted but was too afraid to dream possible."

"All things are possible in the Lord," he said, shifting her hand from his cheek to his lips. He brushed a kiss across the backs of her fingers, then drew her closer. "I know we can't make any promises right now, but I hope you're willing to settle in Westfield so we can explore what God has in mind."

The sun slipped from behind the tall shrubs, and a beam of

light spread across Rich's face. They'd stepped from the shadows into light, and Gerri sensed God had smiled on them.

"How could we go against the Lord's wishes?" she said, her heart smiling. "I'm very willing to stay here and to explore our relationship."

Rich smiled back. "I'm guessing the search will be short, don't you?"

"Very short, and my heart agrees."

Rich's lips met hers in a gentle caress, and Gerri knew that the truth had come into light, and she could see God's plan as clearly as the blue sky.

Thank You, Father, her heart sang. *Thank You.*

GAIL GAYMER MARTIN

Gail loves nothing more than to write, talk, and sing—especially if it's about her Lord. With hundreds of articles as a freelance writer and numerous church resource books, she sold her first novel to Barbour in 1998. Now, she has been blessed as an award-winning, multipublished romance author with seventeen contracted novels or novellas.

Although Gail loves fiction, her worship materials are a direct way of sharing her faith with worshiping Christians. Gail has four **Heartsong Presents** novels and five novellas published with Barbour fiction. She is also a contributing editor and columnist for the ezine, *Spirit-Led Writer*.

Besides being active in her home church, Gail maintains her professional counselor license in the state of Michigan. She is involved in a number of writers' organizations and especially enjoys public speaking and presenting workshops to help new writers. Gail loves traveling, as well as singing with the Detroit Lutheran Singers. She lives in Lathrup Village with her husband and real-life hero, Bob Martin, who proofreads all her work. "Praise God from whom all blessings flow."

At the End of the Bayou

by DiAnn Mills

Dedication

To Kathleen Y'Barbo.
God gives us friends so the winding road
is never beyond our sight.

So do not fear, for I am with you;
do not be dismayed, for I am your God.
I will strengthen you and help you;
I will uphold you with my righteous right hand.
ISAIAH 41:10 NIV

Chapter 1

The headaches had rendered me helpless for another day. I never knew when they would attack. They crept in unsuspectingly, a cruel beast that showed no mercy, only endless pain. I neither saw flashing lights nor felt a prickly sensation at the top of my skull. Nothing. Only incessant, debilitating pain.

This pain and my perpetual search for a cure led me to a new doctor who, after performing all of the usual tests for tumors and such, suggested my migraines might be emotional. Burying my face in my hands, I could only weep.

"I feared this." I brushed back the hair from my dampened face.

"Why, Shelby?" the balding young doctor asked.

"My mother is in an institution for the mentally ill. Her doctors offer no hope for recovery."

"Does she have headaches?"

I shook my head and swallowed the lump in my throat. I detested weak women who resorted to tears rather than logical communication. "No, not to my knowledge."

"Are you overburdened by her care and condition?"

Although his question was poignant, his voice rang tender. Again I said no.

"Many people, especially women, suffer from migraines. You simply need to take the prescribed medication."

"But do these people have mentally ill mothers and a childhood they cannot remember?"

The doctor scrutinized me closely. "Perhaps a therapist is in order."

"I've seen a Christian counselor for years. Still do. I simply don't remember my life before moving to Detroit when I was nearly eight years old."

The doctor sighed. This problem of mine was definitely not within his realm of expertise. He wanted to prescribe a pill and send me on my way until the next monthly appointment. "Perhaps a psychiatrist?"

"I've done that, too." I forced a smile in hopes of hiding my distress.

"Then consider returning to your birthplace."

I shuddered. How many times had those same thoughts entered my mind? My counselor, Mary Linda, who is also my pastor's wife whom I've grown to love as a surrogate mother, has prayed with me about this very thing.

"I guess I have no choice." Already my mind spun with all the arrangements necessary before obtaining a leave from my dental practice. I'd considered selling the Louisiana property left to Mother since I had power of attorney. This way I could take care of both matters.

Leaving the doctor's office, I drove to the private hospital where Mother had spent the last fifteen years. She hadn't recognized me for a long time, and the doctors said she probably did not comprehend anything I said, either. But I had to tell her nevertheless.

The hospital gave exemplary care in a loving environment. The cost did not matter. Each time I entered the foyer and noted the rich mahogany furniture and textured upholstery and made my way down the hardwood halls featuring the finest of oil paintings, I praised God for the facility. Here, noteworthy caregivers and professionals tended my mother with the dignity she deserved. I rested easily knowing their care far excelled what I could do. Today they had Mother in a comfy recliner facing the terrace area where the mid-April signs of greenery sprang up from the cultivated earth.

"Mother, I'm going to visit the old home in Louisiana." I tucked the lap blanket around her waist. She'd just been bathed and smelled of strawberries.

She stared blankly at me and my heart wrenched. Gone were the days when Mother caught the eye of every passerby. Her jet black hair had grown gray and brittle, and those once light blue eyes with flecks of gold now stared dull and listless. The wrinkles in her face had deepened into an image of battle scars. An old friend told me I looked like my mother, and his words filled me with pleasure because I'd always felt she was beautiful. We were petite and never had a problem with weight gain, which had been the envy of my friends.

Since my father died in Vietnam shortly before my third birthday, I barely remembered him. This visit would give me a sense of belonging in my otherwise obscure world.

"I love you," I whispered as I bent to kiss her pale cheek. "Jesus loves you, too, and I believe He wants me to find out what happened in Louisiana. I'm staying until I find what I'm looking for." I tilted my head, seeking a sign that she understood why I must leave.

Two weeks later, I still wondered if I'd made the right decision as I drove a leased sedan from Lafayette, east to the section of Louisiana called Zirondelle in New Iberia parish. The travel agent said it contained magnificent antebellum homes and a rich history.

Already I sensed a slower pace of life, and I felt rather lost—me who always conducted my life according to a rigid schedule. Mary Linda believed this was a coping mechanism developed as a child so no one would know my mother's condition. She urged me to slow down and enjoy life. I tried, but I couldn't afford the luxury of deep friendships. Except for Jesus. My Savior stood as my life and joy. I told Him everything, pouring out all my hurt and disappointment. Oh, I had foster parents who meant well and tried to get me to open up, but I refused. So the social workers labeled me as socially unadjusted. I could only guess their thoughts. I compensated by pouring out my energies into books. Learning became a fascination.

I pressed the automatic window button and allowed the fresh spring breeze to flow over me. The sweet smell of freshly turned earth and the chirping birds eased my troubled thoughts. I couldn't quite label my normally logical emotions. I wavered between excitement, fear, and adventure, like a boat bouncing along the waves.

Glancing at the map, I turned down a narrow, paved road that eventually became a ground oyster-shell surface. A cloud of white dust trailed behind me. I would have called the road gravel, if not for the travel agent who specifically indicated otherwise. Both sides of the road were shaded with huge towering oaks. Deep green moss draped from the trees, and I could detect the scent of water somewhere. I wondered why Mama had to leave a place so hauntingly beautiful, but right then a black snake crawled across the road, and I couldn't get the window up fast enough.

"Snakes, huh?" I said aloud with a laugh. "So in this beauty there's danger?"

Three miles later, I saw the rickety mailbox indicating Shelby Oaks, the entrance to a five-hundred-acre estate. I whipped the car to the left, down a winding, narrow lane covered with the same crushed oyster-shell paving. An eerie sensation tickled at my nape. Dizziness threatened to overtake me, and I fought the overwhelming urge to close my eyes. A huge house rose in sight, a monument to pre-Civil War days. Huge pillars, yellowed and paint chipped, held the ornate roof above the ground like the fingers of a prehistoric creature destined to guard the home. Century-old oaks amidst overgrown grasses and shrubs guarded both sides of the front, and when I studied them, they waved their lofty branches lightly. I didn't know if they were welcoming me or warning me of what I'd find inside.

Foreboding. I shivered despite the warm, humid temperatures.

I'd searched online for Louisiana plantations in the area and found a few, none of which unlocked that abyss of my mind.

Silent grandeur. This one whispered of things I'm not so sure I wanted to know.

Immediately, pain burst from the top of my head—familiar but despised. Often I felt like a prisoner sentenced to a life of torture. Another stab pierced my right eye, blurring my vision and causing me to slam on my brakes. I trembled while reaching for my purse. It only took a moment to retrieve the nasal spray, and it would eventually bring relief. It worked faster than pills and injections and, in times like these, was certainly easier to administer.

I closed my eyes and a few minutes later managed to slip the car into Drive. Slowly pulling into a circular driveway that led up to the veranda, I stopped the car and released a sigh. I had to give into a nap.

Beneath my closed lids, I heard a tapping on the window. *Go away.*

"Miss, Miss," a woman said.

I slid open my eyes through the haze of my medicine-induced sleep. I attempted to lower the window, but I realized the ignition wasn't on. Fumbling for the keys, I finally got the window down.

"Are you all right, chil'?" the woman asked in a sweet voice. Her dialect sounded strange with a hint of French, and I gathered she must be Cajun.

"I. . .will be. Headache."

"Yes, ma'am. I take it you're Shelby Landry?"

I nodded.

"I'm the housekeeper, Mrs. Thibodeaux, and I'm sorry you're having a bad time of it. Can I help you into the house?"

Closing my eyes, I shook my head. "I'll be better in about thirty minutes."

"I'll come back then."

I offered a weak smile. I'd hired Mrs. Thibodeaux through a Christian housekeeping agency listed in the Lafayette phone book. After checking her credentials and finding she lived in the area, I approved her employ and mailed a check and a key to the agency. I hadn't wanted a live-in housekeeper, just someone during the day, more for company than anything else. Luckily she lived in Zirondelle. Along with hiring the woman, I had all the utilities turned on.

True to her word, Mrs. Thibodeaux tapped on my car window exactly thirty minutes later. "Are you better?" she asked. "I've been praying for you."

Although the throbbing had lessened, I still felt miserable. I grabbed my purse and opened the door. "Thank you. I'm so sorry. These nasty headaches never give me any warning." I held out my hand and she grasped it lightly.

"Welcome to Shelby Oaks. Let's get you inside so you can lie down for a while." Again her slow drawl soothed me, and the warmth emitting from her brown eyes eased my nerves.

"I have a huge suitcase in the trunk, but it has wheels. Then I have my laptop and a cosmetic case."

"We'll manage." She linked her arm into mine as though I were an old friend. I liked her immensely. Odd for me, for my skeptic side avoided personal attachments. Oh, I had friends and we did lunches and shopping excursions, but I steered away from letting anyone venture too close.

Mrs. Thibodeaux helped me lift the mammoth suitcase

from the trunk of the rental car and set it on its wheels. My computer case was also on wheels, which meant only the cosmetic case had to be hoisted onto my shoulder. The woman moved much faster than I did, and even with the heavier load and ascending the six steps, she had the double doors opened by the time I reached the veranda.

"I've spent the last week cleaning," she said, "but it does need more."

"I'm sure it will be perfect," I replied, but my legs shook. Nothing about the exterior of the home looked familiar, although I'd spent the first seven years of my life here.

Mrs. Thibodeaux gestured me through the door, and I gasped at the richness of the architecture. Directly inside the polished wooden-floored entrance—with twin pillars so ornately carved, I felt mesmerized by the craftsmanship—she ushered me to a winding staircase leading to the second floor. I glanced up at a myriad of twinkling lights from a chandelier that must have extended five feet wide or more. I imagined the hundreds of prisms glittering at night. To the left of the staircase, I could see floor-to-ceiling windows from a far room. Fingers of light radiated at my feet, sort of a carpet effect as though I were royalty. At least I'd like to think so.

"Would you like me to show you to your room?" Mrs. Thibodeaux asked, smoothing her plain navy dress.

"Oh, yes," I said breathlessly, then glanced at my suitcase. "This is too heavy for either of us to lift, and I don't want it to scratch the wood."

She folded her hands at her waist. "My husband plans to pick me up later. If you can wait, he'd tote it up."

"Wonderful idea."

She picked up my computer case and I followed her toward the stairway. My senses relished in the parlor furnishings on my left and the dining room on the right. All so very old. I anticipated ghosts swirling through the place, although my Christian upbringing frowned on the thought.

"I love the sea-foam green upholstery," the woman remarked, peering into the parlor. "The mahogany wood has done well despite the lack of care."

Yes, mahogany like the wood in Mother's nursing home. "I agree." I marveled at the dining room in the same wood. The china cabinet held a set of dishes I wanted to examine later— a hobby of mine. The table could have easily seated sixteen people. Why did my mother leave this? We'd lived in squalor until I finished college and started my pediatric dental practice. Recently, I discovered she had inherited this house and a handsome sum of money, which I refused to touch.

The home had been named for my father, and me for him. A twinge of alarm sped up my arms. Why couldn't I remember anything about my childhood? What could possibly have happened?

Upstairs, down a long hallway, I followed Mrs. Thibodeaux past four closed doors. Tomorrow I'd explore them. When the door opened to the bedroom obviously assigned to me, visions of a Southern belle danced across my mind, and I was instantly transported into another era. From the delicately embroidered coverlet on the high-poster bed to the dressing table with a muted peach floral chair, I saw only delicate lines seeped in femininity.

"Is this where I am to stay?" I asked in sheer amazement.

"Oh yes. Do you like it?" She tucked a gray lock back into a loosely woven bun.

I slowly turned to every corner of the room, wanting to see it all but not wanting to send my aching head into another whirl. A cherry wardrobe caught my attention, then a vanity dresser complete with a matching beveled mirror and a small sitting stool. A pale blue chenille bedspread covered a four-poster bed. I had taken a step back in time, and I felt drawn yet fearful. "It's breathtaking, like something from a magazine or an old movie."

"The chifforobe will have to do as your closet." Mrs. Thibodeaux called it a "clowset" and I inwardly smiled. I'd never heard of a wardrobe or armoire referred to as a chifforobe, but I intended to pick up some of the colloquial phrases. Mrs. Thibodeaux rested my computer case on the floor, then expertly turned back the bed. "Here, chil'. Rest in the quiet beauty of Shelby Oaks."

The motherly tone coming from anyone else might have sounded contrived, but not from this lady. I glanced into her eyes and saw the peacefulness I'd already guessed. "You told me you prayed for me, but now I see you are Christian," I said.

Her dark brown pools sparkled. The lines in her face widened, assigning wisdom and trust. "And so are you." She chuckled. "My mama doesn't believe a Yankee Christian walks the earth, much less in the Louisiana bayou, but now I can tell her she's wrong."

"Perhaps I can meet her," I said, suddenly wanting to know all about Mrs. Thibodeaux. After all, these were my people.

"She's in a nursing home," she replied in an apologetic tone.

"That would give you and me a pleasant outing. My mother is in a nursing home, too."

She tilted her head. "I grew up around here. I knew your folks, but my mama knew them better."

My stomach fluttered.

Mrs. Thibodeaux fluffed the pillow. "Your mama was a beautiful woman. You put me in mind of Bonnie when I first saw you, and your daddy." She lifted her head. "He looked so good that he made a person's eyes tired. But my mama was acquainted with your grandfather."

I couldn't believe my good fortune. "I do so want to talk to someone who spent time with my family."

"We'll arrange it." She walked to the door. "God has brought you to a good place, Miss Landry."

"Shelby," I corrected. "And your name?"

"Doris." She pronounced it "Daris," making it have such a pretty ring. "I'll leave you now. Dinner will be at six, and I understand from the agency you have several food allergies?"

I nodded.

"I have the list. Later you can give me your favorites."

"As long as it's not on my list of allergic items, I'll eat anything. Surprise me." Suddenly I remembered I'd forwarded phone calls. "Are there any messages for me?"

She pulled a pad from her pocket. "I'm so sorry; I nearly forgot. Mr. Chad LeBlanc phoned. He'll get back in touch with you tomorrow. Says he's a land developer up the bayou, heard the house was vacant."

After Doris left, I crawled beneath the crisp, white sheets

191

and gently massaged my head. Another nap would help before I tended to things in this picturesque old house. I knew the Lord had brought me here and provided a new friend in Doris. Perhaps He'd even brought a developer who might be interested in the property.

If I could only discover the secret of my past.

Chapter 2

I awakened from the nap in my typical ravenous mode. As I made my way down the circular staircase, I smelled something delicious—a mixture of chicken and sausage with onions and something else I couldn't quite figure out. My stomach growled and my mouth watered.

"What is this heavenly smell?" I asked Doris, who was stirring this huge pot. She wore a red gingham apron and looked quite at home in the kitchen.

"My lands, chil', why it's gumbo. Don't they cook where you come from?"

I peered into the pot. "Yes, but I've never eaten anything that resembles this."

"It'll be ready in an hour." Doris replaced the lid. "Won't taste right until then. I checked with your list, and nothing in it should make you sick."

I laughed. "I'm so hungry it wouldn't make any difference." I glanced around the kitchen, and it reminded me of a kitchen in an old black-and-white TV show. I liked it. Stepping to a cupboard for a glass, I found it remarkably strange that I knew just where they were kept. Feeling Doris's gaze, I said nothing but went about the business of filling the glass with water. *I had lived here, and I do remember where the glasses were kept.*

"I'd like to call Mr. LeBlanc," I said. "Did he leave a number?"

Doris pulled the pad of paper from her apron pocket, tore off the sheet with the developer's information, and handed it to me. "Shoo on out of here. I want to pass the mop over the floor before I leave today."

I silently questioned what she meant by passing the mop but then presumed her mannerism was colloquial and I'd better get used to it. Up in my room, I dialed Mr. LeBlanc's number. Normally I punched in phone numbers or pressed speed dial, but not here at Shelby Oaks. This was another world. . .or was it?

"Mr. Chad LeBlanc, please," I said to a female who identified the business as LeBlanc Real Estate and Development Firm. A strange, yet familiar music greeted me for the few moments I waited for Mr. LeBlanc to answer. The instruments were a combination of an accordion, fiddle, and guitar.

"Chad LeBlanc here."

"My name is Shelby Landry, and I understand you tried to contact me at Shelby Oaks earlier today."

"Yes, ma'am, I did." His deep voice rang friendly, and the twang of his Cajun accent appealed to me. "I understand your property may be for sale?"

"Yes, it is. Would you like to take a look at the house and land?"

"Absolutely. Is tomorrow convenient?"

"Can we make it morning?" I asked, trying not to convey my eagerness. Although the place was beautiful, obviously something here had caused my mother unhappiness. The sooner I disposed of the property the better.

"I can be there by ten."

"Perfect."

I hung up the phone, and where I'd been enthusiastic in talking to the developer about selling, now I felt rather bittersweet. The mixed emotions frustrated me. *I lived here, played here. Somewhere in the recesses of my mind are memories of a little girl.*

In the next instant, I elected to do a physical inspection of the grounds. A part of me thought it wise, especially with Mr. LeBlanc's appointment in the morning, but the bigger part of me thought something might trigger what I longed to discover.

I exited the double front door onto the wide veranda. I listened to the sounds of insects, and a warm breeze carried a fragrant touch of spring wildflowers. Inhaling deeply, I noted the rotting boards beneath my feet and the cracked, peeling paint. Vines scaled up the side of the massive two story, and weeds infested the once rich flowerbeds and lush, green grass. My attention focused to the right, where in the afternoon sun, several rose bushes once bloomed. Smiling, I walked toward them, remembering the huge blooms in summer and the way my mother loved them so. Remembering wasn't nearly as painful as I originally thought. In fact, most of it could be quite pleasant.

Glancing upward, I noted a broken window, and for the first time I believed the house looked like an old woman whose beauty lay in the past. Unlike the aged, this home could be restored, but not by me, and I doubted if Mr. LeBlanc held to those ideals either. I ventured on around to the back and found a bit of disappointment in not recalling some childhood game. Perhaps if I'd had siblings, I might have remembered more.

Beyond a line of moss-covered oaks where branches dipped low from the weight, I discovered a swamp below. Bald cypress rose from the water like the pillars on the front of Shelby Oaks. Curious about the legendary Louisiana swamps, I studied the water and thought it closely resembled Doris's gumbo. Just when I considered moving down the bank and exploring the area, a log moved and a pair of eyes glared up at me. *Alligators!* Could the beasts climb up to the house? How could this lovely setting accommodate such a dreadful creature?

I shuddered and decided to forego my little adventure in lieu of completing my walk around the house. The grass and weeds grew above my knees and a bit of fear nearly overcame me. Between the snake I'd passed on the road and the alligator in the swamp, I could easily be persuaded to spend all of my days in the parlor.

Once inside, I made notes of what needed to be done outside, even for the short time I intended to live there. Regardless if Mr. LeBlanc purchased the estate, the grounds should be presentable.

Mr. Thibodeaux arrived and carried my suitcase upstairs while Doris ladled out a huge bowl of gumbo. We said our good-byes and even before their antiquated Ford truck rattled off down the driveway, I sensed utter loneliness. This was rare for me, for most of my life had been in solitude. But all evening I looked forward to eight o'clock in the morning when Doris would arrive. I wanted to hear her gentle voice and feel her presence.

As the evening wore on, I heard countless noises—frightful at times, making me wonder if the house was haunted. I chose to put away my things rather than explore the house. After all, I had the next four weeks to examine all the rooms and discover what encompassed the five hundred acres. I phoned the hospital to check on Mama, then elected to read a dentistry journal.

When the appropriate hour came for me to go to bed, I crawled beneath the sheets as I'd done earlier and did my best to sleep. Instead my mind replayed the events of the day, and the moments ticked back while I listened to the peculiar moans and groans of the house.

I dwelled a moment on Mr. Chad LeBlanc. He had a pleasant voice, somewhere in the range of baritone. Was he single? Handsome? How shameful of me. What if he had a wife and children? *Father, forgive me for such thoughts.* I hadn't delved much into relationships; always Mother's care took priority, and I hadn't found a man who understood my devotion to her. Casting aside my foolish notions about a man I hadn't met, I drifted off to sleep.

Hours later, I wakened sharply, my body drenched in perspiration. I'd been running from an alligator, and the creature hurried close behind. I raised myself and noted the pain in my head again. Another headache. Another cursed headache. Throwing back the sheet and coverlet, I switched on a light and made my way to the bathroom for the medication.

When would this all end?

❧

Promptly at ten o'clock the following morning, someone pounded on the door.

"I'll get it," I said when Doris's sensible shoes clopped across the wooden floor toward the door. A white, four-door luxury sedan stood parked in front of the veranda as if at attention.

A dark-haired man with large brown eyes smiled at me. Admittedly so, he was much too good looking for a single woman to contemplate. Olive skin and a slight build gave him a boyish appeal, although a few lines etched around his eyes indicated otherwise. Pardon my boldness, but he didn't wear a wedding band. I scolded my thoughts and determined to keep the conversation on business and not the wayward musings of a woman away from her pediatric dental practice.

"Miss Landry."

I nodded and he extended his hand, which I grasped lightly. "Chad LeBlanc."

With my invitation, he stepped inside. "I've driven past here a few times, even saw the owner lived in Michigan. It's a classic, isn't it?"

"A piece of the past."

He flashed me a sparkling smile. The man had the whitest teeth I'd ever seen outside of a toothpaste commercial. "My thoughts exactly."

"I assume you're interested in purchasing the estate. I've only been here since yesterday, but I can show you what I do know."

Doris walked into the foyer, eying him curiously. "You look like a LeBlanc from here."

"I am, ma'am."

"Thought so." Doris raised her chin as though she'd placed the last piece of a jigsaw puzzle. "I'm a Thibodeaux. Are you Doc Poot and Lillian's?"

"Yes, ma'am."

She crossed her arms over her ample chest. "Don't let city life take your roots."

I wanted to laugh, but I refused to insult Doris or Mr. LeBlanc, and I didn't understand their ways—yet.

"Do you want a tour of the inside first?" I asked, suddenly wishing I'd taken the time the night before to become familiar with the fifteen rooms.

"I'd prefer the outside, if that's all right with you." He laughed easily and made me feel comfortable, another rarity for such a private person as myself. And, my goodness, he was a handsome man.

"What are your plans for the property?" I asked, leading him out of the front door.

"An inn, I think, with all of the southern hospitality and Cajun charm we're famous for. This is a project for me, a desire to bring back the antebellum period to those who appreciate its beauty."

I felt a grin tug at my lips. "I think it's a splendid idea. I'm not much of a visionary, but I see the potential. Once renovated, it could draw people here from all over the country. There's a problem, though."

He swung his attention my way.

"Alligators live in the swamp behind the house."

"We call swamps a marsh, Miss Landry. Every marsh has

199

gators, and I suspect I'll send the guests who don't pay their bill down there for a swim."

"Mr. LeBlanc!"

He chuckled. "The name is Chad."

"And I'm Shelby."

"How nice to be named for the family estate."

"Actually, I was named after my father who was named after his father."

He cleared his throat. "Gators give the area character and also make some mighty good eatin'."

The thought curdled my stomach. "I'll pass."

We walked along the side and back of the house as I'd done the afternoon before. He examined the rose bushes and pulled up a few weeds. He stood under a towering oak. "I can see picnics on the lawn and flowers growing everywhere."

"And a rope swing on one of those low branches."

"With a gentleman pushing a lady."

I nearly said he was a hopeless romantic, but those words were too familiar. After all, Chad and I were conducting business.

"I bet you remember good times at this house," Chad said.

I hesitated to answer, but truth never strayed far from my path. "I'm sure I do."

A curious look spread across his features, and my face grew warm. "How old were you when you left?"

I sighed. "Seven. . . .I don't want to talk about me. If you're interested in purchasing the property, then make me an offer." Before the words left my mouth, my right eye felt as though a knife twisted inside. Never had I experienced consecutive migraines, although I knew those type existed.

"Are you all right?" Chad asked.

"Just a headache," I managed, doing my best to look pain free and in control.

"Let's get you inside."

Embarrassed beyond my wildest dreams, I moved on around the house to the steps. *I will not stagger like an old drunk.* This trip was to find the source of the headaches, not increase them. I should have stayed in Michigan and contracted the sale via a broker.

"Do you have medication?" Chad asked. Suddenly I noted his hand on the small of my back. This couldn't be happening. I despised weak women.

"I'll be fine in a few moments, and yes, I have medication."

"Do you get these often?" Chad asked.

I fought to keep my eyes open and took a deep breath. "More often than I like, but not enough to stop me from doing anything." That was a partial truth.

"I'll pray for you," he said.

He's a Christian. The realization helped ease my humiliation. "Thank you. I've prayed about the headaches for years."

"I'm sorry, Shelby. A lovely woman shouldn't have to endure the kind of pain I see on your face."

Pity was not what I wanted or needed. I pulled myself from his grasp and mounted the steps to the front door, all the while praying I wouldn't stumble and fall. "Mail me an offer."

Chapter 3

Once again I spent a fitful night dealing with the migraine and the guilt from my curt reply to Chad. My response to his caring attitude reminded me of a spoiled child. I knew why I'd reacted badly. Pity characterized what others felt for my mother, not me. I could take care of myself.

Chad LeBlanc deserved an apology, no matter what the reason for his compassion. According to my pastor, in a sense, I'd flung the words at Jesus, too, and for that, I felt a deep regret.

Doris lifted my spirits with a hearty breakfast of pancakes and sausage while humming a tune.

"You're fattening me up," I said. "Keep going and I'll not have a thing to wear."

The older woman promptly poured me a cup of black coffee; its strong aroma wafted through the kitchen. "Good, and add two spoonfuls of sugar. You're much too thin. Of course the Landrys were always slight."

Immediately my attention clung to her words. "You did know my parents well."

Doris scooped up a generous portion of sausage links and placed it beside a stack of pancakes. "A bit."

Why is she so vague? "I came here to find out about them and sell the property."

A warm brown gaze met mine. "I figured as much. Why didn't your mama come?"

"She's ill. . . ."

Doris knew the truth; I could see it in her eyes. "Poor baby. She'd seen enough in her day. No wonder she moved north."

"You mean with my father dying in Vietnam?"

A peculiar expression swept over Doris's face, a mixture of fear and awe. She hesitated before replying. "They loved each other very much."

Her words brought comfort that my parents were devoted to each other but saddened me in the eventual outcome. I wanted to find a love of my own, and I'd prayed for God to bring me a husband who would love and respect me. I slid into a chair and held my chin in my palm.

"If only I could have seen them together, just once. I don't even have a picture."

Doris used the corner of her apron to swipe at the wetness beneath her right eye. "I imagine not."

"Did you visit them here?" I asked, reaching for the butter.

"A few times. Your granddaddy wasn't fond of visitors."

Sipping my coffee and eyeing the feast before me, I realized Doris withheld information about the situation at Shelby Oaks. I desperately wanted to pry for it all, but Doris needed to trust me first. Best I change the subject. "Would you mind contacting someone to clean up the grounds?"

She tilted her head. "Yes, ma'am. I can have someone out here this afternoon or tomorrow."

I ate in silence, my mind filled with all the things I wanted to accomplish. After thanking her for breakfast, I went straight to the phone in my bedroom to call Chad. I trembled a little and my heart pounded. Confrontation had always been my downfall, and I wasn't sure why. Mama never raised her voice or spoke harshly. Thankfully working with kids left the bitter pill of opposition to someone else.

His card held two phone numbers: his office that I'd used the day before and a cell. I chose the latter, thinking he'd be more apt to answer—and I surely didn't want to dread a second call.

"Chad LeBlanc here."

If I had thought the sound of his voice unnerved me before, it surely did now. "This is Shelby Landry." I braved forward, much like an ant heading up a hill with a load twice its size. "I want to apologize for my rudeness yesterday."

"You were hurting."

"Bad circumstances are no excuse for bad manners, my mama always said. Please forgive me."

"Already have. Are you feeling better today?"

"Yes." I still had a dull ache, but at least I could function.

"Your offer is finished. In fact, I plan to put it in the mail today."

A feeling totally foreign to me embraced my heart. I wanted to see him again. "If you'd like to deliver it, I'm sure there is enough gumbo here for lunch."

He chuckled. "I'd drive to the ends of the earth for good

gumbo. I could be there about eleven."

"I thought your office was in Lafayette."

"It is, but I'm staying with my parents for a few days."

His reply rolled over me like a hot mocha on an icy day. "Good, then I can apologize in person."

I hung up the phone and swung a glance toward the chifforobe. My favorite yellow silk pantsuit seemed to call my name. With my shoulder-length, black hair, I resembled a bumblebee. Laughing to myself, I thought I might sting Mr. Chad LeBlanc. Rather, he'd stung me. I took a little longer with my makeup and then scolded myself. Here I was, Miss No-Nonsense, Scheduled, and Too-Busy-for-Men fussing over which color of eye shadow and a double layer of mascara.

For a moment, I'd forgotten the real reason why I had taken up residence at Shelby Oaks. Once Chad left today, I must begin searching through closets. Tomorrow I'd head into town to see what the public records stated about the property. Old newspapers from the library might trigger something in my memory bank.

Promptly at eleven, Chad arrived. He looked devastating in khakis and a pale green knit pullover. No doubt about it, I was more than attracted to this man. Yet, a note of caution rode with my new feelings. His charm could be deceptive, a ploy for me to sell the estate at a lower-than-market price. The thought ran ice water through my veins.

He grinned, and I tossed away my suspicions. I invited him inside to what Doris called the parlor. She served us sweet iced tea in tall glasses with a floating sprig of mint.

"What do you have rolled up there?" I asked. He'd laid

down what looked like plans on the sofa beside him.

"I thought you might be interested in what I'd like to do here. I've spent weeks, actually six of them, coming by and taking measurements."

"How did you get inside?"

"A window on the back side of the house."

I lifted a brow. "I'm not so sure you should have told me that."

His shoulders lifted and fell. "I wanted to be honest."

I swallowed hard. Honesty swung a pendulum in his direction. "We could spread out the plans on the dining room table." And we did, leaning over his sketches as though examining a treasure map.

I marveled at how Chad had utilized every bit of the home's charm, although I wasn't happy with his initial deception. Bathrooms were penciled in for every bedroom and modern amenities noted for the comfort of the inn's guests. His restoration plans intrigued me. He mentioned the original wallpaper probably lay beneath the existing yellowed paper, and he intended to keep as much of the old as possible.

"I'd like for you to visit when I'm finished, a night free on me."

"We haven't agreed to terms yet," I said.

He stepped back. "You're right. I'm prepared to pay whatever you want." He smiled. "Within reason." He handed me an envelope where he'd handwritten *Shelby Landry* in neat, slanted letters. I appreciated a man who wrote legibly. To me it meant he kept his life in order.

"I'll take a look at it later." I took a deep breath. "When

would you want to take possession, providing I agree to your offer?"

"As soon as possible."

"I need time to search through all the closets and drawers for family memorabilia." I didn't speak the entire truth, but I refused to be dissuaded from my purpose.

"I understand. I'm eager, but in due time."

Several awkward moments passed, and I despise unproductive time. "Again, forgive me for yesterday."

Chad's fingers touched the plans in a deft motion to roll up the sketches. "Of course, Shelby." His gaze met mine and I nearly drifted into Fantasyland. "Could we take a walk before lunch? The road in front of the house dead ends at the far end of the property."

I nodded and we left the house soon afterward. His shoes crunched the oyster shell in the road, and mine sank into the soft grass. Strolling beside him seemed natural. I inwardly expressed my gratitude for his lack of height. My short stature kept me shopping in the petite section and shying away from men who towered above me.

"Do you like fishing?" he asked above the rhythmic hum of singing katydids.

"I've never been fishing in my life." Actually there were many things I hadn't done in my life. As a teen, I'd spent more hours with books than talking with friends. As a result, I communicated rather formally.

Chad startled. "You've been deprived."

I giggled—a gesture not characteristic of me. "The idea of stringing slimy worms onto a hook in hopes a fish might find it tempting doesn't appeal to me."

"Again, I say deprived." He stopped in the middle of the lane leading to the road. "What do you say we go fishing this afternoon? I've got a taste for catfish."

Did I dare say I'd never tasted that either? "Aren't you concerned about snakes and gators?"

"They can go fishing, too."

I laughed, long and hard, and the release felt good.

"You're prone to a more serious nature, aren't you?"

"Guilty, I guess, although children keep me entertained. I'm a pediatric dentist."

Shock registered on his handsome features. "You don't look like a dentist."

I thoroughly enjoyed the conversation. "What does a dentist look like?"

He grinned. "Not sweet and pretty like you. I'd let you pull my teeth any day."

I felt myself grow red and hastily glanced away.

"Ever get bit?" Chad asked.

"A few times. It's a hazard to the trade."

He shook his head. "So what do you say to fishing away the afternoon? I could get us a can of red wigglers—those are worms, for a Yankee gal such as yourself."

The idea of pulling worms out of the earth had as much appeal as a traffic jam in August. However, I did enjoy his company. "I can move my plans to tomorrow."

"Great. I have an old pair of jeans in the trunk of my car, and I always have a couple of fishing poles. In fact, I have some bait, too."

Doubt gnawed at my mind. Had he planned this? Was I being a fool by allowing him to charm me senseless? If he'd been a dangerous sort, surely Doris would have warned me. "Just for a little while. I need to take this fishing venture slow and easy."

We walked nearly a mile to where the road wound around to the top of a bank with the swamp, or rather the marsh, below. I gazed into the muddy waters for signs of those dreaded creatures. Holding my breath, I caught sight of an alligator. "I hate those things."

Chad shrugged. "I hate rush-hour traffic and stress."

"Any of those can kill you," I said. "I think we simply choose our own poison."

"Ah, a philosophical lady."

A droplet of perspiration slipped down my temple and I dabbed it away. So much for the carefully applied makeup. He served as a diversion and nothing more. Tomorrow I'd not accept any calls or visitors.

Noting the walk back, I slipped off my black sandals to allow a soft bed of grass to tickle my toes.

"You just ruined my image of you," Chad said, taking my shoes. "Here I thought you were this sophisticated lady from the north."

"I'm on vacation."

"Really?" He replied as though he didn't believe me, and I refused to look his way to confirm it.

My feigned interest in the overgrown, briar-infested area to the left of us sparked a memory. "A house once stood there," I said, "and it burned." *What more can I remember?*

209

"I recall hearing about a fire here." Chad pointed in the direction of where huge trees must have lined the back to shield the inhabitants from the marsh. He stared at me oddly. "You don't remember the fire?"

I truly didn't, and it frustrated me. "Not at all. I hope no one was hurt. I hate to think I owned the land where something horrible took place." Chad said nothing, and I swung around to peer into his face.

"Why did you really return to Shelby Oaks?" he asked softly.

I stiffened and fought the urge to tell him the matter was none of his business. Never had I revealed my loss of memory to anyone but Mary Linda, my counselor, and the trained doctors who sought to unlock the closed door of my mind.

"I'm sorry," he said.

I blinked and told myself the wetness pooling in my eyes was due to the heat, not a watery display of emotion. First Doris and now Chad held keys to my closet of nightmares. "Talk to me about fishing. I need a tutorial." Sighing, I fanned myself. "A cold glass of iced tea or lemonade sounds good, doesn't it?"

Back at the house, Doris entertained us both with fishing stories, each one claiming a larger catfish than the time before. Her nut brown eyes and deeply tanned skin led me to believe she'd spent enough time in the sun to validate her tales. I laughed until my sides ached and wondered if Mama would delight in Doris. . .and Chad. Odd, I always referred to her as Mother until two days ago, then my childhood fondness drew me to call her Mama. Pushing away the sad thoughts, I concentrated on Chad.

"You best bring out the cornmeal, 'cause we're fixin' to catch a mess of catfish this afternoon."

Doris bustled about the kitchen until I urged her to sit down at the table with us. "I remember when Mr. Thibodeaux used to coax me into going fishing. Mercy, what he wanted was all the stolen kisses he could get."

I felt my flesh heat up hotter than a firecracker. Why, Chad and I were strangers, business associates.

Doris's tone dropped to barely above a whisper. "Bonnie and Shelby used to go fishing. I remember. . .I remember how you could hear them two laughing for a mile. They caused the bayou to come alive with their love."

Such sweet words, almost poetic, and Doris spoke with an air of reverence. "During my stay, I want to hear every story, if you don't mind," I said. "Mama never spoke of this place. I learned about Shelby Oaks when I obtained power of attorney. I never understood why she kept this a secret. This house, the grounds, they're so beautiful."

"To protect you," Doris said, reaching over to touch my arm. "Charm is deceptive, and beauty is fleeting."

Chapter 4

I recognized the Proverbs passage, but why did I need protecting? "What happened here?" I asked. "I have to know. My childhood memories are gone." My gaze moved from Doris to Chad. Desperation assaulted me as though someone pelted my body with rocks.

Doris continued to peer into my face. Compassion poured from every inch of her. "Perhaps it's better you don't remember."

"Whatever happened pushed my mother into insanity. I think my headaches stem from the same thing." I paused and took a deep breath. "I'm afraid I will end up like Mama if I don't learn the truth."

Chad rubbed the back of his neck, and suddenly I realized I'd revealed more of me in a few short sentences than my close friends had ever discovered. Confession was supposed to be good for the soul, but at the moment humiliation oozed through my pores.

"All I've heard is hearsay," he said. "I don't want to say a word without the facts."

The clock from the parlor chimed one o'clock. To me, it

signaled the beginning of the truth, no matter how painful.

"I can tell you about your mama and daddy—when they were together. But I won't speak of other things." Doris stood and moved to the sink.

"Tomorrow I plan to visit the library for old newspapers and check the records office for anything else I can find."

"Would you like some company?" Chad asked.

I studied him—the narrow bone structure of his face and the twist of his nose as though it had been broken. "Why? Is it because of the sale? No matter what I learn, I have no desire to keep this place."

His jaw tightened, and he pushed aside his empty bowl and spoon. "I have no hidden agenda here. I thought we had the beginnings of a friendship. Friends help each other, at least here we do."

I nodded, but my doubts about him resurfaced. Had he searched through the house and found things I should know? His admittance of a friendship sounded foreign to me. A naïve portion of me wanted to label his caring and concern as southern hospitality. Another part of me would like to think he was more interested in me as a woman. But the sensible and skeptical side of me feared he was focusing on a selfish motive. Caution flagged its warning, and my head began a dull ache. I wanted to excuse myself and take my medicine before it grew worse.

"Do you still want to go fishing?" I asked.

"Always."

I tore myself from his warm gaze. "Give me a few moments to change clothes."

While in my bedroom, I took a nose spray. I pulled a T-shirt and jeans from the chifforobe, then brushed my hair back into a ponytail. This inner struggle for and against Chad accompanied the deep need to learn my past. I seemed to be racing against an invisible clock. When I considered the increasing intensity of my headaches and Mama's insanity, I wondered why I spent my time in his company rather than setting my sights on what really needed to be done.

In short, I feared the truth. I could be the tragedy that forced Mama to leave Shelby Oaks. What could a child have done that horrible? I shuddered and reached up to massage my head.

Dear Lord, You have the answers. Be with me.

Chad whistled a nondescript tune as we walked toward the area where bald cypress rested their roots in dirty water. Dressed in worn jeans and a Saints T-shirt, he looked like a true native. We'd driven his car since all the fishing gear lay in the trunk. I hadn't said a word about the conversation over lunch and neither had he. He laughed and teased me about being a Yankee. Then, I heard every bad dentist joke he could muster. From anyone else, I would have been offended—if not downright mad—but I couldn't be irritated with Chad. His carefully put-together words made me see myself and my profession from a different perspective. A humorous one.

I wouldn't have ventured within ten feet of the water without Chad. I saw a baby gator and wondered where its mother lay hidden.

"I'm watching out for you," he said, as though reading my

worrisome thoughts. "Living here they grow fat and lazy. It's the hungry ones or the mothers frettin' over their younguns that you need to watch out for."

He hadn't said a word to ease my frazzled nerves. I'll admit the scene looked picturesque with the hanging moss and abundance of green, but not the threat of danger lurking in every direction.

We sat on a small pier with our feet dangling over the side. I felt like Tom Sawyer or Huckleberry Finn. I thought one wasn't supposed to talk when fishing, that it chased away the fish. So my gaze darted all about me, memorizing the bugs and willing away the wildlife that made my skin crawl.

"Your line will bob when a fish bites," he said. "This first time, I'll reel it in to show you how." He wore a baseball cap advertising an oil company, and his ears peeked out on both sides.

I glanced at the bucket on the other side of him. "How are you going to keep them in there? Won't they jump out?"

Chad chuckled and held up a thin rope that had a piece of metal attached on one end. "This line will keep them good."

"How long do we wait?" I whispered.

"For as long as it takes."

I imagined myself sitting in the same spot for a week. Already bored, I wished I'd insisted on heading into town for research. Except I enjoyed Chad's company.

"She'll be coming around the bayou when she comes," Chad sang, more than a little off-key.

I recognized the tune, but not the words.

"She'll be coming around the bayou when she comes.

She'll be coming around the bayou. She'll be coming around the bayou. She'll be coming around the bayou when she comes."

"I don't think that's the way the song goes," I said with a giggle.

"Hush, there's more. Besides, the fish like it."

"Right." I shook my head in pretended frustration.

"She'll be ridin' a big green gator when she comes."

"Oh no," I groaned, but laughter welled inside me.

"She'll be ridin' a big green gator when she comes."

One look at Chad told me he was loving his rendition of "She'll be Comin' Around the Mountain."

"She'll be ridin' a big green—I have a bite," he claimed. His brown eyes reminded me of a little boy. "Told you the fish liked my singing."

I covered my mouth but couldn't stop the overflow of uncontrollable laughter. "Maybe it bit because you were torturing its ears."

He slid me a sideways scowl. "You're jealous."

About that time my line tugged. "I have one, too! I bet mine is bigger than yours."

"I hardly think so," he said. "But I'll bet dinner."

"You're on!" I concentrated on what I was doing since he couldn't reel in both fish at the same time. He told me what to do and I followed his instructions. I saw his catch first, a huge, rather nasty-looking creature with whiskers that reminded me more of an old, weathered man than a feline. "Look at the size of that thing."

"Yep, this Cajun can land a catfish with his eyes closed.

Be careful though, they can bite."

About that time, I raised my pole out of the water. Mine was bigger! Chad slid his catfish onto the line and grabbed my pole.

"I should have upped my bid," he said. "Now I have dinner to buy."

"Write it off as a business expense."

He lifted his cap and wiped his forehead. "Mama said never trust a Yankee."

"Especially one who was born on the bayou."

We arrived back at Shelby Oaks at nearly four o'clock. Doris met us at the back door and made a huge fuss over our catch. I was anxious to start my search of the house and a little tired.

"Can we do dinner another night?" I handed him a glass of iced tea. "But not tomorrow night, 'cause we have this bayou treat."

"By all means. I don't want you getting sick of me." He grinned, and I nearly landed in a pool of pleasure.

"As long as you don't sing, I'm fine, but I do have things to do."

"How about lunch tomorrow, after we've done a little research about your family?"

"What about your work?"

"I own the land development business, and I took a few days off. Shall we meet at the library in the morning, say about nine thirty?" he asked.

"Sure. I picked up a town map when I arrived, and I have your cell number if I get lost."

"Considering the size of Zirondelle, I doubt if that happens."

After he left, I chose to spend a few minutes with Doris before her husband picked her up. I had all evening to rummage through the house.

"Thank you, Doris," I said while she washed the iced tea glasses. I picked up a towel and dried them.

"For what?"

I loved the sound of her voice. The Cajun accent reminded me of a gentle, rolling stream, although I needed to strain to hear every word. "For your kindness. For telling me about my mama and daddy."

Doris nibbled on her lower lip. Her ample shoulders lifted and fell. "Chil', don't you remember anything at all?"

"No, ma'am." I wanted to cry. "My memory is the real reason why I'm here—not the sale of the property."

She glanced at the clock on the electric stove. "Let's talk a spell." She led me into the parlor and pointed to the sofa. "Aren't there fancy doctors for problems like this?"

"I've been to a few. Some of them suggested hypnosis, but I didn't feel comfortable with it. Honestly, I've spent most of my life talking to Jesus about my lost memory, and I did pray through coming here."

"He is the Healer."

I moistened my lips. "Mama's been in a mental hospital since I was fourteen. She doesn't recognize me or talk."

"I'm so sorry, but I understand why."

Frustration surfaced and I clenched my fists. "I don't, Doris. I remember my eighth birthday in Detroit with Mama, nothing before that. Absolutely nothing."

"So you are determined to find out why your mama left."
She stated my feelings about the matter rather than asked me.
Her sad tone told me what I learned would not be pleasant.

I nodded. "My doctor believes whatever made Mama leave
is the reason for my migraines."

"Wise man, I'd say."

"Will you tell me why we left?" I waved my hand around
the room. "I look around and wonder why anyone would ever
desert this beautiful house and land."

Doris folded her hands and brought them to her lips.
"Shelby, dark, evil things happened to your mama."

"You mean when Daddy was killed in Vietnam?"

"Long before that and long afterwards." Doris paused. "I
want you to learn what the papers said about it all. Read every
word, Shelby. And pray while you're doing it. When you're finished, I'll help you. I'm not the person to talk to, not really, but
there is one still living who can tell you the truth."

I blinked a few times to dispel the signals of one more
headache. How could I make her understand how much I
needed to know the truth?

"I see pain on your face. Do you have another headache?"

I swallowed hard. "The start of one. My medicine is in my
room."

She stood much too quickly, as though needing an excuse
to end our conversation. "I'll fetch it for you."

After Mr. Thibodeaux picked up Doris, I took a nap and
felt refreshed and eager to begin. I set to work looking first
through all the cupboards and drawers in the kitchen. All I
found were manuals on appliances dating back to the fifties.

I fixed a sandwich and took it upstairs to eat while I began a research task that I believed would take several hours or several days to complete.

The furniture pieces in my bedroom were void of anything but my personal belongings. I even looked under the bed and between the mattress and box springs. The bathroom down the hall had cupboards so high that I had to get a chair from my bedroom. I stood on my tiptoes quite precariously, but nothing was there except an old jar of Vicks and a small bottle of Bayer aspirin. The housecleaning service had done a thorough job, but I also realized they wouldn't have thrown away anything if it looked important.

Each room and the second upstairs bathroom proved the same. Nothing remained in them. They were spotless—and empty. My head bothered me with the same dull ache. I'd never get used to the pain. I remembered the apostle Paul prayed for God to take away an affliction, but He told Paul His grace was sufficient. I'd been telling myself the same thing for years, but I didn't intend to stop praying for healing, either.

Close to midnight, I walked into the fifth bedroom, a small room decorated in earth colors—brown and a hideous shade of green, reminding me of an avocado. A double bed, dresser and mirror, and a chest in oak were placed against the walls and resembled the other bedrooms. My head had begun to bother me again and as I stood in the doorway, I thought of simply going to bed. Instead, I decided to finish what I'd started.

Each drawer of the chest was empty. Then, I began searching the small dresser. On the right-hand side at the bottom,

I pulled out a drawer and saw an envelope in the far back corner. I snatched it up and saw it was sealed with a piece of yellowed tape. With renewed enthusiasm, I hurried downstairs to retrieve a butter knife to ease it open.

Standing in the kitchen, my trembling fingers pulled out a photograph. Three young girls and a toddler sat on the front steps of this very house. They all smiled, even the littlest one. The girls were pretty, each one with dark hair and angelic features. I turned over the photograph and read the names: Therez Ann, Lisa Kathleen, Angela Marie, and Shelby Lynn.

Shelby Lynn. I flipped it back over and studied the toddler. Was it me? It had to be. And who were the older girls? My heart pounded. I must have cousins. How wonderful. We could visit, and talk. How utterly exciting. For the first time in my life, I imagined a real family with annual reunions and stories about the past. These girls, now full-grown women, were both a mystery and the object of exhilaration.

I sucked in a breath. A surge of pain exploded in my eye. I staggered, nearly dropping the photograph. This headache had hit me hard. I closed my eyes and moved to the floor. Cradling my head in my hands, I prayed for this torment to end. Was I being punished for something I'd done to Mama? Logic stepped in. My God loved me and wanted the best for me. I begged for release. Slowly the incessant pain dissipated.

Once I focused my eyes, I took another glimpse at the picture. Why wasn't I told about these girls? So many questions and no answers.

Chapter 5

"Do you know what Zirondelle means?" I asked Chad as we mounted the steps to the library—a stately, stone building, weathered with time and grace.

"Mosquito hawk."

"What did you say?"

He laughed. "It means dragonfly, but folks here call them mosquito hawks."

When I thought about the small town with its quaintness and charm, the name fit. "I'll take the Yankee version. It's incredibly peaceful here. I imagine the worst thing ever happening here is the electricity goes off in the middle of a thunderstorm."

"Oh, we'd like to think that."

The way he responded led me to believe otherwise, but of course every community had its share of problems.

With the help of the librarian, I could look at newspapers thirty to thirty-five years old. It occurred to me Chad could save me a lot of time and effort if he'd reveal a little information.

"I understand you know more than what you're telling me," I said. "I have no idea what year or month to look for."

The photograph tucked into my purse came to mind. "And I found this last night. I think I may have cousins." I pulled out the envelope and handed it to him. "I started to ask Doris about this, but I wanted to search through the records first."

Chad stared at the yellowed envelope for a moment, then lifted the photograph from inside. He said nothing; no expression creased his features. "Let's step outside and talk," he said, and placed the photograph back inside the envelope before handing it to me.

Confused, I started to protest, but when I saw his eyes filled with compassion and something else I couldn't quite discern, I swallowed my reply and dropped the envelope into my purse. Once outside in the sunshine, I asked if he wanted to walk, but he declined.

"Why don't we sit in my car?" he asked. "I need to tell you a few things in private."

Suddenly the warm spring day brimming with a hint of flowers and serenaded by birds left me cold and rather frightened. "All right. If you feel that's best."

I liked his car. It had all the extras—leather interior, state-of-the-art sound system, a hundred gadgets—but this morning, the luxury made me feel like sitting in a doctor's plush office waiting for bad news about Mama. I leaned against the passenger side of the door and crossed my arms over my chest. This had to be bad news; I could see it in his face, hear it in his voice.

"I'm ready," I said. "Whatever it is, please tell me."

He pressed his lips together. "Can we pray first?"

The knot in my stomach tightened, and I bowed my head. "Heavenly Father, I want to help Shelby work through her

223

past. The things she will uncover today won't be easy to deal with, but I know You can work them for good."

A chill raced up and down my arms while a dull ache spread across my forehead.

"Be with her and let her feel Your love and comfort. Amen."

What could be this horrible?

He turned to face me. "Remember the walk you and I took at Shelby Oaks?"

"Yes."

"When we turned to head back, you mentioned a house had burned."

My ears began to ring. "Yes. I wasn't sure where the recollection came from. It sort of popped into my head."

"That house. . ." He moistened his lips. "That house was your mama and daddy's. They lived there until he went to Vietnam, and your mama lived there until the fire destroyed it."

"Did it burn before or after we left?" I really didn't want to hear the answer, but I must learn the truth.

"Before."

I gasped. "How awful for Mama! Daddy killed, and her home destroyed."

He paused and glanced out the window at the quiet street. His gaze swung back to me. "The story is worse, Shelby, and I'm not sure how to tell you."

As fearful as I felt, he looked like he needed comforting. I uncrossed my arms and folded my hands in my lap. "Chad, I've had a tough time finding joy in my life. Always, I have trusted God to show me the light in the darkness. When I felt utterly alone in foster homes, God sent me His comfort. He created a need in me to help others and to not drown in self-pity. I understand the things that happened here cannot be good, or my mother wouldn't have left. I am a strong woman, a survivor. Whatever you have to tell me, God will show me how to handle it."

Silence prevailed and I waited patiently.

"The girls in the photograph. . .they are your sisters. They died in the fire. . .in the house."

I sucked in a breath and reached for my purse. Yanking on the envelope, I pulled out the picture and stared through blinding tears at the three smiling girls. *Therez Ann, Lisa Kathleen, Angela Marie. My sisters.* "Poor Mama." My stomach churned and bile rose in my throat. "No wonder she went insane. No wonder she left here."

The haze of a clouded memory crawled through the agony. I saw yellow-orange flames through a window. I heard the cries of terror. I heard Mama scream.

"I wanted a glass of milk, and Mama was in the kitchen making popcorn for us. We heard an explosion and Mama fell, grabbing me as she went down. Glass shattered everywhere. Mama carried me outside and told me not to move. She tried to get back inside for my sisters. The fire roared like a mad animal. I heard crashing, and the flames seemed to eat the house. Mama couldn't get through the fire, and I watched the house burn to the ground."

At last I remembered, and now I understood what blocked my thoughts. No child should remember such terror. I shivered, and Chad reached over and pulled me into his arms. He was a stranger; I shouldn't allow this closeness. Yet, God had

225

given him to me for this moment. The instant I felt his touch I began to cry, not simply a few tears but liquid grief that shook my body and paralyzed all other responses. Such profound grief was foreign. I had no idea how long I rested against Chad's chest, but I soaked his shirt with my tears.

"Cry it all out," he whispered. "Cry until there is nothing left."

And I did, for in the sorrow of losing those I treasured, I remembered the whispers of those around Mama.

"Shelby Lynn has not cried."

"Didn't she love her sisters?"

"For shame, Bonnie, have you given birth to a child with no feelings?"

"I blocked it all," I said between my sobs. "I never cried for my sisters. I tried to pretend they weren't killed. I tried so hard until I forgot."

"God protected you."

"Yes." I caught my breath. "I believe He wrapped His love around me and kept me safe until I could understand." I leaned against Chad's chest until my breathing came easier. He gave me enough tissues to wipe my eyes and nose. "Thank you for being here."

"Thank our God, for He ordained it all."

I nodded, thinking I should sit upright, but the solace Chad offered was as though God chose him as a messenger of comfort. The closeness I sensed for this man nearly pushed me into weeping again. *Thank You, Father. At last I know the truth.*

"I hope one day I can do for someone else what you have done for me," I said, determined to cease the crying.

"Maybe you already have."

My mind spun with children's accidents where I mended their teeth and hugged their parents. Perhaps Chad had more insight than he realized. "I'm ready to tackle those newspapers now," I finally said.

He took my hand, this stranger-friend, and smiled reassuringly. "Last night I talked with my folks about the date. October 1977 is when it happened."

I nodded and swallowed the last of my tears—at least for now. It didn't take long to find the newspaper on microfiche. I tried ignoring the pain around my eyes.

"You have a headache." Chad touched my shoulder. "Do you have medicine with you?"

I excused myself and stepped into the bathroom. Although taking a nose spray was no crime, I didn't welcome an audience. A glance at myself in the mirror confirmed a bad case of swollen eyes and splotchy skin. I lingered a few moments to patch my makeup while a verse from Proverbs about vanity danced across my mind. I tried not to think about the fire and my dear sisters. When I finally could talk to God, He'd help me come to terms with the grief.

By the time I returned, Chad had found the article. "I hope this answers all of your questions," he said. "I've already read most of it."

I eased into a wooden chair—one with a hollowed bottom that must have been older than both of us. The headlines read TRAGIC FIRE CLAIMS THE LIVES OF THREE YOUNG GIRLS. While my gaze took in every word, my emotions played havoc with my senses. I recalled conversations with my sisters. Therez asked for buttered popcorn. Lisa didn't want any, but she asked for a slice of pecan pie from dinner, and Angela wanted her hair braided after she'd eaten the popcorn. I heard their voices, distinguishing each one. Shaking my head to push the thoughts aside, I focused on the article. Later I'd revisit my sisters and all the cherished times I'd missed over the years. I decided to read aloud.

"Fire destroyed the home of Bonnie Landry Tuesday evening around eight thirty, killing three of her four daughters. Cause of the blaze is undetermined; however an investigative report is pending. The girls' charred remains were uncovered by the parish's fire department: Therez Ann Landry age twelve, Lisa Kathleen Landry age ten, and Angela Marie Landry age six. Bonnie Landry, age thirty-three, and four-year-old Shelby Lynn escaped the blaze. The late Lieutenant Shelby Landry II preceded his daughters in death. Shelby George Landry Sr. survives at Shelby Oaks."

An inner nudging caused me to reread the short accounting. I took a deep breath before I braved forward. "It says here the cause of the fire was undetermined. Is there a follow-up?" I turned back to the microfiche and tried to find more information, but there was nothing. "I don't understand."

Chad pulled a chair beside me. "I might be able to help you. Your grandfather was highly influential in this area."

"You mean he kept things from getting into the paper?"

"Exactly."

"Reporters can do a lot of damage." I studied his face—this man whom I'd grown to care about in such a short time. The realization caused me to shiver.

"Cold?"

"No. I suppose my grandfather is dead."

"Yes, about ten years ago."

"Is there anyone who can tell me more?" I felt myself grow pale. "Why didn't the paper say anything about the explosion?"

"I wondered that when you mentioned it before."

"Is there is an official report? I mean, doesn't the law require such a thing?"

Chad said nothing.

"What are you not telling me?"

"According to town rumors, your grandfather had all the documentation destroyed."

"Why? Did the grief of losing his son and then his granddaughters overwhelm him?"

Chad stood and glanced around the room, as though thinking through his reply. He jammed his hands into his jeans pockets. "Let's talk to Doris."

The drive back home gave me time to think. My mind seemed to spin with all the new revelations. I swiped at the tears and kept telling myself I could cry again later in the privacy of my room. If not for Chad driving behind me, I'd have pulled over and talked to God about the whole matter, but then I'd have been there for the next three days. All the years I wanted to remember, all the years I thought Mama's problem was me. She'd never breathed a word about a fire or my sisters.

"Oh, Mama, I ache for you," I whispered. "I ache for myself." Maybe when I told her doctors the truth, they might be able to prescribe a more effective medicine. The more I considered the reality of Mama reliving the truth, the more I wondered if her method of dealing with the tragedy was better.

With a deep sigh, I remembered Mama holding me tight and screaming for God to help. I could not imagine the horror of watching my own children burn to death. I swiped at another tear and took a glimpse in the rearview mirror at Chad. I didn't want to suffocate him with my neediness. Already my emotions were strained, and my heart toyed with a semblance of affection. Love toward a man was foreign, and I'd made certain no part of my life required the luxury of marriage and family. Even with my carefully laid plans, thinking about Chad caused me to long for a home and children.

It's only the heartbreaking news and the stress of digging into my roots, I told myself. If I'd met Chad in Detroit, I'd have ignored him. Placing my new friend in a nice box in the corner of my mind, I concentrated on recalling every moment of the fire. I needed to learn more about my grandfather. My mind had yet to uncover any physical characteristics about him—and it frustrated me.

Chapter 6

I don't have any more to tell you than what Chad already has," Doris said. Her eyes pooled with tears and I put my arms around her shoulders.

"Don't concern yourself with it," I said. "No need to get upset."

"But it was all so horrible. Your mama loved you girls. First one tragedy with your daddy and then the fire." She stiffened. "Evil stalked her, Miss Shelby, and for no good reason except she loved Jesus and your daddy."

"What about the grandfather?" Chad asked. "That's where I thought you might tell Shelby more."

"My mama worked here at Shelby Oaks, not me. She didn't tell tales, my mama, but I overheard her say if it weren't for the money, she'd leave. Old Mr. Landry had an "evil" streak."

Three times I'd heard Doris use the word *evil* in describing my grandfather and the tragedies akin to Mama. "What did he do?" I asked. "I understand he covered up the fire investigation. I thought it was to protect Mama from news reports, but now I'm wondering what else."

Doris trembled, and I urged her to sit down. "I'm sorry, chil'. The man never did a thing to me, but I didn't like the way he always looked at me—as though his eyes saw through my clothes." She tugged on the buttons on her shirtwaist dress and glanced at Chad with a slight flush. "Anything I tell you is gossip, and the good Lord doesn't tolerate a loose tongue."

"I understand," I said. "I surely don't want you to damage your relationship with the Lord."

Doris nodded and offered a faint smile. "My mama, like I said before, is the person to talk to."

"May I talk to her?" I asked.

"Yes, ma'am. I believe it would be good for you to visit with her. She has a heap of things weighing on her heart about your mama and old Mr. Landry."

"When can I see her?" I asked. The old, familiar anxiousness tore through me like a tornado.

"I'll ask her tomorrow when I visit her." I remembered Doris had Saturday and Sunday off; now I knew why.

A few moments later I walked Chad to the door. As much as he'd given me today, I really didn't want him to leave. What an uncharacteristic feeling for me, but I shouldn't dwell on it. I believed my spent nerves would shift back to normal once I came to terms with the fire.

"Thank you again for telling me about my sisters and letting me cry on your shoulder." Peering into his eyes, I wondered if I'd ever grow tired of the understanding radiating there.

"No problem. It felt good to be needed—for something more than interest in a piece of property." Silence prevailed over the next several moments.

"Doris said she'd have the catfish ready by the time she leaves at five," I said, hoping he hadn't changed his mind about dinner.

"Good. I imagine you're tired of seeing me so much."

Actually, I enjoy it. "I was thinking the same thing about you. You have done nothing but baby-sit me since we met."

"I think you've made a mistake. Besides, we're a pair." His words hinted of more than a witty remark.

"Chad," I began, "in a few short days, you have become a dear friend. All teasing aside, I am grateful." At the risk of sounding sentimental, I lightened my tone. "Now tonight, I must learn about your family."

"It's boring."

It won't be to me. "I doubt it."

He promised to be back at five for dinner. I closed the door and leaned back against it.

"Chad LeBlanc is a fine man."

I flushed to see Doris had been observing me from the hallway. "Uh, yes, he is. I barely know him. Why, it's only been a few days."

"Time doesn't have a thing to do with the heart."

I smiled at this dear woman who had stepped into the role as my mother. "I wouldn't lean on any man right now. I'm weak, vulnerable."

"Chil', weak you're not. You're a Landry."

While Doris busied herself, I chose to lie down and just think. I wanted all the memories of my sisters to slowly inch their way into my heart and mind, never to leave again. My journal rested on the nightstand, and I intended to write down every emotion and happening since I first arrived. Closing my eyes, my mind drifted to another life.

"Shelby Lynn, just 'cause you're the youngest doesn't mean I have to make your bed."

"Mama, Shelby Lynn brought that nasty cat inside again."

"Shelby Lynn, you can't be the teacher when we play school. You aren't old enough."

Odd, Mama never called me Shelby Lynn in Detroit; my middle name had gone by the wayside. Therez loved to pretend she was the mama of twelve children. Lisa wanted to be a nurse. Angela dreamed of horses. And I was the youngest, a little girl who never lacked for playmates.

I started to doze off, then I heard the rumbling of lawnmowers and saw the landscape crew had arrived.

Sitting on the edge of the bed, I watched six men gather up tools and head toward the yard to perform their expertise. I'd asked for every bush and flowerbed to be cleaned and new plants fitting for the climate to fill the barren areas. I'd always dreamed of having a huge house and grounds where plants and flowers grew in abundance. Although I owned this estate for only a short period longer, I wanted to see it finished proper.

Chad's bid! In my haste to learn about my family, I had neglected to take care of business. Rising from the bed, I reached for the envelope beneath my journal and tore into it. A smile tugged at my lips. His offer was neither too high nor too low. Quite satisfactory. Tonight I'd tell him of my acceptance. A twinge of sadness settled upon me. In a few short days, the house had grown to mean much to me—even if my grandfather had an evil streak.

I sighed and studied the yardmen. Pediatric dentistry called for large cities, not small towns. I'd never fit in here.

I began my journaling with words that flowed from my mind like a prolific writer. Toys, games, holidays, and special occasions rippled across my thoughts, and all went on paper. I chose to forget what had ended their lives. My sisters were with Jesus. How selfish of me to deny them Paradise. For now, my heart praised God for giving back my memory. I asked Him to take away the headaches, hoping against hope the terror of my childhood had caused them. As earlier in the day, faces, smiles, and voices filled the emptiness inside me. If my mind ever chose to betray me again, I'd simply open my journal.

When the yardmen left, I noticed the time and realized Chad would arrive any minute. Quickly, I grabbed a pale blue pants outfit with a spaghetti-strap knit top beneath the jacket. I flew around the room like a wild woman in search of a treasure. All this for a man, my stranger-friend who had seized a bit of my tender heart.

After I'd touched up my makeup and added another layer of mascara, I took a brush to my hair and pulled the top and sides back at the crown, fastened it, and allowed the rest to fall down my back. I liked the look—sort of a country-sophisticated appeal.

I walked down the winding staircase and envisioned myself in the antebellum era. Of course, I played the part of Scarlett and Chad played the role of Rhett. How delightful of him to bring out the girl in me.

"You look gorgeous." Chad's admiring glance made my whirlwind effort all worth it.

"Thanks, and you clean up quite nicely yourself."

In the kitchen, Doris hustled about setting the catfish dinner on the dining room table. The mixture of heavenly scents caught my attention. Chad explained each dish to me—hush puppies, mustard greens with hunks of bacon, dirty rice, and a jar of pickled okra spears. I'd never eaten any of it, but my mouth watered.

"Are you feeding an army, Doris?" Chad chuckled. "I could have brought half the town of Zirondelle with me."

"I could have handled it," Doris replied. "Trouble is, once I start cooking, I don't know when to quit."

Her husband came shortly afterward, and I invited them to eat, but they had other plans. I insisted they take a plate of food for their supper. I liked Mr. Thibodeaux and his quiet mannerisms, although he could be hard to understand.

All during dinner, Chad kept the topic away from the morning's discovery, and I appreciated it. His flirty conversation and little-boy smile relaxed me, and I responded to his wit in what I hoped equaled his.

"Tell me about your parents," I said, reaching for the mustard greens. I'd never tasted anything so delicious in my life.

"Great folks. They claim they're retired, but nothing could be further from the truth. Both are involved in community volunteer work to assist the elderly who are not able to do for themselves. Dad's a doctor and mom's always been his right-hand lady. They love Jesus, their kids, grandkids, and people."

"I'm envious. They sound wonderful. So how many brothers and sisters?"

He reached for the bowl of hush puppies. "Two older sisters.

One lives in Shreveport with her husband and twin boys, and the other lives in Lafayette with her daughter."

I laughed. "You were the baby—that's how you learned your charm."

"You're on to me." He laughed. "We had a good childhood, not perfect by any stretch of the imagination, but my folks tried hard to instill in us proper spiritual truths and good manners."

"Did you go to college?" I reached for the plate of catfish. It seemed to melt in my mouth, and I was eating entirely too much.

He nodded with his mouth full, and I waited until he could reply. "Yep, University of Louisiana. Majored in finance."

I wanted to ask why he never married. He possessed all the qualities of the perfect husband—if I had been in the market.

"Can't figure out why you never married," he said with a tilt of his head. He lifted his iced tea glass to his lips and smiled.

"Never met the right man," I said all too quickly. "Taking care of Mama is a real turn-off. The hospital does a great job, but I do visit her a few times a week." I didn't mention I paid for her medical needs. I assumed he already knew it.

Chad studied me for a few moments, and his soft gaze made my toes tingle. Without a doubt, he had the longest eyelashes of any human being on earth. "Any man who passed you up needed his head examined. Here we'd call him a *couyon*, a stupid person."

I attempted to act as though his remark hadn't affected me. "Thank you." I took a breath. "What are your hobbies, Mr. LeBlanc?"

"Hmm. I have lots of things I enjoy doing besides my job. Guess those things fall under the category of hobbies. I teach a tenth-grade Sunday school class for boys. I do volunteer work in the inner city with teenagers. I play guitar. Even recorded a couple of CDs. Lead praise and worship for the high school choir at church." He lifted a brow.

"Is Superman stamped across your chest?"

"Not exactly." He shook his head. "I was the town's worst before God got hold of me in college."

"Well, what you've done with your life is commendable." I placed my napkin on the table and lifted my gaze to meet his. Now I understood his compassion. He'd spent a lot of years rescuing the downtrodden. I felt like another trophy.

"Did I say something wrong?" Chad pushed his plate aside.

I feigned confusion. After all, my thoughts were selfish. I wanted Chad to like me for me, not pity my horrible family background or my incessant headaches. "Not at all."

"What about your hobbies?" he asked.

"Not as exciting as yours. I spend lots of time with Mama and play piano for the patients there. I love kids, but my only time with them is in a dentist's chair." I shrugged. "I'm a workaholic, and this month-long trip here is the first vacation I've taken in six years. I occasionally collect old dishes. Other than attend church and Bible study, that's it."

"We have music in common."

Why is he trying so hard? I knew his interest in me fell under his calling to help people. "I had great foster parents who financed piano lessons."

"Most kids aren't so lucky."

"I will always be grateful to them. They led me to Jesus and encouraged me to journal."

He smiled. "Another interest."

"Right. Through the years, my reflections have helped me weather unpleasant situations."

"You're a strong woman, Shelby Landry."

Doris had made the same statement. I'd never considered myself strong. Logical and sensible, maybe. I glanced at his hands and when he reached for his iced tea, I saw the indentation of the guitar strings on his fingertips. "I'd like to hear your music sometime."

"I'm singing at my folks' church on Sunday. Would you be my guest?"

Oh, how I wanted to spend time with Chad. My earlier thoughts of depending too much on him rattled my mind. "Wouldn't I be in the way?"

"Not at all. I wanted to invite you."

Pain crossed my vision. I hated the beginnings of another headache. *Oh Lord! Please take it away!* "I feel like such a burden."

"Please don't. I want you there, and if you don't like the music, the preaching is good."

How could I turn him down? "All right. Tell me where to meet you."

He gave me directions, and I remembered the location of a church fitting his description. We washed dishes and laughed about the kitchen definitely needing a dishwasher. My manicured nails were intact, but my hands resembled a prune.

As I finished scrubbing the iron skillet, Chad crept up behind me. "You are the prettiest dentist I've ever seen," he said.

His warm breath against the back of my neck sent messages good girls don't contemplate. "How many woman dentists do you know?"

"Just one." He laughed low, and the sound of his voice drove me to distraction.

My foster mother warned me about allowing emotions to rule over what God intended for a man and a woman. Up until now, I had no clue what she meant. Here I was thirty-two years old and feeling like a teenager on hormone overdrive. "My point," I said. "You've led a sheltered life."

"Good thing." He touched my shoulder. It felt as though a hot poker had branded me. I cringed. He immediately stepped back. "I'm sorry."

I turned around to tell him it was too soon for all of this. My resolve weakened the moment I looked into his face.

"How long have we known each other?" he asked. "Six months? Six days? Six hours?"

I smiled and wanted desperately to sound sophisticated, although my experience with sophistication came from movies. "Two days and nine hours."

"And twenty-five minutes," he added.

We laughed and it eased the tension thick enough to slice with a hatchet. Love at first sight happened in romance novels and movies, not to real people.

"I think I've known you for a long, long time," he said, not taking his gaze off me.

"I rather feel the same way." The instant I spoke the words, I felt profoundly foolish.

"I'd like nothing better than to kiss you."

Take control. I could almost hear my foster mother's chiding voice. "Can I take a rain check?"

He nodded and grinned. "My ego's deflated, but I'll survive on hope."

"Oh, pleeeeze." I threw the dish towel at him.

He caught it and a mischievous twinkle replaced the heated gaze.

"Don't even think about it," I said.

He took a deep breath. "You're right. I need to head home before Miss Landry asks me to leave." He laid the towel on the counter, and I walked him to the door. We set a time for nine fifty on Sunday morning and said good night. I refused to linger in the doorway, or I'd be cashing in my rain check.

Chapter 7

C had's song reverberated through the small church. Not a sound could be heard but the strumming of his guitar and his song of praise. The words focused on Jesus as the healer, and the simple tune soothed my heart and soul.

Jesus, if my whole journey here was to only hear these words, then I praise You for this moment.

Afterward, I met Chad's parents and nearly laughed at the likeness of him and his silver-haired father.

"Looking at you is like seeing Bonnie at your age," his mother said. She took my hand, and her touch felt like velvet.

"What a beautiful compliment," I said. At that moment I wished I could stay near these people forever.

"And I delivered you." Doc LeBlanc chuckled. "Welcome home, Shelby. Chad here thinks highly of you."

I glanced at Chad and he winked. I blushed lightly at the thought of Chad's dad delivering me. If only the ugliness of my sister's deaths didn't overshadow me.

Doc Poot—as he preferred to be called—and Mrs. LeBlanc

invited me to lunch and I accepted. What an enjoyable time I spent with the three of them. In Detroit, I had a few good friends and certainly treasured relationships at church and my dental practice, but these people ministered to the part of me that belonged to my mama and daddy.

All too soon, the meal ended. I needed to drive home and check on Mama. Odd to call Shelby Oaks home, when a week ago I'd never seen the estate, at least not that I remembered.

"I'm heading to Lafayette this afternoon," Chad said. "But I'll be back on Tuesday afternoon. How about dinner? Won't be fancy, one of the local spots."

"Sounds perfect."

"I'll call as soon as I return."

I thought about my rain check for a kiss.

A lazy afternoon spread out ahead of me. I roamed the grounds around the house and admired what the landscaping company had done. Come summer, the rose bushes would bloom with the vibrant intensity I remembered, and although the white azaleas had seen their prime, the blossoms remaining fairly sparkled.

My gaze kept returning to the site of my parents' home until I gave in to the tug and walked the mile there. The sun showered warmth on my back while bits and pieces of my younger years flitted in my thoughts. Insects sang a lullaby and birds called to each other. I could get used to this. Then I stood alone and gave my attention to the rubble of what was once my home. Poor Mama. If only I could rid her of the tormented memories.

I stayed at the site for nearly an hour, and as I fully

expected, a headache exploded, sending me into a blinding walk back to the house. The answer lay at the site of the fire, and I believed God did not plan to abandon me until I found the answers I so desperately craved.

Once I secured the migraine medication, I took a nap, but not without praying for Mama, my new friends, and the budding relationship with Chad. His song of worship and praise lulled me into thanksgiving for all God had done for me—and all He purposed in my life.

Toward evening, I decided to examine the plans Chad had for the inn. Envy swept through me; his dreams should have been mine. The penciled sketches and his notes to update the plumbing and electrical work did in no way affect the grandeur of Shelby Oaks. Longing settled in my heart for the same things.

While enjoying the last of Doris's gumbo, my cell phone rang.

"Shelby, this is Chad. I'm on the road and wanted to see how you were doing."

My heart raced. "I've spent a quiet afternoon—even walked to the end of the road in hopes my memories might all return."

"I've been praying for you," he said.

I closed my eyes to savor the sound of his voice. "Thank you. I've been going over your plans for the inn. Very impressive."

"I admit I'm anxious—but not at your expense." He paused. "I like you, Shelby, and the thought of you returning to Detroit is not something I want to think about."

How sweet of him. "Reality must hit sometime."

"It depends upon how you define reality."

I wanted to say I'd never forget him, but I felt foolish with such a confession. "Your hopes and dreams for Shelby Oaks are only a matter of time."

"Are they?"

The question confused me. I ignored it and talked about the landscaping, but his hints of more of a relationship stayed with me long after our dinner the following Tuesday night. I couldn't wait to see him on Wednesday. We took a tour of the countryside, and I sensed a peace riding beside him. I loved the beauty of this land, my roots.

"You fit here," Chad said, glancing my way. "For the life of me, I can't picture you as a city girl."

"I'm simply versatile."

"Have you considered staying?" he asked.

My pulse quickened. "Oh, I couldn't. What about Mama?"

"Don't you think you could find a suitable facility for her here?"

I shook my head and commented about a mass of yellow wildflowers blooming beside the road. In my heart, I knew any reason to stay at Shelby Oaks had to do with Chad. These feelings were like a teenager's summer flings. Once back in Detroit, the longing would fade.

On Friday, I accepted a dinner invitation with his parents. They lived in a comfortable, turn-of-the-century home. It had been renovated to its original grandeur, which must be the current trend in this area.

"You're Shelby and Bonnie's daughter," Mrs. LeBlanc said during her visit. "You're proof you can take the girl out of the bayou, but you can't take the bayou out of the girl."

"I've never had such a fine compliment."

Doc Poot cleared his throat and reached for a cup of coffee. "Folks here could use a good dentist. Think about it."

Little did he know I had thought about it—a lot.

"Best idea I've heard in along time," Chad replied and flashed me his irresistible smile. To ease the thought of the inevitable, I considered not seeing him again, but I couldn't. Every moment with Chad hurled me deeper and deeper into a whirlpool of longing. How ironic of me—the logical, no-time-for-romance woman—to experience the joy and heartache of love.

Doris gave me directions to her mother's nursing home, and we made arrangements for me to meet her and Mr. Thibodeaux there on Sunday afternoon. Doris said her mother seemed reluctant to talk to me, and I wondered why.

"May I go with you?" Chad asked on Saturday. We'd spent the afternoon fishing, and I loved every moment of it. "What if a migraine hits you?"

"I can handle myself." My anger rose. Pity screamed across my mind.

"I know you can. What I didn't tell you is I knew your sister Angela. We were in the same grade. We were sweet on each other as children view things. I lost a friend in the fire, and I want to find out what happened."

Maybe Chad had seen me as a helpless, headache-ridden woman, but this new information caused me to rethink my earlier irritation.

"Is Angela why you befriended me?" I asked.

"Partly." He shrugged. "As a boy, I feared the fireplace in winter, candles, Dad's pipe. Never really came to terms with how Angela died. Then the property came up for sale, and I got the notion of an inn. So to answer your question, I'd have to say both."

I took a sip of cola. All of the things I'd learned since I came to Shelby Oaks crept across my mind, and the familiar head pounding began. "What else, Chad?"

"You look like Angela, at least how I remember a little girl of ten. I thought I'd forgotten until I saw you, but the more I've gotten to know you, the more Angela's memory fades." He paused. "Never mind my rambling. I'm a grown man trying to come to terms with losing a childhood friend, just as you are with your sisters."

We didn't discuss any more of the past but kept our conversation on our present lives. Funny the things we had in common. We both enjoyed jazz, longed for a collie but not until we could move from our apartments and found homes of our own, and shared a deep passion for evangelism. I'd never learned so much about a man in my life. When the time came for me to return to Detroit, I'd miss Chad. I missed him just thinking about it.

On Sunday afternoon, Chad drove me to Doris's mother's nursing home. We arrived at the same time as Doris and Mr. Thibodeaux. I'd stuck a notebook inside my shoulder bag so I wouldn't forget a single word. My emotions wavered between anticipation and dread. Whatever this woman chose to tell me, her information provided the last clue to unlock my memories.

"You're quiet," Chad said. "Would you like to pray before we meet Mr. and Mrs. Thibodeaux?"

"I'm too nervous to muster more than a 'Please God, help

me get through this.'" I swallowed my pride. "I'd be honored if you did the praying."

"Father God, we are meeting with Doris's mother this afternoon. So many questions fill Shelby's mind about her sisters' death. Thank You that she is now able to remember her sisters and the love she had for them. Help her to learn the truth and heal her wounded heart. Amen."

A short prayer, an honest prayer, and even before the "amen," I sensed a calming of my spirit.

Doris stated her mother's name was Mae Rousse and sometimes she made sense and sometimes she didn't. "She worked for old Mr. Landry for nearly forty years. I reckon she knows more about him than he did himself."

We walked up a wooden handicap ramp into a metal structure that looked like a portable building similar to the ones schools use when they run out of space. What a contrast from where Mama lived. The smell of mold and urine nearly took my breath away. Most folks kept their animals in better living conditions than this. Right then I vowed to report the facility.

"I know it's bad," Doris whispered. "But it's the best we can do, and I have to work."

"They could clean up things," Mr. Thibodeaux said through a clenched jaw.

I glanced from his face to hers. It *was* the best they could do. "On Monday, I'll make arrangements to have your mama moved to a nicer place."

Doris startled. "Why, Miss Shelby, I couldn't accept your money."

"You're not, your mama is." I turned my head to smile at a

woman sitting behind a desk who sported hair the color of tomatoes and must have been cut by a blind person. Long and short strands stuck out every which way like a rooster's tail.

"We'd like to see my mama," Doris said.

Tomato Head smacked her gum with lips the same color as her hair. "Sure, Mrs. Thibodeaux. She's making sense today."

I wanted to smack the woman. Mae Rousse deserved dignity and respect. Chad must have sensed my rising temper because he took my hand and squeezed it lightly. One look at him and I saw he felt the same anger.

The hallway leading to the residents' rooms needed a good scrubbing, preferably with a toothbrush, and the walls needed paint. I could only guess about the condition of the rooms. I wasn't surprised.

Doris kissed her mama's cheek and introduced Chad and me to her. Mrs. Rousse couldn't have been over four feet ten and probably weighed eighty pounds soaking wet. Her little face reminded me of a dried-apple doll.

"Give me my teeth." Mrs. Rousse covered her mouth. "Cain't talk without 'em."

Chad and I stared out the window while Doris took care of assisting her mama with the dentures.

"Who are you again?"

"Mama, this is Shelby Landry, Bonnie's youngest daughter, and this young man is Chad LeBlanc, Doc Poot's son."

Mrs. Rousse grinned and displayed her store-bought teeth. "Thanks for coming to visit this old woman." Her thick accent caused me to lean closer and listen. The woman's clouded eyes widened. "Did you say Bonnie's little girl?"

"Yes, ma'am. How are you?"

Mrs. Rousse nodded. "I've been better and I've been worse, but I'm content. That's what the Good Book says. I'll make ninety-four on my next birthday."

"Good for you," I replied.

"How is your mama?"

"She's not well." I took a deep breath and took in the dreadful smell of the place. "Mrs. Rousse, I need to know what happened with my mama. Until recently, I didn't remember I had sisters or anything about the fire."

The old woman sat up in bed, and Doris propped dingy pillows behind her. "Sit down by me, *bebe*. I've known things for a lot of years but kept them to myself. Now it's time to do the sayin'."

I obeyed and took her withered, veined hand into mine. "I'm grateful, ma'am."

Mrs. Rousse closed her eyes, and I thought for a moment she'd fallen asleep, but then she opened them and began to speak. "I first went to work for Mr. Landry when your daddy made seventeen years old. Oh, how old Mr. Landry loved his boy. His wife had been dead over ten years, and he took all his love for her and gave it to him. Your daddy was a fine man, tenderhearted and handsome. He and Mr. Landry did everything together. Then, your daddy met Bonnie." The old woman shook her head. "They were in love, and old Mr. Landry fought it all the way to the preacher. He hated Bonnie because she'd taken his son from him." She looked to the right and to the left of her as if someone spied on her. "Your mama was an angel."

She peered at me as though looking into my soul. "Why,

you look just like her, Miss Shelby. She must be right pleased. Back to my story, Bonnie did her best to please old Mr. Landry, but nothing suited him. Well, your daddy took a notion to join the Air Force. Maybe it was to get away from Mr. Landry, anyway I suspect so. As soon as he finished his basic training Bonnie joined him. Good thing, too, 'cause Mr. Landry was mean to her. They had Therez and Lisa and were expecting a third when they got back to Shelby Oaks."

Mrs. Rousse paused and looked out the window. I feared her thoughts had left her. "I remember the day they came home with those precious little girls. Mr. Landry took one look at them and said they didn't belong to his son. Landrys had boys, not girls. Your daddy marched out of the house with his little family and vowed he'd never set foot at Shelby Oaks again. About a year later, Mr. Landry had a big house built for his son down the road from him. He made up with your mama and daddy. They moved in and things seemed to be all right. Then you came along and Mr. Landry got mad all over again when they named you Shelby. Guess your mama and daddy knew there weren't gonna be no boys." Mrs. Rousse shook her head and pressed her lips together.

"The war in Vietnam broke out and your daddy joined back up. Said he owed it to his country. Well, *bebe*, he paid them what he owed in blood. Your mama took it real hard, and Mr. Landry claimed she forced him to enlist. He hated your mama and all of you girls."

"What about the fire?" I asked. If she mentioned one more word about my grandfather, I'd scream. Hating a man went against everything Jesus taught, but I hoped he died in torment.

"He did it," Mrs. Rousse said simply. Her eyes widened. "I ain't never told a soul that. Your pawpaw told me hisself on his deathbed."

"Mama!" Doris's hand covered her mouth. "Fuh shore, for true? What an awful thing to accuse a body, even someone as mean as old Mr. Landry."

Chills raced through my body, and I feared I'd be sick.

The old woman peered into my face. "I'm going to tell you the rest of it. You have a right to hear the truth."

I felt Chad's hand on my shoulder. His touch gave me the strength to hear what Mrs. Rousse had to say.

"He got the cancer. At first, he cursed it like he did everything else, then it scared him. After he took to bed, he must have started thinking about his life and the things he'd done to folks. He asked me to fetch old Preacher Martin. God forgive me, but I listened to Mr. Landry confess to making sure Bonnie's house caught on fire—he did something to her bedroom."

I gasped. "I did hear an explosion. Every night, Mama had all of us come into her room for stories and prayers. That night she offered us popcorn."

"Miss Shelby, I'm so sorry to be telling you this."

"No, go on. I have to hear all of it."

"Mr. Landry said he'd watched the house long enough to know what your mama did. He thought all of you would be killed."

Suddenly, the figure of my grandfather stole into my mind. I covered my mouth and thought I'd be ill.

"What is it, Shelby?" Chad asked.

My gaze swept across him, Doris, her husband, and to Mrs. Rousse. "I saw him from the back door in the kitchen. He stood in the yard. Just when I was about to tell Mama, I heard the explosion." I stiffened, too stunned to cry. "How could one man be so full of hate?"

"He suffered for it in the end," Miss Rousse said. "Once he confessed to all he'd done, he asked Jesus to live in his heart. He apologized to me for all the years of meanness and asked me to find Bonnie for him before he died. Well, I never did. He had his will changed and left everything to her. Toward the end, he had me read the Bible to him. He cried all day long about the things he'd done." She squeezed my hand. "I swear to you, he repented of it all."

"What good did it do when my sisters were dead?"

"You have to forgive your pawpaw, Shelby," the old woman said. "The hate will drive you to an early grave, just like it did him."

I stood from the bed and dropped her hand. I had to get out of there. My head pounded worse than I could ever remember. Right then I wished I'd never returned to Shelby Oaks. My mind had blocked out the horror of the past; I should have stayed there.

I rushed down the hall and out the front door. Fresh air. I needed to breathe, to think, to stop my racing heart filled with more hate than I ever dreamed possible.

"Shelby, stop." Chad's voice rang in my ears, but I kept on running. Screams of my sisters pierced my eardrums. All those years of Mama wasting away in the mental hospital. All the years I spent in a foster home. One man had destroyed a whole family with his hate. He deserved to die, and he didn't deserve forgiveness.

Chad grabbed my arm and pulled me to a stop. "You are a survivor," he said. "Look at me."

I tried, but the crying jag he'd witnessed the day before did an encore performance. "He killed my sisters, and Mrs. Rousse wants me to forgive him?" I couldn't utter another word. Hatred stopped me cold. Chad's declaration of me having strength seemed like a cruel mockery of what I felt.

"Take me back to Shelby Oaks," I said. "I'm going home to Detroit."

Chapter 8

The next day after I returned to Detroit, I phoned Chad. "I'm sorry for the way I behaved. Please forgive me."

"I miss you too much to be angry," he said. "I'm sure you don't want to hear this, but you need to forgive your grandfather."

I swallowed the perpetual lump in my throat. I nearly snapped at him. "I know, but it's hard."

"I'll pray for you. Remember what I told you? You are one strong woman, Shelby Landry. You survived a tragedy and had the courage to face it."

"Thanks," I finally said, not knowing how else to reply.

"There are people here who care about you very much."

My heart ached for something I couldn't have. "We have to be adults about this."

"Define an adult's approach."

The words escaped me. "You have your world and I have mine. I signed and mailed the purchase agreement this morning."

"Are you sure you want to sell the property?"

"Yes, without a doubt. There's nothing there but bad memories."

"Shelby. . .let's e-mail back and forth. I don't want to let you slip through my fingers."

I refused to respond with my own longing. "E-mail is fine."

For the next three months, we discussed everything from church theology to favorite foods. Through Mary Linda's gentle guidance, I found the need and courage to forgive my grandfather. Chad didn't call and neither did I. Yet, the privilege of expressing my thoughts and viewpoints in the way of the written word allowed me to know him quite well. My formal speech lessened, and I became more interested in the people around me.

Chad never mentioned the contract for Shelby Oaks, and I couldn't bring myself to ask. His face lingered in my mind, and when he posted an E-mail, I could almost hear him speaking.

Much to my relief, the headaches disappeared the same day I forgave my grandfather. My doctor was quite pleased with himself, and Mary Linda wept with me. For the first time in my life, I didn't have to manage my life around pain. Always the Scripture stayed before me: *The truth will set you free.* But it had been so hard.

Every time I reflected on those few weeks at Shelby Oaks, a part of me wanted to climb into my car and drive south—to Chad and all the wonderful people who had shown me love.

Chad shared in my healing. His messages added light to my life. I told Mama all about him and what happened at

Shelby Oaks. Her eyes told me she heard and understood, but her condition remained the same.

One morning, while adding a fluoride treatment to a little girl's baby teeth, a hygienist informed me of my next patient. I finished up and offered the little girl her choice in my treasure chest before making my way to the next patient. From the back of his head, I could tell instantly a grown man waited for my services. Adults did see me on occasion, but usually the patient was a woman who had undergone an unpleasant dental experience.

"Good morning," I said and picked up his chart. At the reading of his name, my gaze flew to his face.

"Chad!"

The familiar smile that had haunted me and drove me to distraction for weeks met my thundering heart. "What are you doing here?"

He handed me a stuffed green alligator. "The bayou has come for a visit."

"I see." I inspected the alligator and grappled for an appropriate comment. "Thank you for the addition to my menagerie."

I laughed and trembled. "I'm glad it wasn't a real one."

He rubbed his palms. "How about lunch or dinner—or both?"

"I'm working straight through until five."

"Can I pick you up at six thirty at your apartment?"

"I suppose so." My heart quickened. "I'll give you directions." Later in the afternoon, I scolded myself for giving in so easily. But the mere sight of him had made my day.

The doorbell sounded promptly at six thirty. My knees shook and my pulse went into overdrive. I could barely lift my hand to the doorknob. In my fantasies, I'd imagined him standing in my doorway, but nothing felt as grand as the flesh-and-blood man before me.

"You look beautiful," he whispered.

A smile rose from the tips of my toes. "Won't you come in?"

He stepped over the threshold, and I sensed his nervousness as well. He presented me with a bouquet of yellow and white roses. Odd I hadn't noticed the flowers until then.

"How wonderful. Thank you." I inhaled their delicate fragrance. "I'd like to place them in a vase, if you don't mind."

He nodded and I shakily carried my flowers into the kitchen for the proper container. "How are your parents?" I asked.

"Good. They said to tell you hello." He'd followed me into the tiny area, and once I secured a vase from the cabinet, he turned on the water.

A question burned in my thoughts. "What brings you to Detroit?"

"I came to collect a debt."

Startled, my gaze flew to his rich brown eyes. Chad took the vase and the flowers from my hands and set them on the counter. "Oh, were you successful?"

"I don't know yet."

I fished for something else to say while a flurry of emotions played through me.

He leaned against the counter, and I admired his short-sleeve, light yellow pullover accenting his tan. As I remembered, he looked incredible. "Don't you want to know the debt?" he asked.

"I guess."

"You have something that belongs to me."

I gasped. "What?"

"You come to the bayou, wrap your fingers around my heart, and leave me."

I blinked.

"I came to see if the lady would consider returning what she took." He touched my arm then my hand and pulled me into an embrace.

"I've missed you so," I said.

"Best news I've heard since I stepped on Yankee soil."

Surely he heard my heart hammering against his chest.

"I love you, Shelby Landry," he said. "I think you feel the same."

"I do," I whispered.

"Come back with me to Louisiana as my wife. I know an old estate for sale called Shelby Oaks that I can buy for us. It's near Zirondelle. Some folks say it would make a beautiful inn, and I'm sure we could find a nurse to care for your mama."

"I don't know what to say."

"One thing though, you have a rain check to cash in." His lips brushed across mine: gentle, warm, and tender. "My grandmother says every lucky man finds his love at the end of the bayou."

"I have to agree with her wise words."

"Is your answer yes?"

I reached up to touch his hair and let it weave through my fingertips. "A man toting an alligator all the way from the marshes of Louisiana deserves a yes."

DIANN MILLS

DiAnn lives in Houston, Texas, with her husband Dean. They
have four adult sons. She wrote from the time she could hold
a pencil, but not seriously until God made it clear that she
should write for Him. After three years of serious writing, her
first book *Rehoboth* won favorite **Heartsong Presents** historical for 1998. Other publishing credits include magazine articles and short stories, devotionals, poetry, and internal writing
for her church. She is an active church choir member, leads a
ladies' Bible study, and is a church librarian. She is also an advi-
sory board member for American Christian Romance Writers.

Buried in the Past

by Jill Stengl

Dedication

To three faithful ministers and their wives
who have richly blessed our family
with godly instruction and priceless friendship:
Lloyd and Judy Ashworth, Dave and Phyllis Georgeff,
and Gordon and Denna Magee.
May our Lord bless you all
as you continue your work for Him.

Therefore do not go on passing judgment before the time,
but wait until the Lord comes who will both bring
to light the things hidden in the darkness and
disclose the motives of men's hearts; and then
each man's praise will come to him from God.
1 CORINTHIANS 4:5 NASB

Chapter 1

O of! Found that pothole," Stephanie Keller groaned. Norma, seated beside her in the passenger seat with forepaws braced on the dashboard, gave a prolonged whimper. The tiny car's headlights barely pierced sheets of rain, and its wipers were overwhelmed.

"Do you see any lights? Don't they believe in streetlights around here? I would even accept another flash of lightning."

The dog replied with another whine.

"I know you're just as tired as I am. I believe this day ranks among the longest of my life. How about you?"

After slowing for a puddle, Stephanie reached for the gearshift with her right hand. It wasn't there. "I wonder how many more times I'll make that mistake."

With the knob in her left hand, she downshifted, wincing at the grinding gears. When she let out the clutch, the car gave a few bunny hops and expired.

Stephanie rested her forehead on the steering wheel. "This car hates me." A sob rose in her throat, but she refused to release it. "I passed the stupid driving test, so I know I can drive a right-hand-drive vehicle. Dear God, please help us find the house."

A wind gust rocked the car, and lightning sliced across the sky. Bits of ice slithered down the windshield. Norma shivered and moaned. Stephanie reached over to hug the Doberman's warm neck. "I know, baby, I'm cold and scared, too—but we must be close. I went around that roundabout in the village four times to make sure we got off at the right place. The sign pointed this way to Staneheath Manor, and Haverstane Cottage has to be close by."

Norma pricked her ears. Stephanie glanced up to see a hooded figure drift across the road in front of her car. Huge owlish eyes mirrored the headlights. Stephanie blinked. When her eyes popped open, the figure melted into the hedgerow bordering the lane. Norma stared, growling and quivering.

Stephanie started the car and cranked the heater up as high as it would go. "That's it—I'm officially freaked. We're out of here! Keep your eyes open. It's a flint cottage with a church next door. The man at the filling station said it would be on the right."

They crawled past a jumble of stone buildings on the left. A small sign announced WESTBOURNE FARM AND STABLES. "That place looks inhabited at least, though not particularly welcoming. Maybe the person we saw lives there." *Or haunts there.*

Lightning flashed again, backlighting a square tower. "There! That has to be the church ahead. We're nearly home, Norma. Stay with me a minute more."

Sure enough, the hedgerows gave way, revealing a stone edifice surrounded by an overgrown graveyard. Granite headstones and marble crosses tilted at rude angles. Stephanie felt her face grow slack, and her grip on the steering wheel tightened. "A cheerful place that is, perfectly suited to the weather and the hour. All we need is to see that cloaked person drifting through the graveyard like the Ghost of Christmas Yet to Come."

Beyond the line of trees bordering the churchyard, a signpost indicated HAVERSTANE COTTAGE. Stephanie let her car creep up the gravel drive while she scanned the imposing stone façade. Lightning flashed across the sky, reflecting in the house's windows like the glint of opening eyes. "This is a cottage? It looks like a mansion to me."

Shifting into PARK, she left the engine running. "Norma, I think we made a mistake coming here. Uncle John's letter said he would have the electricity turned on for us, and he said the place should be clean. . . ." Doubt battled hope in her heart and thoughts. "I don't remember passing an inn in the village, and I don't want to drive all the way back to Cambridge tonight." She gulped and switched off the ignition. "Why do I have to be such a chicken?"

Silence filled the car, broken only by Norma's miserable sighs and the patter of rain. "Lord Jesus, I could use some courage right about now," Stephanie prayed aloud. "Please remind me that You're with us."

She tugged her derby hat over one eye and lifted her chin. "Tell you what, Norma: Let's first go inside and switch on all the lights. We'll turn up the heat and find something to eat. Maybe it will stop raining before we have to unpack the car. What do you say?" Scooping up her purse, she located the envelope that one of Uncle John's London lawyers had given her. A rusted iron key lay inside. "I've only ever seen keys like this one in old cartoons. This is an adventure, Norma. Are you game?"

The car's interior light revealed the dog's doleful expression and flattened ears. "Come now. You're supposed to be my brave guard, and look at you!" She opened her car door and popped the umbrella.

After a brief stop in the soggy weeds lining the drive, the pair mounted the front steps and tried the key. It turned with a *thunk,* and the door swung open. Norma pressed her nose against Stephanie's thigh and hung back.

Reaching inside, Stephanie felt for a light switch and found a bare wall. Moving farther inside, she discovered a corner. No switch on the adjoining wall, either. Floorboards groaned at her every step. "I should have brought a flashlight. I should have—" Lightning crashed directly overhead, rattling the windows.

Back outside on the porch, Stephanie breathed deeply, willing her heart rate down to normal while rain cascaded from her umbrella. Her entire body vibrated to the rhythm of Norma's panting as the dog leaned against her knees. "You cannot possibly be hot. It's freezing out here." Clenching her chattering teeth, Stephanie made one more bold move. During that instant of illumination, she had seen a light bulb suspended from the ceiling. Now, with one hand waving over her head, she plunged back into the house.

Her fingers struck a small chain. Stephanie froze, waiting for it to swing back and hit her hand again. As soon as it did, she pulled.

266

The bare bulb cast a dim shaft of light down a narrow hallway. A staircase began almost at Stephanie's feet, rising into darkness above. Debating her next move, she closed the front door. "I don't think it's any warmer inside than outside, no matter what Uncle John said, but at least it's drier. Let's explore the house first, Norma, then unpack the car." She glanced at her wristwatch. "Goodness, it's only six o'clock in the evening! It feels late."

As they roamed through the cottage, Stephanie's spirits plummeted. The rooms were drafty and sparsely furnished. In the kitchen, the tiny refrigerator was unplugged and empty. She found a few cans of unfamiliar food in the cupboards but no can opener.

She looked at Norma and sighed. "At least you won't go hungry. We've got plenty of dog food in the car. I'm always talking about losing a few pounds. Here's my chance."

When Stephanie had unloaded the car and set a few of her belongings about, the house seemed less intimidating. Norma wolfed down a pull-top can of beef chunks. Stephanie nibbled on a pack of crumbled potato chips she'd found in her purse. "At least we have running water, though it doesn't taste good. Tomorrow I must find a grocery store."

She let her gaze roam the kitchen, imagining ruffled curtains at the windows, her china on the oak dresser, and stenciling around the windows. The cottage might have potential as a home if she could survive in it long enough to discover its charm. "At least it's clean," she mused. Not one painting ornamented the walls. No magazines or books—not even any bookcases that she could find. Only a small television brought the sitting room into modern times. She had switched it on but found nothing worth watching.

"Let's make an early night of it, Norma. Maybe I'll lie in bed and read for a while." Stephanie clicked off most of the lights downstairs, leaving the hall light burning. With her overnight bag slung over one shoulder, she picked up her travel case and headed up the dark stairs. Another bulb lit the upper hallway, revealing several closed doors. Behind one door she found a tiny bedroom, scarcely larger than a walk-in closet. The discovery of a small upstairs bathroom cheered her, though it offered no shower, only a claw-footed, rusty tub. Three other rooms were good-sized chambers, each containing a wardrobe, a chest of drawers, and a bed. One of the beds had a huge wet spot on the mattress, and more rainwater plopped as Stephanie watched. Mottled discolorations like giant amoebas blotched the sagging ceiling and part of one wall. She switched off the light, fearing an electric shock.

She chose the room overlooking the front of the house, farthest from the abandoned church and graveyard. After a search, she located bed linens in one wardrobe, but the mildewed smell of them wrinkled her nose. "Another item for my shopping list."

Shivering after washing her face in frigid water, she changed into purple-polka-dotted long johns, a fleece robe, and fuzzy slippers. "Come, Norma." The dog followed her downstairs. "You'll have to do your business without me this time."

Norma refused to step outside the door.

"You'll never last the night."

Norma remained unmoved.

Stephanie popped on a huge pair of rubber boots she had found in the scullery, wrapped an ancient rain slicker over her shoulders, and opened her still-damp umbrella. "You'd better not make a habit of this." She slipped the front door key into the coat's pocket. Thankfully, the rain had stopped. Norma trotted down the steps and disappeared into the darkness.

Stephanie waited on the porch, listening to the drum and splash of cascading water. "Norma?" she called. "If you get lost, I'm not coming after you tonight." What would she do if the dog didn't return?

Lightning flashed.

A figure in a hooded raincoat stood at the base of the steps. Stephanie shrieked.

"Are you Sir John Haverstane's American relative?" a deep British voice asked.

"I'm Stephanie Keller, his niece. Who are you?"

Norma came running, stopped short when she saw the intruder, and erupted in a flurry of barking, backing up until a shrub blocked her way. "Norma, hush," Stephanie ordered, her voice quivering. The dog quieted.

The man switched on a flashlight and aimed it at his own face. Stephanie saw dark-rimmed glasses, a neat mustache, and chin whiskers. "My name is Larkin. I live down the road. Sorry to disturb you, Miss. We saw lights in the cottage and came to investigate. I'm thankful we didn't ring the constable."

Norma approached Mr. Larkin hesitantly. He held out his hand to the dog and allowed her to sniff it. Her stubby tail wagged. "Beautiful girl. Is she friendly to other dogs? We have two corgis."

"Norma likes other dogs, but she especially likes cats. I had two back home. I gave them to my neighbor. They were old and wouldn't have adjusted well to a move," Stephanie babbled.

"And where is home?"

"Here, now. I used to live in California."

Norma pricked her ears and growled. Footsteps crunched on the drive, and another flashlight approached. "Who is it, Dudley?" called a woman's voice. Two corgis rushed toward Norma, and the three dogs sniffed each other in greeting.

"Sir John's niece from America. Pardon me, but I have forgotten your name."

"Keller. Mrs. Stephanie Keller."

"Mrs. Keller, this is my stepsister, Pat Walden-Hoff."

"Where's Mr. Keller?" the woman demanded.

Stephanie tried not to reveal irritation. "I'm widowed."

"Convenient for you. Relations are like carrion crows." Pat Walden-Hoff's light beamed straight into Stephanie's face. "Soon as His Lordship is taken ill, up pop the relatives. This one no doubt sees herself as lady of the manor."

Stephanie squinted. "My uncle asked me to come."

"He won't be asking anymore," the woman snapped.

The flashlight's beam shifted away from Stephanie's eyes. "Be polite to our new neighbor, Pat." As Mr. Larkin pushed the woman's arm to one side, Stephanie glimpsed her scowling face. "She is alone in a strange country and no doubt frightened."

He turned back, and his glasses glinted again. "Your uncle recently suffered another stroke and has difficulty speaking. He shares a room at the rest home with my father, so I see him frequently."

"I work there," Pat added. "I don't imagine you'll be need-ing employment. As soon as His Lordship passes on, you'll be in clover." Envy laced her voice.

"That is not our business," Mr. Larkin said. "However, our neighbor's welfare is. Mrs. Keller, I know the cottage was cleaned recently, but I doubt there is much food. Why not join us for tea tonight? I made lamb pie. We have plenty."

Lamb pie and tea seemed an odd combination, but Stephanie's empty stomach was in no mood to quibble. "You're very kind. If you will wait a moment for me to change. . . Please step inside. Your dogs may come, too."

After a short, terse consultation, the two mounted her steps and stopped on the mat in the entry hall. Three dogs pushed past and thundered up the stairs, yipping with excitement. "You keep your house cold," Pat remarked. She pushed back her hood to reveal cropped red hair and a deeply lined face. Spying Stephanie's purple-spotted pajama legs, she lifted one penciled brow.

"I turned the heaters on, but they don't seem to get warm. I'll be only a moment." Stephanie hurried upstairs. She threw on black jeans and a scarlet knit top with crocheted bell sleeves and tucked her hair beneath her black derby. The hat was a thrift shop find; she thought it emphasized her eyes, and it concealed her messy hair.

Pat sat alone on the stairs when Stephanie returned. "My stepbrother is playing Good Samaritan and turning on your heat. You had all the wall switches off." The woman's tone held amused contempt.

Mr. Larkin entered the hall. "If I light your water heater

now, you should have hot water by morning."

"Thank you. It's upstairs in a hall closet."

As soon as he was out of hearing, Pat spoke. "Don't get notions about my stepbrother."

Stephanie regretted accepting the tea invitation. Starvation would be preferable to this woman's company.

"Religion is his life. He preaches and farms and reads too much. Doesn't want a woman." Pat smiled with her lips only. "Beneath all that kindness and courtesy, he's cold-blooded as a fish."

Chapter 2

The storm still flashed in the distance when Stephanie shut Norma inside the cottage and accompanied her new neighbors to their house. "You'll need to purchase an electric torch," Mr. Larkin said in his quiet way, "for taking your dog out at night." His flashlight illuminated a path for Stephanie, and he guided her around the deepest puddles. Pat tromped on ahead with the corgis at her heels.

"You can see my cottage from your house?" Stephanie asked, looking up at his shadowy face.

"And you can see our farm ahead. We are your nearest neighbors. My stepmother and Pat live in the house. I live in a flat beside the stable. At one time the farm belonged to tenants of the Staneheath estate."

Winter-bare trees framed the farmhouse, bowing and groaning in the wind. Shrubbery draped over the garden wall, its branches scraping the stones like skeletal fingers. Stephanie's skin prickled as Mr. Larkin pushed open the gate. A quick glance up, and she saw a curtain drop over an upstairs window. "Uh, maybe I should wait until tomorrow to visit. Your stepmother might not appreciate an unexpected guest."

His reply sounded reluctant. "She never appreciates guests. Freda is emotionally unstable. Take nothing she says seriously; she is harmless enough. Talk about the dogs if she seems hostile." After a short pause, he added, "I should have told you earlier, but I was afraid you wouldn't come."

He was right on that score. Stephanie felt disoriented enough without having to face a lunatic woman. But something in his voice prevented her from leaving. His hand supported her elbow as she climbed the front steps. She wanted to pull away, yet at the same time she liked his courtesy.

He hung her raincoat beside his in the entry and arranged their boots on a mat. Other dripping garments already lined the wall and floor, and muddy paw prints embellished the cracked linoleum.

A cream-colored fisherman's knit pullover and brown tweed slacks suited Mr. Larkin's lanky frame. "I'll introduce you to my stepmother before I bring the food over from my flat. I seldom eat here, but today is Freda's birthday, so I prepared a meal to share." He left Stephanie in the sitting room with the promise of his quick return. She heard his footsteps ascending creaky stairs. "Freda?"

The house smelled old. Although several lamps lighted the room, it felt dim and drab. Soiled carpeting matted the floor. The corgis already curled up on two armchairs near a tiny fireplace. Stephanie sat on the sofa and wished she'd stayed home with Norma.

Mr. Larkin returned, leading a stumpy, gray-haired woman by one arm. The dogs sat up and seemed to smile, their ears pricked. A flowered dress sagged on the woman's bulgy yet angular figure, and thick eyeglasses magnified her staring eyes.

"Who's this?"

Mr. Larkin spoke distinctly. "Freda, meet our new neighbor, Stephanie Keller. Mrs. Keller, this is my stepmother, Freda Walden-Larkin. While you two ladies become acquainted, I'll fetch the meal from my flat. Pat is already bringing the trifle."

"I can help," Stephanie offered.

"No need. You're our guest." His smile revealed good teeth. Light reflected off his glasses.

"Where's your husband?" Freda asked as soon as Mr. Larkin left.

"He died four years ago."

"Natural causes?"

"Pneumonia. He had been unwell for many years."

"No children?"

Stephanie shook her head.

"What do you do?"

"Until recently, I owned a small beauty shop. I enjoy styling hair and helping ladies learn to apply cosmetics."

"Pat used to do that job at the funeral home. Her patrons never complained."

"How—how interesting." Stephanie's mouth felt dry.

Those staring eyes never wavered. "You like animals?"

"Very much. I own a dog. Your corgis are handsome dogs."

Freda's lined features softened. "Torville and Dean are sister and brother. Named them after the Olympic ice dancers. Dean lost his hearing though. Getting old, like me. The queen raises corgis. Best dogs in the world. Don't start thinking Dudley will marry you. He doesn't need a woman."

Stephanie blinked, thinking she had missed a vital transition in the conversation. "Dudley?"

"My stepson. If you want an affair, try one of the English Legacy fellows or someone from town. Dudley can't marry."

Stephanie's face burned. More than anything, she wanted to escape from this dreadful house and these bizarre people. "I have no interest in your stepson, I assure you," she said stiffly.

"They all say that. But I saw you watching him. Your first marriage was unhappy. You want babies before you get too old. You look like a short Sophia Loren. Are you Italian?"

What was this woman—a fortune-teller? Her guesses hit too close to home. "On my father's side. My mother was English. She was Sir John Haverstane's younger sister."

"So you say."

To Stephanie's relief, Pat appeared in the doorway. "Tea is served."

Oddly enough, no tea appeared on the table during or after the meal. Stephanie picked at a serving of bland lamb pie, sipped thick-tasting milk, and devoured a cherry trifle. "That was delicious," she said honestly, dabbing her lips with a linen napkin. "You make good desserts."

When Mr. Larkin turned to smile at her, for the first time no light glared upon his glasses. His mild blue eyes expressed pleasure. "Thank you. In other respects I am an uninspired chef, but I enjoy concocting sweets."

"Mrs. Keller needs to go home." Freda's gruff pronouncement held disapproval.

"She's no danger, Mum," Pat said. "Plump and married before. It won't last."

"I'll escort Mrs. Keller home. She is undoubtedly tired tonight." Dudley Larkin rose. "I'll wash up later."

After stammering a passable farewell to the women, Stephanie followed her host to the front door. He held her raincoat while she slipped her arms into its sleeves. "You must have borrowed Sir John's mac and wellies," he observed.

"If you mean the slicker and boots, I found them at the cottage. Tomorrow, I need to purchase new ones in my size." Despite her best efforts, her voice wobbled.

"I apologize, Mrs. Keller. I had no idea they would be so rude."

She turned to meet his gaze. "They seem protective of you."

His voice was subdued. "Not of me. Of this house and my inheritance. They scarcely know me. Dad married Freda before he discovered her problems. And Pat. . ." He shook his head. Brown hair dangled near his cheekbones and straggled over his collar. He looked underfed and melancholy despite his ruddy cheeks.

A sad smile tugged at his lips as he donned his raincoat. "Come. This house is no place for you. I should never have brought you here." He held the door as she exited. "Like a lamb into a den of lions."

"Then why did you invite me?" Stephanie watched him close the front door.

His raincoat rustled as he turned. She heard him draw a deep breath. He switched on his flashlight, and for a moment she looked into his eyes. "Foolishness. You are a believer in

Jesus, aren't you, Mrs. Keller?"

"How did you know?"

"I guessed by your kindness and restraint, your pure vocabulary even in moments of duress, and your 'amen' after my prayer at tea. Pat or Freda might already have told you that I minister to a small local body of Christians."

Stephanie paused while he opened the garden gate for her. "Pat told me you were religious. You're a vicar? Or is that the right term?"

"I dropped out of seminary years ago, so 'minister' is more what I do than what I am. I'm a farmer and a jack-of-all-trades. If not for Jesus Christ, I would be a lonely and frustrated man."

A cat crossed their path and melted into the hedgerow. Moonlight glimmered through fleeting clouds and reflected from puddles in the rutted road. A wailing wind tossed the treetops. Mr. Larkin's tone and topic suddenly switched. "I should like to escort you to visit your uncle tomorrow when I visit my father. I believe you should also purchase a cell phone. You have no telephone at Haverstane Cottage; Sir John refused to have one hooked up."

"I know. To be honest, I have never spoken to my uncle. He communicated with me by letter and through his attorneys."

"At one time he was a strong man in mind and body, but in his later years he has seemed debilitated by unreasoning suspicions. He insists upon sharing a room at the rest home with my father, though he could certainly afford privacy. I believe he—"

After a pause, Stephanie prompted, "You believe. . .*what*?"

"Nothing I need to say. Tonight let me give you my cell phone in case of emergency." He unhooked the phone from beneath his pullover and handed it to her.

"Thank you again." Keeping her gaze away from the old church and graveyard, Stephanie shivered in the icy wind. "Is there something I should know? Am I in any danger? I've had the strangest feeling about this place ever since I arrived. . . ." She hesitated, realizing that Dudley Larkin was nearly as odd as his relatives. What man could develop normally while saddled with a name like "Dudley"? Maybe he was too gentle and soft-spoken to be real.

"I've had the strangest feeling about this place for many years," he said. "I had a happy childhood, but after I returned from college. . ." He stopped and shook his head. "Despite my love for the farm and friends, I would leave in a moment if not for my father who needs me. Since I must stay, I strive to be content and leave the future in God's hands. I hope you will trust me, Mrs. Keller, but I realize that trust requires time to develop."

"You are truly kind, Mr. Larkin." Haverstane Cottage seemed less intimidating when she approached it this time. Norma's welcoming bark gave it a homey feel, as did the lights Stephanie had left on.

"I hope you can bring yourself to address me as Dudley. The name probably sounds archaic to you; it belonged to my grandfather."

Something in his tone made her smile. "I'll call you Dudley if you'll call me Stephanie. And I appreciate all your help. Settling into this new country, new town, and new house will require time, I'm sure, but friends will help ease the transition."

He waited on the step until she located her key and

unlocked the front door. Norma rushed out to greet her, gave Dudley a sniff and a wag, and headed for the lawn. "I believe Norma will like it here. Anything is better than the kennel in London. The house already feels warmer. Thank you again, Dudley, for dinner, for your assistance, and for your offer of friendship." She extended her cold hand.

Instead of shaking her hand, he took it and bowed over it. "Good night, Stephanie. Welcome to my country and to my world." He pulled a paper-wrapped parcel from his jacket pocket. "For your breakfast. I'll drop by in the morning to see how you're getting on. Remember to ring me if you need anything. My number is entered in the cell phone."

"To be honest, I don't know how to use a cell phone."

He stepped into the lighted entryway but left the front door open while demonstrating the use of his phone. As soon as she felt sure she could use the device in an emergency, he took his leave.

Stephanie wandered through the house in an exhausted daze. In the kitchen she unwrapped her parcel to discover two small brown eggs, several slices of meat resembling bacon, and a few crumbling biscuits dotted with bits of dried fruit. "What a sweet man!" she whispered.

That night, after reading several chapters of a dull novel, she switched off her lamp and listened to the clicking wall heater. Wind moaned around the eaves, and water still dripped, hopefully outside. Norma snored contentedly, having worked her way inside the capacious slumber bag.

Lord, thank You for bringing us here safely. Please bless Uncle John and help me to bring some joy back into his life. Sometimes my life has seemed overwhelmingly difficult, but at least I have good health. How sad he—

A sound caught her attention. It sounded like laughter somewhere outside, wild and mocking. Was she imagining things? Norma crawled out of the bag, stood alert on the mattress, then launched herself off the bed and propped her forepaws on the windowsill. The Doberman's ominous growl rumbled.

"What is it, Norma? A bird? A hyena?" Silly questions, but the sound of her own voice helped keep her calm. More from the need to touch Norma than from any desire to see the source of that fearful noise, she climbed out of bed and approached the window.

The laughter repeated, and Norma ran to scratch at the bedroom door. Gripping her dog by the collar, Stephanie opened the door, switched on the hall light, and followed Norma's lead to the leaky room at the back of the house. She threw open that door, and light from the hall made a rectangle upon the hardwood floor. Nothing unusual met her gaze, but Norma ran to the side window, reared up to look out, and flattened her ears. Instead of barking, she gave a long whine.

Stephanie stood just inside the door with her back against the wall. "Norma, you're scaring the daylights out of me." She didn't dare switch on the light—not with that soaked ceiling.

The dog's fixed stare seemed to follow something outside. Although she knew she would regret it, Stephanie ran to join Norma at the window.

Below lay a gray, threatening world of tumbled stone walls, of wind-tossed trees, of sweeping shadows. Norma trembled beneath Stephanie's hand. Following the dog's gaze, she saw a figure moving along the overgrown hedge that divided the cottage from the graveyard. Before her startled eyes, it vanished. Norma woofed, glanced at Stephanie, pricked her ears and flattened them again, then turned and ran from the dark room.

Moments later, Stephanie huddled with her dog inside the slumber sack. She considered calling Dudley, but what good would that do? Long into the night she prayed and wept and feared.

Chapter 3

Morning light poured through the windows and woke Stephanie far too early. She pulled her covers over her head and felt smothered. The close air smelled of dog.

With a disgusted huff, she wriggled out of the sack and sat on the edge of the bed, scratching her head with both hands. The hardwood floor beneath her feet showed promise of beauty. Her gaze lifted. Beneath the age-blackened finish of the corner wardrobe she might, with the help of elbow grease and steel wool, discover an antique treasure. Plaster moldings, mostly intact, framed the door and windows. Maybe this venture wasn't hopeless after all. Black despair always faded to gray in bright morning sunlight.

"Lord Jesus," she whispered, "I was terrified last night, but now I'm not sure why. Maybe someone was out for a stroll— maybe two people laughing at a joke as they walked home from the pub. I'm scared enough about real life. No need to add ghosts to the mix. Lord, please give me courage. My past can't be changed, but You've given me a whole new life to live in this fascinating country. Give me grace to endure disappointment, genuine love for each person I meet, and wisdom to live as You want me to live."

She picked up her travel bag and staggered to the bathroom. No shade or curtain here either, but unless she stood in front of the window, no one could possibly see her from outside. She turned on both spigots in the old bathtub, trying to ignore the rusted gouges in its enamel coating. Deep groans rumbled from the bowels of the earth. The floor shook, and water spat from the faucets, making Stephanie jump. Again it spat, then sputtered, and twin gushes of brown, metallic-smelling water poured from the spigots. The right-hand stream cleared, but the hot water continued to burp and grumble. When she had almost given up hope, it paled to a golden hue. Steam dampened her face.

Stephanie bathed in the ancient tub—a difficult chore without a sprayer to rinse her thick hair—and returned to her bedroom. For some reason, blue jeans didn't suit her mood. She opted for a black skirt and a fuzzy fuchsia sweater. "What do you think, Norma? Do these flat shoes make my legs look chubby?"

The mound of bedding heaved. First the dog's black muzzle slid into view, then her mournful brown eyes. She eyed Stephanie but made no noise.

"Wise of you not to comment that my legs *are* chubby," Stephanie said. "Oh, go back to sleep. What good are you?"

Plenty of spray conditioner helped tame her hair, which was still recovering from a disastrous highlighting experiment. Reddish streaks did nothing to enhance its natural frizzy dark brown or to hide its encroaching gray. She probably ought to cut it off, but her heart wouldn't allow such a drastic move. In uncompromising daylight, it looked worse than ever. "Oh beautician, beautify thyself," she muttered. With a resigned sigh, she braided it into a thick rope and hid it beneath her signature derby. A fringe of bangs escaped to soften her forehead. "I feel twenty-two on the inside but look forty-two on the outside, no matter what I do. Better to look my age than older, I suppose."

I wonder how old Dudley is? The thought crept in unbidden. "Stop it, Stephanie!" She scowled at her reflection.

After applying her makeup, she met her own gaze in the wardrobe mirror, tried to smile, and swallowed hard. "Please, Lord, I need wisdom about people. Help me know whom I can trust. English people are so different; sometimes I have no idea what they're thinking. Help me know what to do and where to go. I imagine I'll be talking to You all day long, so no sign-off this time." She scooped her Bible from the bedside table and headed for the door.

A long sigh caught her attention. She paused to swat the lump in the bedclothes. "Come, Norma, you slug-a-bed."

The dog slithered out of bed and followed her downstairs and into the kitchen. Seeing light in the back hall, Stephanie discovered a windowed door. "Look, baby, you've got a walled-in playground out here. Very overgrown, but think how pretty we can make it come summer."

While Norma explored her domain by daylight, Stephanie heated breakfast. A knock sounded at the front door. Glancing at her watch as she hurried to the entryway, Stephanie realized she had left the cell phone upstairs.

Dudley and an adolescent boy waited on the front steps. "Good morning. Sorry to come unannounced, but I did attempt to ring you earlier." With his hair combed, wearing fresh clothing, Dudley looked like a new man.

"I must have been in the bath." Her face grew hot, and she shifted her attention to the gangly boy. "Hello."

"This is Colin Bant. He works for me. I thought I should introduce him in case you need a handyman about the place to trim the shrubbery, repair the gates—anything you need done. Colin's a good worker, and honest."

"Pleased to meet you, Colin."

"Mum." He shook her hand. "Fo' pound sn'our."

She looked at Dudley. He nodded. "Four pounds an hour is a fair rate."

Stephanie smiled at Colin. "Okay. My yard is a mess. When can you begin work?"

The boy barely opened his mouth. "Now, 'f you want. Brought tools 'long."

"His tools are in the back of my Land Rover," Dudley said.

Thinking of the few pound notes and coins in her purse, Stephanie decided she could always write a check. English money would take getting used to. "That would be fine. Perhaps you could begin with the lawn, although I'm certain it's wet after that storm."

"All trum the 'edges." He trotted down the steps and began to pull tools from the Land Rover parked in the drive. Norma gave a few tardy barks from the backyard.

Stephanie eyed Dudley's gray tweed trousers and his jacket

with leather patches on the elbows. Out for a morning call, yet he looked ready to instruct a college class.

He cleared his throat. "Colin is a man of few words. I asked him to accompany me as a chaperone of sorts, but he prefers action."

"I'm not sure how I'll cope when you aren't here to translate for me," Stephanie admitted. "Please, won't you come in? I was cooking my breakfast. Have you eaten?"

"I have, thank you."

An awkward pause, then both spoke at once.

"Last night I—"

"Would you—"

"Go ahead," Dudley said.

"I need help with an appliance in my kitchen. At first I mistook it for a dishwasher."

He nodded soberly then turned around. "Colin, your help is required."

The boy left his stack of gardening tools and trotted back up the steps, flinging stringy black hair from his eyes. Both guests scraped their shoes before entering Stephanie's house.

"The kitchen is this way," she said.

Dudley paused to survey the sitting room. "Not many furnishings. Sir John left most of his belongings in the big house. English Legacy owns them now."

"Place is a tomb," Colin remarked.

"When did my uncle sell Staneheath Manor?"

Dudley's eyes focused sharply on Stephanie's face. "Nearly two years ago. I gather he failed to inform you."

"If you're thinking he deceived me, that's not the case. I

never expected wealth and glamour. Uncle John's attorneys tell me he wants me to care for the cottage while he's hospitalized. Maybe he'll be able to come home now that I'm here to care for him. I have experience caring for invalids."

"You have no family back home to miss you?" he asked.

"None. My parents died long ago, and I've been a widow nearly four years. Norma is my only family. And, to save you the trouble of asking, I have no children and no brothers or sisters. A cottage in Cambridgeshire sounded like a fairy tale when Uncle John's lawyers wrote and asked me to come. I knew my mother had relatives in England, but until recently I had no idea her older brother was lord of a real manor. My grandparents disinherited my mother when she ran away to marry an American serviceman—my dad."

"I smell bacon," Colin said clearly.

"My breakfast!" Stephanie dashed to the kitchen.

At Stephanie's request, Dudley let Norma inside and introduced her to Colin. While the two males petted the dog and chatted about recent local events, Stephanie ate what remained of her breakfast. At the mention of church, her ears pricked. "Do you use the church for services?" she asked while rinsing her plate at the sink. In response to their quizzical looks, she pointed out the window at the gray stone tower.

"That building hasn't been used for a century. We meet at a community center in the village," Dudley answered.

"Why hasn't the church building been used?"

"I believe a Haverstane ancestor had a falling out with his vicar, and the living was never given to another clergyman. When your uncle sold Staneheath Manor to English Legacy, a private organization dedicated to preserving our national heritage, he retained possession of the church along with the vicarage, this cottage. A pity, since English Legacy might have restored the church to its former glory. It is sixteenth century, I believe, like the manor. Tudor era. The cottage is Georgian, of course."

Stephanie nodded as if she had a clue what he meant, then opened the round door of an appliance beneath the counter-top. "Before I forget to ask, can you tell me what this is?"

"It's a washing machine," Colin said in a "duh!" tone, "for clo'es."

She stared at him. "In the kitchen. And I suppose there's a clothesline outside."

They both nodded.

"Well, I'm sure I'll adjust. It's like going back in time or. . . well, like moving to a new country, which is exactly what I've done. All bridges burned! No return."

"I'm pleased to hear it," Dudley said. "Last night I offered to take you with me to the rest home. I plan to visit my father there this morning, and I have a few hours available in case you need a local tour."

Colin snorted. "He worked like a dog all morning t' free up the rest o' the day."

Although he ignored the boy's remark, Dudley's face reddened. "Now tell me, is anything in the house in need of repair?"

"One of the upstairs rooms sustains a waterfall and a thriving mildew colony, and the bathroom has no shower," Stephanie said.

"Mind if we take a look?" Dudley rose. "I can't give you an

estimate without a thorough inspection, of course, but I should like to gain a general impression."

"Please, go on up and survey the disaster. This is great! Every woman should have a handyman for a neighbor if she possibly can swing it."

This time Dudley returned her smile. He and Colin headed upstairs while Stephanie straightened her kitchen. She could hardly wait for her shipment of boxes to arrive. How nice her mother's china would look on that antique china dresser! This cottage had unlimited potential for charm.

A short time later she climbed into Dudley's Land Rover, wrapping her fleece jacket around her shoulders. "My California clothing is inadequate for English weather, I'm learning. This wind has a bite. How can Colin work outside in his shirtsleeves?"

"He's used to it. You might find a few warm jumpers and cardigans in town, but for serious clothes shopping you'll need to try Cambridge." Dudley put his Rover in gear and headed up the rutted driveway. "Colin's bicycle is at the farm. He'll head home when he finishes trimming your hedges. I told him to leave the tools in my shed."

As they turned onto the road, Stephanie noticed horses and sheep grazing in the pasture across the way. A fat gray horse lifted its head and whinnied at the vehicle. Dudley made a sudden U-turn and pulled close to the fence, rolling down his window. The horse ambled over, reached its neck over the rails, and snuffled in his face. Dudley's glasses fogged over. Grinning, he patted the horse's furry neck. "Meet Pookah. She's expecting a foal come spring."

Stephanie laughed. "You baby your horses as badly as I baby my dog. Tell me more about your farm."

Pookah drew back, gave a hearty snort, and walked away, swishing her tail. Dudley pulled off his glasses and cleaned them with a handkerchief. Stephanie watched in disbelief. A handkerchief? This man was out of his time period, for certain.

"I raise hunters as a sideline, and we keep a few Suffolk sheep. I do co-op farming with several nearby farms, sharing equipment and labor. We raise sugar beets, carrots, and Swedes, along with some hay." He put the Rover in gear, checked for traffic, and made another U-turn back onto the road.

"Swedes?"

He smiled. "Swedish turnips. You might know it as rutabaga."

"Rutabaga I've heard of, though I'm positive I've never eaten it." Stephanie chuckled. "You said 'we.' Do Pat and Freda help you?"

He glanced at her. "By 'we,' I meant my neighboring farmers and myself. Pat works at the rest home."

"Is she a widow?" Stephanie watched farmland flash past.

"Her husband disappeared twenty-five years ago. Investigators found his name on the passenger list of an airline flight to Australia, but he was never found. Probably changed his identity. He and Pat were unhappily married."

Stephanie recognized vast understatement in that last remark. "Might he be dead? If I were her, I would want to know."

"I was away at school when all this occurred, so I know few details. I need hardly say that Pat is disinclined to discuss the matter." He pulled into a car park behind a sprawling brick building.

"We're here already? That didn't take long," Stephanie said. "I'm glad this place is so close, since I plan to visit Uncle John often. He must be a lonely man. I wonder why he never married."

Dudley opened her car door, then the rest home's entrance door. He seemed pensive, Stephanie thought, as he announced their arrival at the front desk. The nurse waved them on.

The unpleasant odors of disinfectant and body waste weighted the atmosphere. Stephanie heard a woman babbling as they passed an open doorway. Memories of Reece's last hours weakened her knees, and she felt uncomfortably warm.

Dudley ushered her into a room divided in half by a curtain. "Your uncle appears to be sleeping," he said, nodding toward the section to their left. A blanket-swathed figure lay in shadows.

To their right, daylight brightened the chamber, and an elderly man greeted them with a smile. "Dudley, my boy, so good to see you! And who is your lovely companion?"

Stephanie stepped forward, smiling, to take his trembling hand. His entire body quaked, and his voice quivered, yet his welcoming manner removed any awkwardness.

"This is our new neighbor at Haverstane Cottage. Stephanie, may I introduce my father, Philip Larkin? Dad, this is Mrs. Stephanie Keller, Sir John's niece from America."

Mr. Larkin patted her arm with his free hand. "My dear, you bring pleasure to my old eyes. Sir John is blessed to have such a charming relation."

"Mr. Larkin." At a loss for words, Stephanie simply returned the older man's smiles. He resembled Dudley, having the same slender frame, sharp features, and attentive expression.

"When did you arrive?"

"Last night. Your son was kind enough to invite me to tea, so I met your wife and stepdaughter."

"I see. And how do you like Haverstane Cottage?" A restrained urgency colored the question.

"I found it rather cold at first, but I believe it will become a comfortable home, given a little time and a lot of repairs. I've always wanted to live in the country."

A uniformed figure slipped behind them into the adjoining area, and Stephanie wondered if her uncle had awakened. Mr. Larkin loosened his grip. "I must not keep you, my dear. Sir John will wish to meet his niece."

The curtain beside them was hauled back, revealing Pat Walden-Hoff's stony face. "His Lordship is awake. Don't expect him to talk, and don't exhaust him. I'll return soon."

Stephanie turned toward the other bed. Staring gray eyes captured her gaze, the right eyelid drooping. Muscles worked in the man's sunken face; a moan issued from his lips.

"I thought she did only service work here," Stephanie heard Dudley murmur after Pat left the room. "Delivering meals and cleaning."

"You know Pat—always looking for something more to do."

"Would you like me to move you to a different home, Dad? The more I see of this place, the less I like it. We might sell off some stock and—"

"No, lad. I'm fine here."

Gathering her courage, Stephanie approached her uncle's bed, produced a shaky smile, and grasped his withered left hand. "Uncle John, I'm Stephanie Keller, your sister Josephine's daughter. I've come to stay with you and keep you company. I hope you like dogs. I own a Doberman named Norma, who was supposed to be a watchdog but turned out to be a big baby."

Sir John blinked, and his gaze moved to Dudley. Stephanie read dislike in the older man's expression and felt a need to explain. "Mr. Larkin welcomed me to the neighborhood and brought me here to see you. I have an appointment with your solicitor, Mr. Graham, here in town this afternoon; I met with your lawyers in London before I drove up. They helped me open a bank account and get my driver's license and, oh, ever so many things!"

Her uncle's steely gaze returned to her face. She rattled on, "I must thank you for providing for my easy transition. You have been extraordinarily generous and thoughtful. I—I was unaware of the severity of your illness. Mr. Graham's letter assured me it was a mild stroke, but after my arrival here I learned of your second stroke. I hope and pray you will recover quickly and be able to join me at Haverstane Cottage. I enjoy cooking and homemaking, and I promise to prepare all your favorite meals once I learn how to shop."

Behind her she heard Dudley conversing with his father. At least she had only one witness to her nervous babbling. "I shall enjoy decorating the house and cleaning up the flower garden, and I'm hoping we can do something to fix up the old church. Right now it's an eyesore and a disgrace, what with the weedy graveyard and the missing windows. Dudley Larkin is a minister, you know, and I think it would be lovely to fix up that old church and sell or lease it to a congregation that will put it to proper use once more."

The hand she held tightened its grip until she tried to pull free. "You're hurting me, Uncle John. Is something wrong?" The gray eyes pierced her, and a groan escaped his drooling mouth. "Are you in pain?"

His head barely moved from side to side.

"Do you need a nurse?"

He shook his head again.

Dudley appeared at her side. The furious gaze shifted to him, and Stephanie suddenly sensed evil in this pathetic old man. "Uncle John, what did I say to upset you? Was it the church?"

He nodded.

"We won't sell it unless you want to. I was just talking." Stephanie cast a pleading look at Dudley and tugged at her imprisoned fingers.

"Sir John, you are hurting Stephanie," Dudley said firmly. "She came here out of filial affection for her uncle. I advise you to nurture her trust and regard lest you lose them altogether."

The tortuous grip relaxed, and Stephanie snatched her hand away. Sheer hatred pervaded the glare Sir John directed at Dudley.

"Would you like me to pray for your uncle?" Dudley asked.

"Yes, please." Stephanie shifted closer to his comforting presence. He laid one hand on her shoulder, the other on Sir John's, and bowed his head.

"Our Lord and Father God, we request Your healing presence in this room. Touch Sir John's broken body and disquieted spirit with Your compassionate hand. We know that You love this man and desire his fellowship. We ask that You awaken his understanding of Your grace and fulfill his inmost desire, the secret longing of every man and woman for peace with You. Give him courage to understand and accept Your sacrifice of love on his behalf, that he may enter into Your presence here on earth as well as hereafter. In the blessed name of Jesus Christ we beg mercy upon this man. Amen."

When Stephanie opened her eyes, Sir John stared blankly at the ceiling. His breathing seemed uneven. Dudley gave her shoulder a gentle squeeze, then left her alone with her uncle.

"Dear Uncle John, I shan't disturb you longer today since you seem distressed and tired. I promise to return tomorrow and every day to visit. Is there anything you need? Would you like a radio or a CD player to listen to?"

He turned his head to meet her gaze. Suspicion and confusion filled his eyes. "Are you all right, Uncle? Would you like me to read to you? I have my New Testament here."

His gaze focused beyond her shoulder, and he abruptly turned his face toward the wall. Dismissed, Stephanie stepped away from the bed. Pat Walden-Hoff bustled over to pull the curtain. "Next time try not to upset him so much. Anyone would be upset at the sight of that absurd hat. What are you trying to do, finish him off so you can inherit?"

Stephanie reached up to touch her derby. "My uncle is worth far more than any amount of money. I plan to take him home with me as soon as he is able."

"You're living in a dream, luv. He'll never leave these walls."

Dudley stepped forward, caught his stepsister by the arm,

and ushered her into the hallway. Stephanie heard their angry voices. She cast a pleading glance at Mr. Philip Larkin, who looked equally concerned, then slipped around the curtain to bid her uncle farewell.

"I hope you don't believe anything that woman said, Uncle John. I came here for you, not for wealth. I deposited money from the sale of my house and beauty shop in California into my new account at Barclays Bank, so you needn't worry that I came to sponge off you. After we repair the cottage, we can live simply, maybe plant vegetables and keep a cow and some chickens. It will be an adventure."

Sir John's hand groped toward hers, and she allowed him to clasp her fingers again. His face worked, and guttural noises came from his mouth. "Don't try to talk, Uncle. You'll tire yourself."

Turning red, he raised up on one elbow. With great effort he formed his lips and uttered, "Cu'ss. Ch–ch. Deh–th." He fell back on the bed.

"Did you say 'church'?" she asked.

He nodded, eyes closed.

"Cu'ss. Curse? The church is cursed? I don't believe in such nonsense. The church belongs to the Lord. You needn't fear for me, Uncle."

He moaned.

The curtains rustled, and a nurse entered the chamber. "Visiting time is over, ma'am. Lord Haverstane must sleep now." She began to prepare an intravenous feeding bag.

"Good-bye, Uncle John." Stephanie took one more look at his gray face and crept from the room.

Chapter 4

Late that afternoon, the Land Rover rolled up the cottage driveway. As Dudley switched off the engine, Stephanie flopped back against the headrest. "What a day!" She rolled her head to the side and gazed at Dudley. "I can never thank you enough for chauffeuring me everywhere. Now I feel able to survive in this country."

His mustache lifted at the corners when he smiled. "Good."

"I don't see Colin anywhere, but my hedges look much better. I can't believe it's getting dark already."

"I'll bring your supplies to the door if you'll carry them to the kitchen," Dudley offered. "Are you hungry?"

She straightened her hat. "I'm still full from lunch at the pub."

After her purchases covered the kitchen table and overflowed to the floor, Stephanie met Dudley at the front door. "That's everything," he said. The hall light reflected from his glasses.

"Thank you so much. Putting it all away will keep me busy for some time, I should think." She handed him his cell phone.

"Thank you for lending me this."

"May I return this evening and escort you for a walk around the property?" he asked. "The night will be cold but clear."

"Norma would enjoy that." Stephanie looked at her watch. "Why not call me on my very own, brand-new cell phone, and we'll decide then? You needn't feel obliged to entertain me, Dudley. I've kept you from your work all day."

"Once I complete my chores, I have no other pressing engagements."

Hearing sincerity in his gentle assurance, Stephanie agreed on a walk. Maybe she would find opportunity to ask him about laughing midnight trespassers. After a day in Dudley's company, after meeting his friends and parishioners around town, and especially after hearing him pray, she could no longer suspect his motives.

When Dudley returned with the two corgis, Stephanie and Norma were ready. "It gets dark so early," Stephanie commented. "I feel as if we're taking a midnight walk, but it's just past seven."

"I brought my torch. In winter our days are short, but in summer we have daylight past ten at night," he said, waiting while she closed the cottage door. "You're in northern latitudes now." He wore a leather coat over his jacket, and a fedora that might have belonged to his grandfather, judging by wear and tear.

Dudley offered his arm. Stephanie linked her gloved hand through the crook of his elbow, and they strolled down the drive and into the lane, following the bobbing circle of light from Dudley's "torch." The cold winter sky arched above the naked treetops. Something yipped mournfully in the distance. Norma pricked her ears, gave a *woof*, and hurried back to Stephanie's side. "You big chicken," Stephanie chided.

"Tell me about yourself, Stephanie."

His smooth, elegant voice disturbed her peace in delightful ways. "What do you want to know?"

"When did you give your life to Christ?"

"As a child. A friend invited me to Sunday school, and there I first learned about Jesus."

Before long, Dudley had learned most of her life story. He was a good listener: sympathetic, interested, responsive. The ideal minister.

"I don't blame Reece for being angry. He was an ambitious, athletic man before the accident, rising in rank on the police force. Being a quadriplegic nearly drove my husband insane, I think." Stephanie hadn't said a word about Reece's vicious tongue, yet Dudley seemed to know.

"He was blessed to have you, and in his heart he must have realized it. No woman could have done more for him."

"I did my best. These last few years, since I opened my beauty shop, have been easy in comparison." Would he hear the relief in her voice and despise her?

"Don't feel guilty, Stephanie. You loved and served an ungrateful man for twenty years. Release the past and enjoy the future God has provided."

She looked up at his face, barely visible by starlight. "Thank you." Joy bubbled up and burst into a smile. "I will. Now it's your turn to tell your life story."

"Not much to tell. Twenty-some years ago I studied at Cambridge, intending to make a name for myself in the Church of England. Then I actually met Christ. My ambitions crumbled beneath me, my girlfriend left me, and my father fell ill. I returned here and took over farming the land."

"And your church here?"

"Entirely the Lord's doing." His voice held a smile. "A few old friends accepted Christ and desired teaching. They asked me to study God's Word with them. Over the years New Life Christian Fellowship has grown to sixty or more people, all starving for spiritual food."

"How wonderful! And how strange that you left the organized church yet became a minister anyway." She wanted to hear more about the girlfriend but didn't dare ask. "But why would you study for the ministry before you met Christ?"

"Money. Career. Prestige. My girlfriend's father was a bishop. She had plans for my future, plans that did not include farming."

"I'm sorry."

"Better to learn sooner than later that she loved the career, not the man. Once I developed moral convictions and attempted to live the faith I professed by asking her to marry me, she expressed her scorn in unequivocal terms. Although her rejection stung my pride, I cannot claim heartbreak. My interest in her was equally shallow, I fear."

They strolled in silence for several minutes. Stephanie realized they had passed the graveyard and Westbourne Farm. "Which way is it to Staneheath Manor?"

"Just ahead is a public footpath that leads past the house.

Tomorrow, if you like, I shall take you to see the manor and meet the director of its restoration, Jack Hartwell. He visits New Life Christian Fellowship occasionally."

"I would like that. I wonder if Mr. Hartwell could give me information about restoring the old church building. I think it should be used for meetings again. My uncle may not want to sell the place, but maybe we could lease it or rent it to your church after it's refurbished a bit."

"A bit?" Dudley sounded amused. "Not only is the building near ruin, but your uncle will certainly object. He hates anything to do with God and the church." He assisted her over a stile, whistled for the dogs, then drew Stephanie's hand through his arm before they walked on.

"You never know what God can do in people's hearts," she said, trying not to overreact to her companion's old-world courtesy. "I'm going to start praying for Uncle John's salvation and for God's will concerning the old church. He put me here for some reason, and I want to be available to carry out His plans."

Dudley's elbow pressed her hand against his side. "Stephanie, you're an amazing woman. Please know that I have no desire to discourage your dream. I want to be part of God's plans for you in every way possible."

Stephanie blinked, wondering if he realized how his words might be construed. Although Dudley had been attentive throughout the day, giving freely of his time for her convenience, she had detected no hint of sentiment in his courtly manner. Only a fool would build air castles upon the kindness of a godly minister.

"Thank you." She cleared her throat. "I should have known God would provide me with friends here. You've been wonderful to me today, beyond the call of pastoral duty. No wonder your church is growing strong with you as its pastor."

He said nothing until they topped a low rise. "There lies the manor."

Stephanie gaped, unable to conceive of her mother growing up in such a mansion. Moonlight revealed towers and turrets, many dark windows, and layers of scaffolding. "I never realized. . ."

"You will enjoy seeing it in daylight tomorrow." He whistled the dogs close again and continued along the footpath. "Would you like to look through the church building tonight or wait until morning? We'll pass it on our way to the cottage."

A little thrill chased up Stephanie's spine. "Is it safe?"

"I believe so. I haven't been inside it for years, but I played there often as a child."

"Your parents allowed it?"

"We children never asked permission to trespass. Why spoil the fun?"

Although she liked Dudley's dry humor, Stephanie's courage faltered as the crumbling edifice came into view. "Do any of your old playmates still live around here?"

"Two of them, Alf and Ray, helped me begin New Life Christian Fellowship—along with their wives, of course. If you join us for worship this Sunday, I'll introduce you." Dudley helped her over a stile in the fence around the graveyard. The corgis scooted under the fence rails. Norma ran back and forth along the fence, whimpering, until Stephanie coaxed her over the stile.

Dudley's flashlight beam played on the building's outer walls. "Requires a crew of good stonemasons; even then, the structural integrity of the tower is questionable. The carpentry will require more time and expense. I imagine the floors need replacing, and I know the doors and frames do." He evaluated the church as they approached, estimating the cost of windows, plumbing, and electric wiring. "And of course we must apply for permission to restore a historic building."

Stephanie's heart sank as he spoke. "So you don't think my idea will work? I wouldn't begin to know how to do any of that."

"No, but Jack Hartwell knows. He's heading up the restoration of the manor. If you want information, Jack's your man. Your source of information, that is," he amended quickly.

"If you'll help me talk to him, I'll do it."

"Done." Dudley led the way up stone steps and through the jagged maw of a doorway. "Avoid the doorframe or you'll get splinters. As I recall, the vestry is intact though badly weathered. It smells musty in here—probably dry rot."

Wooden floorboards groaned beneath their feet. Stephanie's heart leaped to her throat, and she barely restrained herself from clutching Dudley's arm.

"That sounds discouraging," he remarked in his usual tranquil tone. He aimed his flashlight into the auditorium, causing an outburst of flutters and squawks. The entire structure seemed to groan and rumble.

Stephanie shrieked, stepped back, and almost fell. Dudley

caught her by the arm and hauled her upright. "Starlings, I believe. Maybe bats. Are you all right?"

"Y–yes." Her heart pounded.

"You don't sound it. Take a moment to recover, luv. Sorry to cause you such fright."

She reminded herself that "luv" was a common form of address in this country; he meant nothing by it. She suddenly wanted to cry.

"Stephanie?"

She shook her head, trembling in every limb.

He led her outside and pulled her down to sit beside him on the broken steps. "I should never have brought you here at night. I apologize."

The self-recrimination in his voice snapped Stephanie back to life. "It's not your fault. We had a busy day, and I'm still tired from all the traveling and such. I'll be fine once I get back to the cottage."

"Calm yourself, Stephanie. No evil can harm you. The Lord is near, and so am I."

She stiffened her spine and focused on the white circle beaming from his flashlight. "I'm fine. What makes you think I'm frightened?"

"The fact that you sound like a forty-five being played at seventy-eight gives me a clue."

Stephanie's chuckle came out more of a cackle. "You're revealing your age, Dudley." She rose and steadied her wobbly legs. "And I'm revealing mine by understanding what you mean. I must have watched too many scary movies if a flock of birds gives me the willies. You'd think the Frankenstein monster had popped up to eat me from the way I acted."

Dudley called the dogs to heel and escorted Stephanie through the graveyard, over another stile, along the lane, and to her door. "He never ate anyone, you know," he said as she turned to face him.

"Who?"

"Frankenstein's monster was a sympathetic character, not a cannibal. You ought to read the book, but not now." He smiled. "Tonight I would recommend *The Wind in the Willows*, or something equally benign."

"I've never read that either."

"Perhaps we can read it together sometime. Good night, Stephanie." He touched his hat brim and nodded.

❧

Norma and Stephanie snuggled together beneath a new fleece blanket and dozed through a gardening show on television. The host's posh accent reminded Stephanie of Dudley, and she thought back over the day. "He's such a gentleman, Norma. I didn't know men like that existed anymore."

The dog sighed and moved her head to rest on Stephanie's shoulder. Suddenly her ears pricked, her head lifted, and she let out a sharp bark. As Norma struggled to rise, Stephanie heard running footsteps outside, then a pounding at the door. "Stephanie!" Dudley's voice called.

She threw off the blanket and rushed to answer, thankful she'd changed into sweats instead of a nightie. As the door opened, Dudley thrust his cell phone at her. "It's the hospital. They've been trying to contact you. Your phone must be turned off."

Stephanie took the phone but held Dudley's gaze. "My uncle?"

He nodded.

She lifted the cell phone to her ear. "This is Stephanie Keller."

Chapter 5

Seven months later

There. That was the last weed. "If any more show up today, I'll scream." With a groan, Stephanie sat on her heels and reached up both hands to rub her aching shoulders, still holding the garden spade. Beside her on the grass, Norma snoozed in the sun.

"You're dropping dirt on your back," a gruff voice said.

Norma scrambled to her feet with a startled bark. Freda Walden-Larkin stood at the garden gate; her two corgis peered between its slats. Despite the summer heat, a chill trickled down Stephanie's spine as she met the woman's impassive gaze. . .or perhaps it was cold soil. Good thing she hadn't tucked in her T-shirt.

"You gave me such a start!" She brushed off her back and summoned a welcoming smile. "Isn't this a lovely morning? Come in and visit. I was just thinking about a tea break." Her joints crackled as she rose, but the squeaking garden gate drowned out the noise. At least she hoped so. "How have you been?" Stephanie was determined to be pleasant. Visits from Freda and Pat tended to test the limits of her tolerance.

"Same as ever." Freda patted Norma and glanced around. "You've been hard at work, I see."

"Yes." Stephanie lifted her hat to push back sweaty curls and surveyed her flower garden with pride. "Dudley and Colin helped me plant these climbing roses. The old ones were dead." She knocked dirt from her trowel and her spade. "Come inside and I'll make tea."

Leaving the dogs in the garden, Freda followed Stephanie into the kitchen. Stephanie studied the older woman for signs of approval, but none appeared. The kitchen was now an English homemaker's dream, the ideal blend of charm and practicality. Thanks to Dudley and Colin, the entire cottage became more welcoming and livable each day. If not for its inescapable view of the church tower, Stephanie would have adored her home. But soon, Lord willing, that eyesore would become an ornament.

Freda sat at the table and waited.

Stephanie hung her derby on a wall hook, then tied a flowery apron over her soiled gardening clothes. As she washed her hands, a fresh breeze lifted the ruffled curtains framing the kitchen window. Outside on the green lawn, Norma rolled on her back, four paws kicking, while the corgis sun-basked nearby. Joy and thankfulness welled up in Stephanie's heart. "I love summer!"

Freda grunted.

While waiting for the water to heat, Stephanie arranged

red-currant scones, Devonshire cream, and gooseberry pre-
serves on a tea tray. After much trial and error, and the help of
sympathetic friends from church, she felt she had mastered the
art of scone-making. "Do you enjoy cooking?"

"No."

At least when Pat dropped in to visit, she talked. Mostly
gossip and rudeness. And she always ate a great deal and out-
stayed her welcome.

Gossip or grunts. Some choice.

*Dear Lord, please give me patience with Freda. She needs You,
whether she wants You or not.*

"I visited your husband yesterday." Stephanie again
attempted to open a conversation.

"Why go there, now that your uncle's dead?"

"To see Mr. Larkin, of course."

"Why can't you be satisfied with the Haverstane fortune?
Your uncle conveniently died the very day you met him—a
woman with nothing to hide would have had his sudden death
investigated."

Stephanie's hands stilled. "What are you implying? The
doctors said he had another stroke."

"The story is all over town about how angry His Lordship
got during your visit. You must have told him your plans for
the old church."

Help, Lord! Did she really just accuse me of killing Uncle John?

"Sir John had no use for religious drivel," Freda ranted on.
"You Christian types are all alike; you talk charity while keeping an eye out for your own gain. If it's land you're after, I'll
have you know that Dudley shares his inheritance with me; you

310

can abandon hope in that direction. Too bad you can't get your hands on the manor, but marrying Mr. Hartwell wouldn't get you a title."

"Mr. Hartwell?" Stephanie could only stare as her stomach shriveled into a hard knot. "I don't know what you're talking about, Mrs. Walden-Larkin."

"You came here because Sir John promised you land and money, right?"

"Partly. Mostly I came because my uncle was family. I wanted a place to belong and someone to belong to."

Freda huffed.

Patience. Love. Patience. Love. And to think, I wanted her to talk.

"You don't have to believe me," Stephanie said, "but it's true. I can't say that I loved Uncle John, for I met him only once. But I'm thankful I have that one meeting to remember. Dudley prayed over him. My uncle might have reconciled with God before his death. I can hope, anyway."

Freda laughed, though her expression revealed no mirth.

Stephanie poured hot water into her teapot and placed it on her tray. "If you think I inherited a vast fortune, you're mistaken. Uncle John invested the remainder of his estate these past few years, owing to wise business counsel, so I can be comfortable for life if I live frugally. I can afford to refurbish this cottage, but if we are to repair the church, we must have assistance from English Legacy." None of this was Freda's business, yet Stephanie felt compelled to inform her. She carried her tea tray to the table. "It has been allowed to decay, and I haven't the funds to repair it myself."

An unladylike snort expressed Freda's contempt. "What would English Legacy want with that old church? The countryside is full of them, all alike. Dudley is a fool. No doubt he filled your head with his fool ideas."

Stephanie watched Freda pour her own cream and sugar. Drawing a deep breath for serenity, she admitted: "Actually it was my idea. New Life Christian Fellowship needs a facility; I own an abandoned church building. The coincidence was too great for me to ignore. As it stands, the church is an eyesore and a potential safety hazard. Something must be done; why not repair the old place? If God wants us to use the building for worship services, He can make it happen. I see no harm in asking English Legacy for help. Mr. Hartwell has been encouraging and helpful."

"So I hear. Recently divorced, isn't he?" Although Freda spoke around a mouthful of scone, her voice held an ironic note.

Stephanie fisted her hands in her lap. "Mr. Hartwell thinks we can work something out to make the restored church accessible both to the public as part of the Staneheath Manor tour and to New Life for Sunday and midweek meetings. It might become popular as a wedding chapel. It has beautiful lines and stonework, and one of the old stained-glass windows is intact."

Freda's eyes narrowed behind their thick lenses. "Dudley didn't tell us the whole story. I don't want tourists tracking through our property."

"I don't see any reason why they would trespass on your land. We can clear a large car park beyond the graveyard, and

312

the footpaths leading from the manor to the church lie on Staneheath land. I believe the Lord supplied Mr. Hartwell, for I knew nothing about obtaining permission to renovate a historic building, and neither did Dudley."

The scone Stephanie had dolloped with cream and jam now looked unappetizing. She picked at it and sipped her tea, trying to think of neutral ground for conversation. The entire scheme of renovating the old church suddenly seemed irrational.

"Where is Dudley?"

Stephanie blinked but followed Freda's lead. "I don't know. I imagine he's working on your farm. Tonight is Bible study, but you know better than I do what he does all day."

Freda gave another gusty laugh. "I seldom see him anymore. Some people are taking odds on when he'll move into this cottage."

Stephanie imagined slamming her tea tray over Freda's head. But no, she wouldn't want to take the chance of denting the antique tray.

She didn't attempt a smile. "Dudley often helps me in the garden or brings men to work on the house, but he never comes into the cottage alone. As a minister, he must be extra careful about appearances. Our friendship is strictly platonic."

"I know that." This time Freda's laugh held amusement. "He wasn't particular about appearances during his college days. He shared a flat with a woman for a year or more, and him studying to become a clergyman, so it wasn't religion what changed his ways."

Although Stephanie had suspected as much from Dudley's account, the revelation hit her hard. What other secrets lay buried in his past? "That was before he met Jesus Christ," she said.

"Something happened to him, that's certain. He hasn't noticed women since Elizabeth gave him the boot. Pat says he's a eunuch and should study for the priesthood. She says he must have been injured playing rugby and didn't tell us. . . ."

Stephanie rose and began to clear away her tea things before she spoke any of the hot words circling inside her head. Crude talk on television or radio or out of the mouths of rebellious teens no longer surprised her; but adult women should know better. How had this woman survived into old age? Miraculous that someone hadn't knocked her off years ago and pleaded emotional self-defense. No jury could possibly convict.

Freda pushed back her chair. "Go home, Mrs. Keller. You and your ridiculous hats and Puritan ways don't belong here, and you'll never belong." She stuffed the last of a scone into her mouth and exited into the back garden. Stephanie heard her call the dogs.

For a moment Stephanie stood beside her little table, staring at the remains of tea. Familiar feelings of inadequacy, unworthiness, and loneliness rushed into her heart. She'd been fooling herself all these months, imagining she could ever be part of this community. Even people at church, although they seemed friendly and accepting, probably gossiped about Stephanie and her acquired fortune. Her friendship with Dudley aroused undesired speculation.

Someone knocked at the front door and Norma, still in the back garden, barked. Mr. Jack Hartwell of English Legacy waited on the front porch. A portly man in his early fifties, he sported a full head of iron gray hair and large brown eyes. "Mrs. Keller, I have news. Our renovation request has been approved."

Stephanie clasped her hands below her chin. "Yes! This is wonderful news! Thank You, God, and thank you, Mr. Hartwell. I know our request would still be on the bottom of someone's 'in' pile, or maybe even in their 'reject' pile, if not for your influence."

He hemmed and hawed, smiling modestly all the while. "Might you be willing to dine with me tonight, Mrs. Keller? By way of celebration, of course."

"I thank you for the invitation, sir, but a small-group Bible study will be meeting at my house this evening. You are more than welcome to join us." She smiled to ease the rejection.

His face fell. "I think not. Perhaps another time?"

"Perhaps." Stephanie hoped the man hadn't expected some kind of payoff from her in exchange for his help with the planning permission. The suspicion dampened her enthusiasm.

Stephanie sat in one corner of her new sofa. Norma snoozed on the floor near her feet. Guests filled every available chair and sofa cushion, all engrossed in a vibrant discussion of scripture. Dudley had a way of making God's Word real and accessible. Though quiet and restrained in his private life, give the man a Bible or stand him behind a pulpit, and the Holy Spirit's fire transformed him. After Bible studies and church services, Stephanie's heart burned with desire to learn and to grow and to surrender her life for God's service. Although many of her questions about God and faith and scripture had been answered these past few months, many more questions remained in her life.

Why had God brought her to England? Was it truly so important to renovate the old church building? New Life Christian Fellowship seemed to be thriving—gaining in attendance, community impact, and spiritual maturity with each passing week. They were crowded in the community hall, lacking proper facilities for a children's program or nursery, yet why make changes to a ministry God was blessing? A traditional church building might actually impede the church's growth rather than enhance it.

After Dudley closed the study with prayer, Stephanie helped the other ladies prepare snacks in her kitchen. She wanted to tell about Jack Hartwell's news, yet the timing must be right.

"Stephanie, you've done wonders with this old place," Emma Bant said as she poured hot water into the teapot. "Colin told us what a disaster it was when you moved in."

"Much of the credit for its improvement goes to Colin. He's a fine young man, Emma."

Emma smiled her appreciation. "He was going wild until Reverend Dudley took him in hand. Sometimes I still wonder, but we're beginning to see evidence of God's work in the lad. He even speaks more clearly now and stands up straight."

As Stephanie strained to do a mental translation of Emma's thick British accent, she smiled at the reference to Colin's improved speech.

"Where did you find your barley-twist sideboard, Stephanie?"

Peggy Masters asked. "And I love your hall tree. Did you refinish them yourself?"

"Yes." Stephanie relished the compliments. "I'm addicted to antiques. Especially 1920s and '30s oak. I found the sideboard at a second-hand shop and the hall tree at an estate sale. Both were in sad shape. I love rescuing furniture."

Joyce Conninger gave her a fond smile. "You're a blessing to us all, Stephanie. Seeing this house and our village through your eyes has renewed my appreciation for our heritage."

"I never would have thought an American could fit into Staneheath village life," Peggy Masters said.

"None of us did," Joyce put in. "But then along you came with your sparkling smile and your ready laugh and your lapdog big as a horse, and our resistance collapsed like a house of cards."

"You look lovely tonight in that red blouse. We always thought Dudley would remain a bachelor to the end of his days, but—" Emma jumped and turned to stare at Joyce. "What, 'ave I spoken out of turn?"

Joyce chuckled. "Let the man speak for himself in his own time, luv."

Stephanie pretended incomprehension. Dudley had given her no reason to foster expectations. Considerate, attentive, polite, he was. But, romantic? Unfortunately, no.

When the ladies returned to the parlor, they found the men discussing Staneheath Church. "The entire floor will need replacement," Ronald Masters said, "and most of the other woodwork. Dry rot and woodworm have spoiled it all."

"Must do something soon," Alf Bant stated. "Town council's murmurin' about traffic jams in the town center every time our

317

fellowship has an activity. I fear they'll not renew permission t' use the community center for church meetin's come summer."

"I have news," Stephanie said as she set a tray of savory snacks on the brassbound trunk she used as a coffee table. All eyes turned to her. Crossing her arms, she licked her dry lips and smiled. "Jack Hartwell dropped by today to announce that our restoration request has been approved, and English Legacy is ready to discuss terms."

Cheers and applause broke out. Alf swung his cloth napkin above his head. "Answered prayer! God 'as prepared a way."

"I'm still uncertain about this," Peggy Masters said. "Even if the building can be repaired, will it be suitable for our purposes? I'm afraid we might be jumping at the first opportunity that offers itself instead of waiting for God's best." She gave her husband a pointed look that raised questions in Stephanie's mind.

Ronald shook his head as if to cut her off. "Nothing says we can't move if a better situation offers itself. As chair of the planning commission, I intend to set a time to conference with Mr. Hartwell at the earliest possible date. We'll present our options to the church body and request a vote."

Stephanie watched and listened as these founding members of New Life Christian Fellowship continued to discuss plans, concerns, and options. Once, Dudley met her gaze and smiled. Warmth spread through her. She had taken pains with her appearance that evening, painting her fingernails and her toenails, smoothing her recalcitrant hair into a french braid, applying makeup and even a dash of her favorite vanilla perfume. Pleated white slacks accentuated her waist and camouflaged her hips. Strappy white sandals revealed her tanned feet. And her silky cranberry red blouse was the most feminine and flattering garment she had ever owned.

Did Dudley even notice?

As the study members departed later that night, Stephanie accepted hugs from the other women. Despite Freda's words, she felt kinship with these people. If the women ever did talk about her, she believed their words would be kind. And the men treated her like an honored sister—with respect.

When Ronald and Peggy returned to the kitchen to collect their dishes, Dudley turned to Stephanie. "Thank you for hosting the study tonight."

She shook his warm hand, but he didn't let go. "I should be thanking you, Pastor. You've done so much to welcome me into this village and into your church. You've done more than anyone else to turn this cottage into a home. I don't know what I would do without you." He let her talk, all the while studying her face and eyes. She found it difficult to breathe. "I mean to say, all the repairs and improvements you've made, and your biblical leadership, and you're so kind."

His grip tightened, but when they heard Ronald and Peggy talking in the parlor, Dudley released her hand and stepped back. Ronald appeared first, shaking his head. "Reverend, my Peg insists we should let you know about her mum. You know Doreen Markham?"

"Of course." Dudley's brows drew together. "Is she ill?"

"Hearty as ever, thank you, Reverend," Peggy stated. She set her empty bowl on the hallstand's seat and donned her cardigan. "The point is this: Mum tells us she plans to bequeath her property to New Life Christian Fellowship. Her cottage and that fine, large building beside it. Twenty-five years ago, my father built an automobile repair shop, but then he took ill, and my brothers had no interest in running his business, so the building stands empty all these years."

Ronald broke in. "She knows Peg and I don't need it, seeing as how my parents left us the farm and all, so she wants the church to have the place, in gratitude for your kindness in repairing her roof and plumbing last year, I believe."

Dudley pressed one knuckle against his pursed lips while supporting his elbow with his other hand. Stephanie recognized his perplexed mode.

"The shop would convert into a fine large church building, Reverend, and there's plenty of land around it for growth and for car parks." Peggy's gaze shifted to Stephanie. "We're not meaning to disturb your plans, luv, but the church needs to know its options."

"Not that Doreen is ready to pop off anytime soon," Ronald observed, again shaking his head. "It might be years, Peg, and the church needs a place now."

Dudley rubbed his knuckle back and forth across his mustache, regarding the floorboards with a fixed stare.

Stephanie felt adrift. "What are you thinking?"

He glanced her way with a brief smile. "Little of consequence. Our future is in the Lord's hands. Let the church be fully informed, then pray on the matter and decide."

"But what are we to do in the meantime?"

"Pursue all options with enthusiasm. God will make our path clear in His time, Stephanie."

Dudley walked out the door with Ronald and Peggy,

giving Stephanie no opportunity to tell him about Freda's morning call. "Dudley, wait!"

On the second step, he turned. Light from the newly installed porch lamp glinted off his glasses.

"Will you come with me to meet the English Legacy representatives?"

"Certainly," he said. "Whether or not New Life votes to use your old building, I'll be pleased to see the place restored to its former grandeur."

Norma bounded past, thumped down the four steps, and began sniffing in the shrubbery. Stephanie descended a step, sliding her hips and hands down the handrail, and inclined her upper body ever so slightly toward Dudley. "Norma thinks we're going for a walk."

Dudley's hand glided up the rail toward hers as if drawn by a magnet, then it moved to adjust his glasses. "Not. . .not tonight, Norma." He coughed. "Good evening, Stephanie."

She watched him stride away through deepening shadows and smiled.

Dudley noticed. He definitely noticed.

Her smile faded.

"Notice" was all he ever did.

When her cell phone rang late that night, Stephanie answered sleepily. "Hello?"

Harsh breathing chilled her blood.

"Who is this?" She sat up in bed. Norma groaned.

"Let the dead rest. If you disturb their slumber, they will disturb yours."

"What are you talking about? Who is this? Hello?" Silence met her ear. After switching on her bedside lamp, she wrote the caller ID number down in the margin of her Bible study notes.

She folded her phone and glanced around her bedchamber. The same hostile chill of her first night in Haverstane Cottage trickled through her veins.

Chapter 6

The following morning dawned clear and golden. Stephanie rose early, surprising herself. She dressed in a pink velour exercise suit, twisted her hair up and stuffed it under her favorite hat, then set out toward the old church. Norma yipped like a puppy, sniffing at a rabbit hole, bounding ahead to tree a squirrel.

Months earlier Stephanie had found a break in the hedge near the spot where the laughing phantom had disappeared that first night. Common sense told her that the person had ducked into the bushes. Had the "ghost" intended to scare her away? A human enemy was just as frightening as a haunting spirit, and potentially more dangerous.

The stone tower looked no less ominous by daylight. Stephanie's steps slowed as she drew near. "Lord," she prayed aloud, "why does my heart feel weighted whenever I see this building? It's supposed to be Your house, but it feels evil to me. Any number of phone calls can't make me believe in ghosts or curses or things like that, but something about this place gives me the willies."

"Fancy meeting you here, Stephanie, my dear, looking charming as always."

As soon as her heart returned to its proper place, she turned to stare. "You just about scared me to death! What are you doing here at this hour, Mr. Hartwell?"

He skirted a marble monument to approach her. "Sorry about that. I came out early to scout around. I've got several meetings planned with executives today, concerning the possible addition of this place to the Staneheath Manor tour. I don't suppose you'd consider selling outright?"

"The church? Actually, I might." The more she thought about New Life Christian Fellowship meeting in this crumbling ruin, the less she liked the idea. But how could she let her church family down now by rescinding her offer?

"Your cottage was mentioned at our meeting as an ideal location for a gift shop. Plans are already underway for a garden center, using Sandringham House as our model. I expect a generous offer will soon be made to you for the entire property."

"Sell the cottage!" Stephanie paused to reconsider her immediate objections. With the proceeds from the church and cottage, she might purchase a cozy place on the outskirts of town.

No stone tower in sight. No Freda or Pat to pop in for unpleasant visits. No graveyard next door.

What would Dudley say?

Why did it matter what Dudley might say? He was merely her minister, and she would see him each Sunday behind the pulpit whether she lived in town or remained in the country.

"I might be convinced to sell—for the right price. However, I need time to think and pray about this."

"Of course." Mr. Hartwell grinned. "If you have no objection, we'll send a building inspector and a work crew out here tomorrow to estimate cost of repairs. I confess, the more I see of the place, the more I wonder if restoration will even be possible. We may end up leaving it a picturesque ruin."

"Mr. Hartwell, may I ask you an odd question?"

His face brightened. "Anything, luv."

"Does this building give you a sense of. . .of evil?" Put into words, her feelings sounded foolish, yet she had to know.

He tilted his head and pursed his thick lips. "No more so than any other ruin in this country. Most every castle was the scene of a heinous crime at some time in its history, anything from treachery to torture."

"But this was a church!" Stephanie protested.

Mr. Hartwell laughed. "A church controlled by the Haverstane family, which distinguishes it from all others. The family shared a disdain for religion almost unparalleled in this country's history. As the tale goes, the last vicar of this parish angered his patron. Shortly thereafter he disappeared, and some claimed His Lordship murdered the poor fellow. No body was ever found, however. More than likely the clergyman moved on to a more profitable living in another parish."

Stephanie frowned at the idea of having a murderer for an ancestor. "The inscriptions on these gravestones have weathered so badly that I can't read them. Are any of my relatives buried here?"

"Unlikely. None of your legitimate relations, anyway. They'd be buried in the vault near the manor, where your uncle was laid to rest. The last Haverstane." Mr. Hartwell sounded regretful.

"No wonder my mother wanted to leave this place," Stephanie observed with a shudder.

They strolled on through the graveyard and back to the main road where Mr. Hartwell had parked his red Jaguar. He helped Stephanie through a broken place in the fence by placing both hands on her waist. Irritated, she slipped out of his reach and turned back to glare. He heaved a theatrical sigh. "You cannot blame a man for trying, luv."

"Oh yes, I can."

Across the Westbourne Farm fields, a horse and rider approached at a smooth canter. Stephanie, recognizing Dudley astride a bay hunter, waved to him. "Good morning!"

To her surprise, the horse jumped the hedge and ditch alongside the road and approached, snorting with each breath. Dudley's cool gaze moved from Stephanie to Mr. Hartwell and back. "Good morning." His voice sounded tight. Sweat streaked his face beneath his riding helmet and dampened his short-sleeved pullover. The horse pawed at the dirt and clanked the bit between its teeth.

"Is it now?" Mr. Hartwell said, grinning. "Your filly has excellent lines, Parson. Nicely rounded quarters. Pretty face. Hot-blooded. You're a lucky man." He opened his car door and climbed in. "Until tomorrow, Stephanie." He gave her a broad wink and drove away. The engine's purr faded out of hearing. Only the horse's breathing and a robin's song broke the silence.

"Tomorrow a work crew and inspector are coming to find out what repairs must be done to the church," Stephanie said. An unpleasant memory occurred. "Dudley, have you given my cell phone number to anyone?"

Behind his glasses, his eyes narrowed. "No. Why?"

"I received a strange call last night. A harsh voice told me to leave the dead alone or they would disturb my peace. I wrote down the caller ID number, but I haven't yet given it to the police."

His lips tightened. She saw muscles bunching in his bare forearms. "Do you have time to talk this morning?" he asked.

"Yes."

He motioned for her to circle to his horse's left side. "Come around, and I'll pull you up behind me. Let me turn Brogan over to a stableboy, and then I want the full story."

Stephanie gulped. She desperately wanted to ride behind Dudley. She desperately did *not* want to ride behind Dudley. The animal was enormous. Her head barely reached its shoulder. "Um, I can walk and meet you at your stable." Horses were scary. This horse, in particular, was beyond scary.

Dudley gave a short nod. "All right."

The horse moved away, increasing its pace until it cantered smoothly along the dusty road. Stephanie called Norma to heel and followed. "Dudley is acting strange today," she told the dog. "I wonder what's wrong."

When she approached the stable, the sweaty horse, bereft of saddle and bridle, ambled along beside Colin Bant. He turned and waved. " 'Ello, Miz Kelluh."

"Hello, Colin. That is one big filly."

He snorted like a horse. "Brogan's a gelding, nowt a filly."

"Oh." She felt ignorant. . .which she was. "Mr. Hartwell called it a filly."

"He knows Brogan's a male 'orse. You sure 'e weren't talkin' about you?" Without giving her a chance to respond, he commented, "Eh, my dad says church might start meetin' at the ol' ruin behind yer 'ouse."

Still puzzling about Hartwell's comments, Stephanie fell into step beside Colin. She kept her distance from the horse. "Not until after it gets repaired, of course."

"I don't want our church t' meet there." Colin spoke with more animation and clarity than Stephanie had ever heard from him.

"Why not?"

Dudley emerged from the tack room, smoothing back his sweaty hair. Months ago, at Stephanie's suggestion, he had told the barber to crop his thick mane short. The style suited his angular features, unlike his former unkempt look. "If you'll pardon my attire and dirt, we can take a quick walk and discuss this phone call." No smile softened his expression.

"Just a moment, please, Pastor Dudley. Colin is telling me something important." She turned back to the boy, feeling no little pride in her acquired ability to decipher his speech. "Why don't you think New Life should meet in the old church, Colin? To me it seems wasteful to let the building stand empty when it might be useful again."

Colin gave Dudley a penetrating look. "Group of us talkin' t'other day. You know the verse you preached about few weeks back, Rev'nd, the one about puttin' new wine into old wineskins? We think you shouldn't put New Life into that ol' buildin'. It stands for all the worst things about religion in England, rituals and rules and dead people. Our church stands for Jesus Christ and new life."

Dudley and Stephanie exchanged glances. "An interesting point, Colin," Dudley said. "I had never thought about the building in that way. Now if you'll excuse us. . ."

Colin nodded. "Rev'nd. I'll mow yer grass tomorrow, Miz Kelluh."

"Thank you, Colin."

Stephanie summoned her wandering dog and set out to match Dudley's long stride. After a moment he slowed his pace. "I'm sorry, Stephanie." He rubbed his mustache with one dusty knuckle. "I've forgotten my manners." She heard him heave a quick sigh. "That was the longest speech I've ever heard from Colin."

"I think he may be right, Dudley. I was walking around the old church again this morning, and it gives me such an oppressive feeling. For the longest time I thought it felt that way because it's in ruins, but I'm beginning to think it holds some evil secret, and that threatening phone call increased my fears."

"The phone call came last night?"

"Or early morning. I'm not sure." Again she described the short conversation. "I've given my cell number to only a few people."

"Including me."

"I don't suspect you, Dudley. I know you better than that. Don't I?" In his jodhpurs and high black boots, he seemed. . . different. Less the cleric and more the man.

"I hope you do. Stephanie, I am. . .inept at expressing my feelings. I want you to know that—"

She waited in suspense for him to find the words.

"—that I would never do anything to harm you. If ever you feel frightened, at any time of the day or night, please ring me. I wish. . . Perhaps, in time. . ." He gave his head a little shake. The ghost of a smile flitted across his face. "Rest assured of my high regard for you and my deepest concern for your safety and happiness."

Wide-eyed, she nodded. "I'm resting assured. I care a lot for you, too, Dudley."

His face and neck reddened. As they approached the end of the long drive, a car passed on the road. Stephanie told Norma to sit and stay. Looking up at Dudley's abashed expression, she wondered if the man were capable of feeling romantic love. After months of association, she knew he was the soul of kindness and consideration, but not all men were intended to marry. Perhaps this stumbling assurance had been his way of warning her that he could never offer her more than friendship.

"You'd best return to work, and I have gardening to do. Don't bother escorting me home. Remember, the meeting with English Legacy is set for Friday, after they have time to assess the probable costs involved in the project. Mr. Hartwell will give us an exact time later. He told me this morning that they might offer to buy my entire property and use the cottage as a gift shop."

Emotions flickered across his face, but Stephanie couldn't identify any of them except irritation. He nodded and rubbed one hand around the back of his neck. Sweat trickled down his temple, and the sun highlighted the gray in his ruffled hair. "Are you seeing him often?"

"Mr. Hartwell? No. I met him this morning by accident.

I would never plan to meet anyone dressed like this." She looked down at her pink sweat suit and grinned.

"You're always lovely. If ever Hartwell refers to you as a filly again, minister or no, I'll throttle him. Good day." Dudley touched his forehead, turned on his heel, and walked back up his driveway.

Later that day, the local constabulary informed Stephanie that the mysterious phone call had come from a call box in the village just outside the Bear and Boar Inn. They could do little besides offer to keep a close watch on that particular telephone.

Washing up her few dishes, Stephanie admired her garden by evening light and pondered Colin's words. Should the New Life Christian Fellowship begin to meet in the old building, the formal atmosphere might infect the worshippers with its heavy, legalistic traditions. On the other hand, the group of new believers might restore life and light to the old structure. The lack of potential for growth bothered her most. The building had no facilities appropriate for children—she had already volunteered her cottage for Sunday school classes, but how long could that last?

After much prayer and thought, she decided to sell the property to English Legacy. Although she would miss her cottage, there were many others of equal charm in the nearby villages. She could have the fun of restoring another garden using the experience she had gained.

Her only real regret would be leaving Dudley behind. No longer would she glimpse him riding pell-mell across the countryside on a great horse or see lights shining from the windows of his flat as she drove past. No more walks across the fields with Norma and the corgis, arm in arm with her courtly gentleman, talking about the Lord and His plans for the fellowship. When Stephanie pictured Dudley's smile, tears burned her eyes and overflowed down her cheeks.

Impatient with herself, she brushed the tears away. "All good things must come to an end, Norma," she told the sleeping dog. "I must put distance between myself and Dudley. I've grown far too fond of him. All the good intentions I had when I arrived in this country about keeping emotionally free didn't help. Worst of all, I think he knows. Today he was trying to let me down gently." She heaved a long, trembling sigh. "No matter what anyone says, friendship between a man and a woman doesn't work. Somebody's bound to get hurt—and in this case the somebody is me."

Stephanie spent the evening reading her Bible and discussing her future with God. Her love for Dudley, her confusion about the property and plans, everything poured out during that conversation. Although no direct answers popped into her mind as she prayed, peace filled her heart. She could live without Dudley's love. She could survive another relocation, if necessary. Wherever God required her services, she would go. The one absolute necessity in her life was Jesus. Without Him, she knew she would wither up and die.

But it was hard, so very hard, to give up Dudley.

Norma approached the sofa and laid her head on Stephanie's knee. "You need to go out, baby?" Stephanie hopped up and stretched her arms and back. "I've been sitting still for hours. I think I'll go out with you and admire my roses by moonlight."

In the garden, instead of admiring her flowers, Stephanie folded her arms and gazed at the moon. "Lord Jesus, I didn't go looking for Dudley, but despite my best efforts. . .well, okay, my half-hearted efforts to keep him out, he managed to sneak his way into my affections. From now on I'll have to barricade my heart against men, I guess. I'm too susceptible and imaginative. I see interest where none exists, and then I get humiliated. If I didn't have You to depend on and to love me no matter what, my life wouldn't be worth living. But with You as my companion, I know I can move on and start again."

Norma's sudden bark brought Stephanie down to earth. "What is it, girl? You gave me such a start!"

The Doberman put her front paws on the gate and stared down the lane toward the old church. As Stephanie approached, she heard Norma's rumbling growl—a rare sound. "Is someone out there?" Sudden fear made her grasp the dog's pink rhinestone collar and pull. "Come inside, Norma."

As soon as the door closed behind them and Stephanie let go of the collar, Norma ran through the sitting room and charged up the stairs. Stephanie heard her scrabbling claws on the hardwood floor overhead. Of course, she had to know what had riled her dog. Reluctantly she followed Norma upstairs and into the back bedroom. Even with the overhead light switched on, she could see the reason for Norma's agitation: A light glowed in the empty windows of the old church.

Chapter 7

Stephanie telephoned Dudley. While waiting for him to answer, she kept her eyes glued to the church. "Dudley? Someone is inside the church building. I see a light in the vestry. It can't be the inspector; he's not coming until morning."

"Does it look like an electric torch or a lantern?"

The sound of his calm voice soothed her nerves. "It burns steadily. If it's a torch, it's a big one," she said.

"It might be Pat, though I don't know for certain. She and Freda both seemed inordinately disturbed when I told them about the building inspection. You'd think the old place belonged to *our* family by the way they've been acting. I'll walk over to the church directly and see what's what, all right? Don't worry."

"Take the dogs with you and ring me as soon as you find out anything," Stephanie ordered.

"Agreed." He hung up without a good-bye, but Stephanie had become accustomed to that habit months ago. From a front window she watched for his torchlight, heaving a relieved sigh when she spotted the bluish-white spot bobbing along his drive.

When he entered the church grounds, the hedge concealed him from view.

Holding her cell phone, she waited for it to ring. After ten minutes had passed, she dialed Dudley's number. No answer. She dialed his flat. No answer. Quelling panic, she dialed the main farmhouse.

Freda answered. "He took the dogs and went for a walk. How should I know when he'll be back? No wonder he runs when he sees you coming if you pester him like a fly."

Stephanie heard a commotion in the background and a dog's yelp. The connection ended suddenly.

Sucking in her lips, she paced the room and considered her options. She could panic and telephone the police. She could rush over to the church and. . . Peering through the window, she realized that the church was now dark. Dudley must have gone home.

She dialed his cell phone. No answer. She dialed his flat. No answer.

"Lord, where is he?" she prayed in rising desperation. Certainty built in her heart: Dudley was in trouble.

"Norma, we've got to find Dudley." Stephanie hurried downstairs and pulled on her shoes and jacket before she could reconsider. She picked up her own flashlight and switched it on, then turned it off. The moon would light her way until she reached the building. No need to advertise her approach.

Norma stuck to her side like flypaper as she hurried up the lane to the break in the hedge. The gravestones seemed luminous, and the black window holes in the ruined church stared back at her like empty eye sockets. Stephanie fixed her attention

335

upon her goal and kept one hand on Norma's solid back, thankful for the dog's company.

Facing the empty doorway, she swallowed hard. Maybe this was a fool's errand. Maybe she should sneak home and never admit her silly behavior to a living soul. When Norma started whimpering, Stephanie nearly jumped out of her skin. "Don't chicken out on me now, baby. I need you."

The dog pulled her toward the church and up the steps. Stephanie switched on her flashlight as they stepped through the doorway. The beam fell upon a figure outstretched on the floor. "Dudley!" A sob strangled her cry. On his white shirtfront, a dark, wet stain spread. Pain contorted his features.

Norma nuzzled Dudley's face while Stephanie fell to her knees beside him. Even if he were dead, she couldn't leave him here alone. She caught his hand and felt a weak grasp. His eyelids fluttered. All fear forgotten, she unbuttoned his torn shirt and found a bleeding, bubbling wound in the right side of his chest. She tugged off her jacket, folded it into a tight square, and pressed it hard against the puncture. Using one hand, she dialed the emergency number on her cell phone. After stating her name and location, she begged, "Please send the police and an ambulance, and hurry!"

Dudley groaned and gasped. Stephanie wiped her streaming eyes on her own shoulders. "Dudley, you must live. Your church needs you. Your farm needs you. I need you." Keeping pressure on the wound with one hand, she caressed his cheek. "I'm so sorry I sent you here!"

Norma rose and disappeared into a dark corner with a *ticktick* of claws. Suddenly she made a weird moaning sound and hurried back to cower at Stephanie's side, shaking like jelly.

"I don't need you to freak me out, Norma. Please don't do that again."

In the dreadful darkness of those interminable minutes, Stephanie sensed a comforting presence. "Lord, You're with us here, aren't You? No matter what happens, I know I can trust You. Evil will not go unpunished. Dudley is Your servant, Your beloved child. I know You'll care for him."

Dudley's eyes fluttered open. "Stephanie, no!" He grimaced, coughed, and turned his head from side to side. "Ahhh." His agony brought a new onrush of tears to her eyes. Then his face relaxed and his body went limp.

"Dudley!" She pressed her hand to his blood-smeared chest and felt his rapid heartbeat. She wanted to hold him close and keep him warm but dared not release the pressure on his wound. Her arms ached, and a cramp pinched her leg. When would that ambulance come?

Then she heard furtive footsteps and her heart nearly stopped. Slowly she turned her head toward the open doorway. Against the background of the moonlit churchyard she saw, in silhouette, a square figure wearing a dress. Then, a beam of light caught her straight in the eyes.

"You!" A husky voice sneered. "If you hadn't come here, none of this would have happened!" The light flickered aside as the woman rushed up the steps.

Cringing, Stephanie hovered over Dudley. Approaching footsteps echoed on the wooden floor. A powerful hand grabbed her hair and jerked her head back. For an instant she looked into Pat Walden-Hoff's contorted face and frenzied eyes. Light flashed on a steel blade. A deep roaring sound filled her ears.

Abruptly her hair was released. Overbalanced, she fell backward on Dudley's outstretched legs. Hoarse screams echoed off the stone walls. A flashlight beam bounced across the ceiling as Stephanie rolled and scrambled to her hands and knees.

By the beam of her own flashlight, which she had placed near Dudley's head, she saw Pat staggering backward. A writhing, twisting, snarling dog dangled from her forearm, jerking it from side to side. *Clang!* A knife hit the floor. The woman struck at Norma with her free hand, shrieking in fury and pain. Again, Stephanie glimpsed Pat's wild-eyed face.

"Norma, no!" Stephanie shouted. The Doberman released her hold, but Pat, unbalanced, reeled backward and vanished from sight. *Thud!* A horrified scream dissolved into a despairing wail, rasping sobs, and incoherent mutterings, then a deep groan and silence. Stephanie stared into the darkness, every hair on her nape standing on end.

Norma posed in the feeble spotlight with her back arched; her lips curled to reveal long white fangs. Growls still rumbled in her chest like distant thunder.

Wailing sirens filled the night. Stephanie began to sob in earnest. She leaned over Dudley and resumed pressure on the pad. His skin was cold, and he shivered.

As if looking through a fog, Stephanie gave place to the medical technicians, holding Norma by the collar as she backed away. Soon, bright lights filled the vestry and policemen swarmed like ants. Stephanie mechanically answered questions and watched the proceedings. Attention seemed to focus on a rectangular opening in the corner of the floor where Pat had disappeared. Its wooden door leaned against the wall.

Wide-eyed policemen crowded around as a pale-faced medic climbed into the hole. Disembodied voices drifted to Stephanie's ears. "Is she dead?"

"Not dead, fainted."

"Have you ever seen anything like it?"

"Not me. Hope I never do again." Cameras snapped.

"Who do you think the other one is. . .or was?"

"Not in my job description to figure that out." More cameras snapped.

"Okay, let's get a stretcher over here."

Feeling her legs giving way, Stephanie leaned against the stone wall and slid down to a sitting position. She looked up to see the medics carry Dudley away on a stretcher. A wet nose touched her cheek. She turned to rest her face on her dog's shoulder. "Dear God, thank You for Norma."

Eight days later, Stephanie rolled Philip Larkin's wheelchair into Dudley's flat, navigating sharp turns with some difficulty. Norma pushed ahead, eager to greet Dudley. "You're looking much better," Philip commented. "Got your color back."

"Yes, Dad. I'm feeling human again. It's good to see you out and about." Dudley, propped on his sofa against mounded pillows, closed his newspaper, and let it slip to the floor. His right arm still hung in a sling, and a gray pallor defined his cheekbones. When Norma shoved her muzzle into his good hand, he ruffled her ears and hugged her head while the dog's stubby tail wagged. The two corgis hopped off the sofa to greet their guests.

"Hello, Stephanie," Dudley said. "Thank you for bringing Dad. Come sit here beside me."

"Hello, Dudley." Stephanie met his warm gaze, determined to read nothing into it. "Thanks, but I'll just sit here beside your dad." She slid into a chair, and Norma collapsed at her feet.

Philip reached over to pat Stephanie's hand. "This young lady is good medicine. She tells me you've been getting the best of care."

"I have more company than I deserve and enough food to last me through the winter," Dudley said. "The ladies from church come by daily to clean my house and prepare my meals, and the Bants have been caring for my stock. Alf and Colin are at the stables, and Emma and her daughter Sarah are somewhere around the place. They might be cleaning at the main house."

A shadow crossed Philip's face. "Marrying Freda was the worst mistake I ever made," he mumbled, lifting a trembling hand to his brow. "God forgive me for inflicting this horror upon you, son. And upon you, my dear." He clasped Stephanie's hand.

"You couldn't have known, Dad."

"My family was partially to blame," Stephanie said.

Without ceremony, Alf and Colin entered the tiny flat, smiling and smelling of horse. " 'Ello, Stephanie. Mr. Larkin." Alf nodded to Stephanie and shook Philip's fragile hand. "I saw you arrive and thought this'd be as good a time as any to 'ear the straight story about what's been going on around 'ere. I've read things in the paper, but I'd rather 'ear it from you. Is it true Pat fell into an 'ole with a skeleton in it?"

Dudley and Stephanie exchanged concerned glances.

"You deserve to hear the truth, Alf, as does everyone else in the village," Philip said as firmly as his quaking voice would allow. "I'll not be coddled."

Slowly, with some assistance from Dudley, he related the sad tale, some of which was new to Stephanie.

Not long after Philip married Freda, her mental and emotional imbalance had become apparent. Medication seemed to keep her malady under control, and Philip had resigned himself to a lifetime of caring for his erratic wife. Freda's daughter Pat and son-in-law George Hoff soon moved into the house, against Philip's wishes. George seemed content to live off Philip's reluctant generosity while Pat worked at various jobs. She had been an attractive young woman then, forceful and ambitious, although she'd had difficulty keeping a job for any length of time.

Unknown to Philip, Pat became acquainted with Sir John Haverstane, eighteen years her senior, and began a tempestuous affair. Pat had decided to rid herself of George. If she were free, she believed, Sir John would make her Lady Haverstane. After contriving elaborate plans to make George's disappearance look like desertion, she killed her husband and asked Sir John to help her dispose of the body.

Philip could only guess at Sir John's horror when he learned of the murder. Apparently fearing implication, he had informed Pat of a niche beneath the vestry floor of the church, in which

341

clerics of the past had concealed implements for secret Roman Catholic services. After helping her hide George's body, Sir John had washed his hands of any involvement with the homicidal woman.

Then Philip became ill. Dudley returned to care for the farm, but he had been unable to care for his father's needs, as well. Freda and Pat insisted upon placing Philip in a rest home, ignoring Dudley's objections. Philip had been just as happy to escape.

"Even a rest home was preferable to life with Freda," he admitted sadly. "I let Dudley shoulder that burden for me."

"I wanted to help you out, Dad," Dudley said. "You couldn't have known, any more than I did, that Pat was dangerous. I thought she was simply obnoxious and eccentric like her mother. Pat and Freda both often took long walks at night."

"Nearly scaring me to death on more than one occasion," Stephanie inserted.

Dudley nodded. "That was their intent, no doubt. I suspect they felt a need to keep watch over the church and prevent anyone from exploring it too closely. Pat threatened you, and we can speculate that she also made threats, maybe even attempts, against Sir John's life. His paranoia probably had some basis, in fact. When he was placed in the rest home and Pat got a job there, he clung to Dad for protection against her. Not that it did him any good. Investigators are now suggesting she might have hastened his death with her threats."

"The poor man," Stephanie shook her head, fighting back tears. "I'm sure I brought on his final stroke with my suggestion of restoring the old church. He knew the body would be found."

"More likely he feared Pat's retaliation against you, Stephanie," Dudley said. "For all his faults, I believe Sir John wanted to make amends for his past by helping his one surviving relative."

"I agree," Philip said. "Although Sir John professed to despise Christians, he and I talked a good deal before he became paralyzed. He anticipated Stephanie's arrival with more genuine pleasure than I had ever before seen in the man. At the end of his life, he finally experienced the joy of generosity to another."

Stephanie's tears overflowed. She dug in her purse for tissues, aware of Dudley's troubled gaze upon her.

"But what'll 'appen to Freda and Pat now?" Alf asked.

Philip heaved a quivering sigh. "I imagine they will be institutionalized. Freda freely confesses that she knew about the murder and approved. When Dudley told them about the building inspector's coming, they both panicked. I have no idea what Pat planned to do with George's body or how she intended to move it."

Dudley spoke up. "The corgis—unintentionally, of course—warned Pat of my approach. I remember nothing after I stepped through the church doorway."

"After Pat stabbed Dudley," Philip continued, "she took the dogs home with her and told Freda what she'd done. Freda told her to go back and finish the job. Pat found Stephanie tending Dudley's wounds, and she admits her intent to kill them both. Even now, Freda is angry with Pat for bungling her duty and getting caught. Neither one regrets anything else."

"They're insane, Dad," Dudley reminded him.

"I blame myself for bringing her and her fiend daughter

here." Philip's voice cracked. "I never dreamed that my hasty, foolish second marriage would lead to this."

"Don't punish yourself for mistakes of the past, Dad," Dudley said. "God has forgiven you, and He has protected all of us in amazing ways."

"God used Norma," Colin spoke up, "to protect you and Miz Kelluh."

Norma lifted her head and looked at Stephanie, ears pricked.

Dudley smiled. "The heroic dog."

"Didja see 'er photo in the papers?" Colin asked. "Norma got a medal for courage."

"But she wouldn't sit up or look at the camera," Stephanie said with a chuckle, still wiping her eyes. "She melted on the floor like an octopus out of water." Norma flattened her ears and laid her muzzle on Stephanie's foot.

"Quite a dog, she is," Dudley said. "All it took was a threat to you, Stephanie, to bring out all her Doberman courage. I'm jealous, I'll confess. A chap would like to play hero sometimes rather than give all glory to a dog."

The other men laughed.

"I think she used up her lifetime quota of courage in one fell swoop," Stephanie said. "She's been a trembling lapdog ever since and hardly allows me out of her sight."

"Another cause for envy."

Stephanie laughed with the others while puzzling over Dudley's remarks. Ever since his return home from the hospital, she had found his company disconcerting. Why did he gaze at her with such entreaty and hope in his eyes?

Still chuckling, Alf rose and brushed off his overalls. "Run and tell your mother we're off to 'ome, Colin." He shook hands again with Philip. "Thank you, Mr. Larkin. I pray God'll grant you many 'appy years to come." He glanced from Dudley to Stephanie and grinned. "All three of you."

As soon as the door closed behind the Bants, Philip heaved a sigh. "I intended to cheer you, Dudley, not depress everyone with the sordid story of my failings."

"Alf asked for the story, Dad. I don't think it will be necessary for you to tell it again, since the newspaper will carry the pertinent facts for all to read. Recent events have sparked national interest in Staneheath Manor."

"Mr. Hartwell is delighted," Stephanie said. "English Legacy upped its offer on the church and cottage property, eager to profit from the scandal."

"Hartwell." Dudley spoke the name with distaste. "He's after more than financial profit. Wish I'd never introduced you to him." A blanket slid off his legs as he struggled to sit up.

"That introduction did start a string of calamities," Stephanie agreed, rising to tuck the blanket back in place. Dudley submitted silently to her ministrations. "But God has also used it for good. At least George Hoff can have a decent burial, and Pat and Freda will never murder again. Me? I just want out of that place as soon as possible." When she tried to back away, Dudley caught her hand and held it firmly.

"But where will you go, my dear?" Philip asked. "We cannot do without you."

She studied their clasped hands. "I don't know. I had thought of looking for another cottage in the area, something with a garden I could fix up."

Dudley cleared his throat. "Alf tells me that Peggy Masters's mother now wants to donate her property to New Life directly. She will move in with Ronald and Peggy, so the church can take possession of the cottage and auto shop as soon as legal ends are tied up. If you will marry me, Stephanie, I'm ready to sell Westbourne Farm and move to the new vicarage. Alf Bant offered us a good price for the land and buildings, and he'll stable my horses."

Stephanie met his gaze. "Marry you?"

Philip cleared his throat. "If you'll hand me that newspaper and wheel me into the kitchen, Stephanie, I'll entertain myself while you two discuss this matter."

Dazed, she followed his directions, then returned to the book-lined sitting room. Dudley hunched over with his head in his left hand, his glasses dangling from his fingers. He glanced up, red around the eyes, still gripping his hair. "Stephanie, I thought—I hoped you shared my feelings. Have I offended you?"

"But you've never said a word. . .I thought you knew that I had fallen in love with you and were trying to let me down gently. . . ."

"Let you down?" Joy lighted his eyes, and he attempted to stand.

"No, don't get up, you'll hurt yourself!"

"Then you'd better come closer," he said through tight lips, lifting his left arm invitingly.

Stephanie sat beside him. He slumped back against the sofa, taking her with him. "Frustrating to be so weak."

"I'm thankful you're alive. They had to sew a lot of things back together inside you. Give yourself time." Stephanie slid her arms around his trim waist, and his grip tightened.

"I wanted to ask you to marry me months ago, but who could bring a wife into. . ." He sighed. "The situation we had. And you know about my past."

"My past is nothing to brag about either, dear man. The Lord has brought good out of the whole mess," Stephanie said. "Our past sins are buried and gone forever—washed in the blood of Jesus. 'Old things are passed away; behold, all things are become new!' "

She tilted her head back to inspect his face. "Dudley, I want your father to come live with us in the new vicarage. I can care for him while you're out ministering. Does the cottage have a fenced-in garden for the dogs? I hope there are plenty of good footpaths nearby."

"Plenty."

"The cottage is thatched, isn't it? I remember seeing it on that corner when I drove past and thinking it was the sweetest thing. Oh, Dudley, this will be so much fun!"

"I agree," he said, and kissed her before she could say another word.

JILL STENGL

Jill lives with her husband, Dean, and their family in the Northwoods of Wisconsin. They have four children and a busy life. Tom is an Air Force Academy cadet, Anne is in college, Jim is in high school, and Peter is Jill's last home-school student. Jill loves to write books about exciting times, historic places, and unusual people—and animals somehow sneak their way into most of her stories. The Stengls lived in England for seven years while Dean served in the Air Force, and Jill enjoys setting many of her stories there. You may correspond with Jill at jpopcorn@newnorth.net.

A Letter to Our Readers

Dear Readers:

In order that we might better contribute to your reading enjoyment, we would appreciate your taking a few minutes to respond to the following questions. When completed, please return to the following: Fiction Editor, Barbour Publishing, Inc., P.O. Box 719, Uhrichsville, OH 44683.

1. Did you enjoy reading *Hidden Motives*?
   ❏ Very much—I would like to see more books like this.
   ❏ Moderately—I would have enjoyed it more if _____
   _____
   _____

2. What influenced your decision to purchase this book?
   (Check those that apply.)
   ❏ Cover   ❏ Back cover copy   ❏ Title   ❏ Price
   ❏ Friends   ❏ Publicity   ❏ Other

3. Which story was your favorite?
   ❏ *Watcher in the Woods*   ❏ *At the End of the Bayou*
   ❏ *Then Came Darkness*   ❏ *Buried in the Past*

4. Please check your age range:
   ❏ Under 18   ❏ 18–24   ❏ 25–34
   ❏ 35–45   ❏ 46–55   ❏ Over 55

5. How many hours per week do you read? _____

Name _____

Occupation _____

Address _____

City _____ State _____ Zip _____

E-mail _____

If you enjoyed

HIDDEN MOTIVES

then read:

OLYMPIC MEMORIES

Four Stories of Inherited Athleticism and Love

Olympic Dreams by Melanie Panagiotopoulos
Olympic Hopes by Lynn A. Coleman
Olympic Goals by Kathleen Y'Barbo
Olympic Cheers by Gail Sattler

HEARTSONG ♥ PRESENTS

Love Stories
Are Rated G!

That's for godly, gratifying, and of course, great! If you love a thrilling love story but don't appreciate the sordidness of some popular paperback romances, **Heartsong Presents** is for you. In fact, **Heartsong Presents** is the premiere inspirational romance book club featuring love stories where Christian faith is the primary ingredient in a marriage relationship.

Sign up today to receive your first set of four, never-before-published Christian romances. Send no money now; you will receive a bill with the first shipment. You may cancel at any time without obligation, and if you aren't completely satisfied with any selection, you may return the books for an immediate refund!

Imagine. . .four new romances every four weeks—two historical, two contemporary—with men and women like you who long to meet the one God has chosen as the love of their lives. . .all for the low price of $10.99 postpaid.

To join, simply complete the coupon below and mail to the address provided. **Heartsong Presents** romances are rated G for another reason: They'll arrive Godspeed!

YES! Sign me up for Hearts♥ng!

NEW MEMBERSHIPS WILL BE SHIPPED IMMEDIATELY!
Send no money now. We'll bill you only $10.99 postpaid with your first shipment of four books. Or for faster action, call toll free 1-800-847-8270.

NAME _____

ADDRESS_____

CITY _____ STATE_____ ZIP_____

MAIL TO: HEARTSONG PRESENTS, P.O. Box 721, Uhrichsville, Ohio 44683
or visit www.heartsongpresents.com